I0637529

THE ZHORE DECEPTION

CHRISTINE POPE

Dark Valentine Press

THE ZHORE DECEPTION

978-0692488577

Copyright © 2015 by Christine Pope

Published by Dark Valentine Press

Cover design and interior layout by Indie Author Services

Visit www.christinepope.com for more information
or to contact the author.

THE ZHORE DECEPTION

ONE

TRINITY KNOX SAT IN A STERILE CHAMBER PRECISELY TEN FEET square. The only furniture the room contained was a plain steel table and two steel-framed chairs with mesh seats. She tried to sit as quietly as possible while she waited in one of those chairs, eyeing the empty one across the table from her with mounting dread. Sooner or later someone would come in and take that empty seat, and that, she knew, was when the real fun would begin.

There was no sign of any surveillance devices, which of course meant nothing. The designers of a facility like this one would have made damn sure that every bit of tech was carefully hidden. However, the smooth, uninterrupted gray-beige surfaces of the walls and ceiling didn't mean that every movement, every breath she took wasn't being recorded.

So she sat quietly, hands folded on the table in front of her, and stared into what she hoped looked like the middle distance. Not that there was much of a middle distance in a room as small as this one. However, schooling her features to a careful blankness helped a little to hold back the panic within her, the small frightened beast inside her ribcage that threatened to burst out and show her captors how truly terrified she was.

She'd really screwed up this time.

How could she have been so stupid as to confide in Caleb Prescott, of all people?

Because she'd thought she was in love with him. And he'd told her that he loved her. That was her first mistake, she supposed. Caleb was one of the rare few she couldn't read. His thoughts were opaque to her. And she'd appreciated that quality, because it meant there was an aura of mystery around him. She'd never catch him thinking that her ass was too big or her nose too long, or any one of a myriad of faults that a man might comment on during any given day. No, Caleb had said she was beautiful, and he loved her, and then, one night after making love, she'd confessed her big secret.

"I can read minds," she'd told him, and his eyes had widened in the darkness.

"No shit. Seriously?"

"Seriously."

A flash of his teeth. He did have very white teeth. "So what am I thinking right now?"

That had been awkward. She'd had to explain that there was one person in a thousand—maybe one person in ten thousand—whose thoughts were invisible to

this strange talent of hers. And he'd looked skeptical…
of course he had…until the next day at work she proved
she wasn't exaggerating to him, by reciting word for word
what their supervisor had said to Caleb at a closed-door
meeting regarding the latest security upgrades to their
computer systems.

Caleb hadn't doubted her after that. No, he was
very enthusiastic about her "amazing talent." Problem
was, it didn't take long before he was scheming, thinking of ways he could use that talent to benefit himself.
Of course, he was smart enough not to put it that way.
He talked a lot about how the corporation was corrupt,
and how it would never miss a few measly million units.
Then he'd gone on to explain how they could be away
and off-world before anyone could figure out what had
happened, and living a life of luxury on Eridani or some
other planet that didn't have an extradition agreement
with the Consortium. After all, Trinity would be stealing
the passwords right out of their supervisor's own mind.
How could anyone ever detect that kind of intrusion,
since there would be absolutely no hacking involved?

Trinity had known it was wrong. She'd resisted for
a while. But she was so desperate to believe Caleb—
to believe in his love for her—that eventually she'd
given in. It was victimless crime, wasn't it? Maybe their
supervisor, Lisanna Cruz, would get her hands slapped
for funds disappearing from her department without a trace, but because she was in fact innocent, there
wouldn't be anything that the authorities could actually

pin on her. Besides, Trinity could desperately use some of that money herself. When her mother had died halfway across the country, she'd left a mountain of debt as her sole legacy, and Trinity was doing the best she could to pay it off with the tiny amount she had left after covering her expenses each month. Half a million units could do a lot to erase that debt.

The problem was, once the funds were in his hands, Caleb promptly disappeared. Yes, he had planned to go off-world…without Trinity. There was a whole galaxy full of interesting women waiting for him, so why would he want to saddle himself with dead weight like her?

And how kind of him to drop a little note to the local authorities explaining exactly how she'd done it.

When she'd first been arrested and locked up in a cell at the main jail facility in Barstow, she'd cried tears of fear, of anger, of self-recrimination. What an idiot she'd been. She should have known better than to trust Caleb. Didn't she have the example of her own mother to show her that placing your trust in a man was the quickest way to a broken heart and an empty bank account, or worse? And yet Acantha Knox had gone from partner to partner, always thinking the next relationship would be "the one." Right until the end, when she'd been murdered for her vehicle and the contents of her wallet, and not a whole hell of a lot else. There hadn't been anything left.

Now, though, as Trinity waited in this room that frightened her because of its cold functionality, she didn't weep. Dry-eyed, she stared at that fixed point in the middle distance, the one she'd chosen because she hoped it would make her look untroubled by her current predicament. What else could she do?

This wasn't a police station, or a holding tank for low-level criminals. No, she would have bet her cut of the take she never received that this was some kind of government facility. Everything was just a little too clean, a little too polished. The guards who'd escorted her to this room had worn no insignia, not one badge or patch to show who they worked for. And that frightened her more than anything else. People were brought to places like this so they could disappear.

She swallowed, then couldn't avoid startling as the door hissed open, sliding into a cavity hidden inside the wall. A man in his early thirties, some ten years older than she, entered the room. He wore a dark gray suit and had eyes almost the same gray, piercing against his tanned skin.

Some women would have probably found him handsome, but Trinity reflected that she was done with handsome men. They just weren't worth the trouble.

The newcomer carried a black plastic file in one hand. He set it down on the tabletop before pulling out the empty chair and sitting in it. The entire time, those dark gray eyes were fixed on Trinity, and something about the way they scanned her face sent a cold little thrill down her spine.

Maybe it was a mistake, but she couldn't help pushing out a small ping, just to see if his thoughts would be as opaque to her as Caleb's had been. To her surprise, she could hear him quite well.

I suppose you wanted to find out if you could enter my mind. Yes, you can…but only those parts I will allow you to see.

Her mouth must have dropped open, because he smiled. "Yes, Ms. Knox. I'm not like your erstwhile lover. On the other hand, I'm probably not like anyone else you've ever met, either. I've been trained to block the sections of my mind I want to keep concealed from people with your particular…talents."

Trinity finally found her voice. "Trained? Trained by whom? I thought the Consortium government didn't even recognize psi powers."

"Officially, no." He pulled some papers out of her file, and her eyes widened. She couldn't recall the last time she'd seen anyone use actual physical paperwork. Everything was digitized and electronic. Far more efficient that way.

And hackable, she supposed. Maybe this faceless agency had decided that it was safer to commit sensitive data to paper, records that could be easily—and permanently—destroyed.

"By the way," he went on, after organizing the paperwork in front of him, "my name is Gabriel Brant. I've been assigned to your case."

"So you're my attorney?"

Another smile, although it was only a slight lift at the corners of his mouth. It never reached those gun-metal eyes of his. "No. I'm your…well, let's just call it 'caseworker' for now. You have no need of an attorney, Ms. Knox, because you will not be put on trial."

"I won't?" she asked, a sort of disbelieving relief beginning to flood through her. "What, you mean the charges have been dropped?"

"There were no charges," Brant said smoothly. "All record of your involvement with the TransCal embez-zlement case has been expunged. In fact, Ms. Knox, all record of *you* has been expunged. Mr. Prescott is being tracked as we speak—it seems he was headed to Iradia—and that should clean up most of the mess."

She didn't reply to that revelation, only pressed her lips together.

An eyebrow lifted. "Not a very social person, are you?"

In response, Trinity gave Brant a stony look. No, she wasn't a social person. Moving every six standard months at a mother's whim could do that to a person. What was the point in trying to make any sort of con-nection if it was merely going to get ripped away when you were just becoming comfortable with someone? There had been men before Caleb, but he was the first Trinity had ever confided in.

And the last, she thought drearily, although she was careful to keep that part of her mind walled off, beyond her captor's reach. *I kind of doubt Mr. Brant is going to give you the opportunity to have any more love affairs.*

Brant appeared nonplussed by her lack of reaction. "Very well. Moving on. I would like you to provide more information about your father's identity. Since your mother's records show no sign of the kind of psychic talent you possess, we would like to know if it came to you on the paternal side. Unfortunately, your birth records have your father listed as 'unknown.'"

"That's because my mother probably didn't know," Trinity replied, not bothering to keep the bitterness out of her voice. "She was too busy partying to keep track."

Gabriel pulled an old-fashioned ballpoint pen out of his jacket pocket and made a notation on the paper in front of him. "She never described him? Never mentioned where he was from?"

"No."

"And you never asked?" The eyebrow went up again. "Never tried to pick it out of her mind?"

God, no. Trinity supposed she might have done such a thing, but invading her mother's thoughts was something she could never bring herself to do. Well, except for that one time, but she learned her lesson on that one and afterward left well enough alone.

She shook her head, and Gabriel wrote something else down. "We'll try to find a match through the genome database."

That was something she supposed she could have done herself, if she'd been willing to pay the price, or take the risk of discovering something she would have been happier not knowing.

Considering the losers her mother had picked up throughout Trinity's childhood, she really didn't want to know. In her mind, she'd always imagined her biological father as some handsome, dashing type—maybe a spy—who had a brief passionate fling and then had to move on. If he'd known of her existence, of course he would have made sure to be a part of her life, but since Acantha Knox had kept her existence from him, he'd never returned.

It was a nice romantic fantasy. Trinity knew that was all it was, though. For one thing, her mother would have had to get black-market shots to counteract the birth control meds all women on Gaia were given, just to avoid little "accidents" like Trinity Elizabeth Knox. Acantha had known what she was doing. Why, though…that was something that Trinity had never dared to ask. Had her mother thought she could keep this particular lover around by having his baby, or had there been something special about him, something Acantha wanted to ensure lived on in his child? Those questions had danced around in Trinity's head her entire childhood, but she hadn't been able to summon the courage to demand that her mother give her the answers. Instead, she'd let her daydreams take the place of the truth. Better to have a pleasant fantasy than an ugly reality, especially when her life already had its fair share of ugliness.

She'd never had any close friends. How could she, when her mother had dragged her to a new city at least twice a year ever since she could remember? And as her gift developed and grew, she isolated herself even more. A friend was someone you were supposed to confide in, and she didn't dare take that risk, let alone face the problems of being friendly with someone whose every thought she could read. Once she was done with her mandated fourteen years of school and working as an admin, Trinity had moved out on her own and tried to build some kind of a life that was hers and hers alone. That had never seemed to work, though, maybe because she still couldn't allow herself to get close to anyone. Men were different—you could be intimate physically without revealing anything of yourself, your true self. Besides, she'd always been able to hear what they were thinking about her, and that sort of unvarnished truth was the kind of thing that could drive a stake right through the heart of a romance.

Until Caleb. If only she'd been able to see into his black heart as well, she probably wouldn't be here.

"Good luck with that," Trinity told Gabriel Brant, placing her hands flat on the tabletop. Maybe her father hadn't even been from Gaia, but from Nova Angeles or New Chicago or someplace even farther away. He might not be in the database at all. She had far bigger things to worry about. Voice flat, she went on, "It sounds like I don't exist anymore. I suppose that's your call. But now that you have me, what do you plan to do with me?"

Brant cocked his head to one side and studied her carefully. She didn't flinch, but gazed back at him, noting his fine straight brows, his strong nose. Yes, he was very good-looking. For all she knew, he'd been chosen as her handler just because he was so attractive. But if the people pulling his strings thought she was going to fall for him and then be easy to control because of that, they didn't know her very well.

At last he smiled. Well, smirked, really. She knew the difference. Then he said, "You, Ms. Knox, are going to be our secret weapon."

Zhandar entered his counselor's office at the agreed-upon time, precisely one hour before noon. Because their relationship as counselor and counselee was considered intimate enough, she had allowed the hood of her robes to drop down around her shoulders, and her black hair gleamed with bluish highlights under the light streaming in through the bank of windows that overlooked her balcony garden.

Counselee. On other worlds, he would have been referred to as Rozhara's patient. That was not the way on Zhoraan, however. Wounds of the mind were not seen as a sickness, but rather as a temporary condition, one that could be overcome with the proper guidance and compassion. This was why he had been assigned to Rozhara, although he had begun to wonder how much longer she would have continued their professional relationship if she were not under instructions from the local council to do so for as long as necessary. Perhaps once Zhandar would have taken some pride in the notion that the council found him valuable enough that he required such cosseting, but now he was only impatient, thinking these sessions a waste of time better spent elsewhere.

"And how are you, Zhandar?" Rozhara inquired, once they had seated themselves on a pair of low, soft divans near the windows.

"Fine," he said shortly, gazing past her to the welter of plants in their self-sustaining beds. The *lizhain* were looking a bit droopy; he made a note to check on their watering tubes once his session with Rozhara was done. Not that performing such a task was really his responsibility, but it would help to distract him, and he'd been sorely in need of distractions lately.

"Merely fine?" she probed, green eyes keen.

He could sense the worry coming from her, overlaid with a hint of skepticism. They had had this conversation too many times before.

In the past, he might have tried to tamp down his frustration, which he knew must be radiating from him in waves. Now, though, after coming to see Rozhara for nearly a year, Zhandar had decided he wouldn't bother any longer. This was an exercise in futility, and they both knew it, even if his counselor refused to see that particular truth.

"I am a good citizen of Zhoraan," he said in ironic tones. "I rise every morning and bathe myself, then go to do the work that benefits everyone who lives in this city. What more is needed?"

"Healing, Zhandar," Rozhara replied, sadness tinging the word.

"It has been a year. I believe I am as healed as I will ever be."

Without speaking, she rose from her divan and went over to the window. It was a fine spring day, with lacy bluish-green clouds fanning out across the skies and a bright, fresh breeze playing with the leaves in the garden. And not just Rozhara's garden, but the gardens on every balcony and rooftop, bringing life and energy to Torzhaan, the capital of their province. Zhandar knew well enough how all those gardens functioned in the living organism that was their city, as it was his task to keep them all running at the optimum levels required for health and vitality.

After a long pause, Rozhara turned back to him, her hands open and turned toward him, a gesture of trust, but also of pleading. "Yours is a loss no man should have to suffer. I understand that. Elzhair is gone, and yet you show no sign of healing, of beginning the next chapter in your life."

"And what is this 'next chapter,' precisely? I have met no one else who is *sayara,* whose heart speaks to mine. Perhaps I never will. Most of us are blessed to have only one such connection in our lifetime."

"Most…but not all. Such connections—such second chances, as it were—are rare, but they are not unknown.

Of course your chances of meeting someone else who is compatible are lower if all you do is stay here, continuing the same routine, day in and day out. I've urged you many times over the last year to take a sabbatical, to travel and open your eyes to new vistas, new situations. And I am urging you again. A fresh perspective can be very helpful."

Perhaps Rozhara was right, but Zhandar didn't wish to leave Torzhaan. At least here he had some sort of purpose when he awoke each morning. The city breathed more easily because of his work. That had to be of some value.

He would not admit to Rozhara that he also wanted to stay because here he had reminders of Elzhair around every corner. The botanical gardens where they had walked and talked of his beloved plants, the holo-theater where they went to view compositions made of both light and music. Yes, it was painful to pass by those places and know she was gone, and that the dream they'd discussed so often had died with her, but better that than to be alone in a strange new place, unanchored, with nothing familiar to hold to.

It had been a risk, but one which Elzhair wanted to take. And things had gone well at first—at least she was able to conceive a child, something that fewer and fewer of his world's women had been able to do. The first few months had been uneventful, the doctors saying that she was healthy and everything was proceeding well.

But then she had fallen ill, the child she carried seeming to sap her strength with every passing day. Although they understood the gravity of what they were asking, Elzhair's doctors had at last urged her to give up the child, for them to perform the necessary surgery to save her life. She had refused, and told Zhandar that their child was more important than she was, that their child was the future.

He'd pleaded with her, saying that they could try again when she was well. Oh, how he had begged her. He knew their world was going into a decline, and that without enough children, his race might someday cease to exist altogether, but in those last frantic moments, all he could think of was how much he loved her, how his world would end without her by his side. Weighed against that, their child did not seem nearly as important as an existence with Elzhair absent from it.

Being Elzhair—stubborn, wild, passionate—she hadn't agreed with him, had held onto her life for as long as she could, thinking that if she persisted, their child might be able to survive on his own. In the end, though, she had gone, taking their unborn son with her. And Zhandar had been left with nothing.

"My mind says that you are right, Rozhara," Zhandar began, the words heavy, slow. She didn't move, but only remained there by the window, watching him carefully, perhaps in the hope that this time he might tell her something different. "But my heart says I must stay. The work supports me, fulfills me. In this place and time, it is all I am. Can you understand that?"

A nod, but at the same time, she sighed. "I do understand. But I do not agree. We all feel your pain, Zhandar, for your pain, at bottom, is Zhoraan's pain as well." She paused then, her gaze straying outside to the garden, and the plants and flowers shimmering and dancing in the springtime breeze. "But that pain is no excuse not to get on with your life. I cannot believe that Elzhair would want you to remain as you are forever."

He wanted to fling back at her that she had not known Elzhair, and so Rozhara could not have any idea what the other woman would have wanted. But he knew that his counselor had seen Elzhair's profile, had known of his late wife's loving heart, her compassion, and so was not speaking out of hand. It was true. Elzhair would not have wanted him to become the automaton he'd been for the last year, functioning but not living.

"Not forever, Rozhara," he allowed at last. "But for the foreseeable future, I fear."

TWO

"ZHORAAN," GABRIEL BRANT SAID, SWITCHING ON A HOLO-projector. At once a 3-D image of a blue-green planet shimmered into the air in the center of the conference room. Two moons, smaller than Gaia's own satellite, orbited the world. "You've heard of it, I suppose."

"Yes," Trinity replied cautiously. After her initial debriefing with Brant, she'd been led from that small interrogation room to, not a cell, but a small suite complete with a separate bedroom, sitting area, and refrigeration unit. There were pouches of water in the refrigerator but nothing else, and in the closet in the bedroom, she found several changes of clothing, all in her size. She wouldn't question where all this had come from or why it was being provided for her; apparently her status as a "secret weapon" was enough to merit special treatment.

And now it seemed she was to find out what being a secret weapon entailed. But Zhoraan? What did they expect her to do on that mysterious alien world? She'd never even been as far as Gaia's moon. She knew absolutely nothing about interacting with alien races.

"I'll speak frankly with you, Trinity," Gabriel said. He wore another of those not-quite smiles, and she wondered if he intended them to be ingratiating. If that was the case, he'd missed the mark by about a kilometer. All those smiles did was get her hackles up, especially since she couldn't read him unless he allowed her to. "The Consortium's mission is to expand into the galaxy, to ease the burden of over-population through colonization."

She nodded but didn't speak. That was common knowledge. More than once she'd considered joining a colony herself, just to get away from Gaia, to get the fresh start that even moving to a new city didn't seem able to provide her. Every time she'd gotten close to applying for colonist status, however, she'd backed out at the last minute. The psych evaluations and physical testing were well known to be rigorous, and she worried that the Consortium's doctors and psychologists might somehow ferret out her secrets, might realize there was a little more to Trinity Knox than what you could see from the outside.

"The Zhore, on the other hand," Brant went on, "have always more or less remained on their own world, save for the very occasional traveler here and there. That is why, until recently, we haven't paid them much mind, except to make the usual diplomatic overtures. Our energies were consumed in fighting the Stacians, and, to a lesser extent, the Eridanis."

"The Eridanis?" Trinity echoed, surprised. "But I thought they were our allies."

A smirk. She was beginning to really hate those, especially since she knew he was wearing that sarcastic smile because he thought her foolish and naïve. "The Consortium has no true allies, Trinity. We pay lip service to the treaties we have with the Eridanis, but because they are building their own empire—albeit slowly—we must view them as competitors for the same resources. Which brings us to the Zhore."

The projected image shifted, this time showing a dark, sullen-looking world covered in gray clouds. "This is a colony planet called Lathvin IV. And on this world, something extraordinarily disturbing took place approximately six standard months ago."

"What?" she asked. The place was clearly undergoing intensive terraforming, judging by its cloud cover. Had some sort of environmental catastrophe taken place there?

"You may not be aware of this—Lathvin IV is an obscure little planet—but our colonists there have had to share that world with some of the Zhore, as there is an ongoing dispute as to which government had first rights of colonization. So humans live, if not precisely side by side with the aliens, at least in close proximity to them."

That sounded ominous, and she could tell she wasn't going to like where Gabriel intended to steer the conversation. At the same time, she was beginning to realize that Gabriel Brant was one of those men in love with the sound of his own voice. But since she wasn't locked up in a prison cell, or being sent to the MaxSec prison on Titan, she figured it was in her best interests to indulge him and appear absorbed by what he was saying, although every instinct was telling her to get the hell out.

Not that her captors would actually let her go.

"A little more than a standard year ago, one of the young female colonists on Lathvin IV went to live with one of the Zhore, for reasons we still haven't been able to adequately determine. And some time after that, she bore a child to this Zhore, a son."

That revelation made Trinity sit up a little straighter in her seat. "Wait—humans and Zhore can have sex? But they're aliens!"

Well, strictly speaking, all of them were—the Eridanis and the Stacians as well. But at least everyone knew what an Eridani or a Stacian looked like. They were humanoid, if not exactly human stock. Anyway, humanity had been interbreeding with the Eridanis for generations now. Trinity had no idea whether any human had been brave enough to have sex with a Stacian. They were a fearsome-looking warrior race, bigger than humans, but still recognizably humanoid—two legs, two arms, two eyes, a nose and a mouth.

The Zhore, on the other hand...as far as Trinity knew, no human being had ever seen what a Zhore looked like. They could be hiding anything under the black hooded robes they wore at all times. To think that a human woman had actually slept with one of them, let alone had borne him a child—well, that was something she would have never thought possible.

"Yes, alien," Brant said. "But apparently not *too* alien. We still couldn't get any real information on their appearance, though—this young woman and her family were being remarkably close-lipped about the whole thing. Bringing any of them in for questioning would have sparked a diplomatic incident, since it seems she married this Zhore, and is now bound to him by his home world's laws. You see the difficulty."

Trinity nodded. Her brain was still trying to digest the concept of marrying a Zhore and bearing his child, but she could tell that Gabriel didn't want her to interrupt with what he no doubt would consider foolish questions.

"Three standard months ago, however, we had a stroke of luck. One of our operatives on Bathsheva was contacted by the leader of a mercenary clan there. This man said he had something we might find of value."

Again Trinity nodded. Brant might be a closed book to her, but every once in a while she got the faintest glimpse of one of those pages. Right now, that little glimmer meant he wanted her to acknowledge how clever he was, but in a way that wouldn't interrupt the flow of his narrative.

As for Bathsheva, she didn't know much about the world, except that it was in the outer territories, and supposedly a rough planet populated by a number of inter-related clans, most of whom seemed to be weapons-for-hire of some sort. It probably was the kind of place where the Consortium would have operatives placed, not only to hire mercs when the situation warranted, but also to keep track of who else was hiring them, and why.

Gabriel continued, "That something was the body of a Zhore."

She definitely hadn't been expecting that bit of information. Forgetting that she was supposed to be Brant's rapt audience and keep her mouth shut, she asked, "What was a Zhore doing on Bathsheva?" True, the secretive Zhore didn't keep completely to their home world, but on the other hand, it seemed that those of its people who did venture out into the galaxy generally chose more civilized places, such as Nova Angeles or Eridani.

"We still don't know for sure. What's important is that we were able to procure a Zhore for study purposes, and also to hack his tech to see if we could find anything valuable."

"Wouldn't the Bathshevans have already done that?"

At her question, Brant scowled. Clearly, he didn't want her acting as if she could form a single independent thought. She was supposed to be his puppet, no more.

Well, we may have a little problem with that, Mr. Brant. I'm not quite as stupid as you think.

Although, after the way Caleb had gulled her, she could see why Gabriel Brant had a fairly low opinion of her intelligence.

But then—well, she didn't know exactly what his title was, but she'd already begun to think of him as her handler—he gave her an indulgent smile and replied, "That's against their code, Ms. Knox. If a Bathshevan has something he wants to sell, he has to ensure that it's unsullied, untouched. Which means the Zhore handed over to us was in perfect condition, except for the injuries that took his life, and the handheld he carried was likewise undisturbed."

"Injuries?"

"Apparently he was set upon by what the Bathshevans refer to as a *xeno,* or outsider. One who is lawless, outside their clan structure. The motive was simple robbery, most likely, but the *xeno* was chased off by members of the clan who contacted us. They could do nothing to save the Zhore's life, but, being practical people, they recognized the body's worth. And so it came to the Consortium."

Brant pushed a button on the handheld. "I think you'll find this very interesting."

The image of Lathvin IV, which had been swirling in the center of the room the entire time, looking like the planetary equivalent of a very bad bruise, switched over to a dark human form lying on a gurney.

No, not human, Trinity realized. *Zhore.*

He—and it was a he, despite the long silky black hair that had been arranged to lie neatly on either side of his head—was definitely alien. The skin was black as well, but seemed to gleam faintly with the sort of rainbow reflections you might see on an oil slick. Looking closer, she saw that those reflections came from thousands of tiny scales, much smaller than anything she'd seen on a snake in a zoo. The Zhore male's nose was long, his chin proud. His hands, lying next to his still body, were also covered with scales, the nails black and flat.

Alien, but oddly, strangely beautiful. That shimmering skin couldn't obscure the finely honed planes of his face, just as the shapeless hospital gown someone had put on the corpse couldn't hide the width of his shoulders, the strong muscles of his legs and arms.

And staring at him, knowing that he'd died far from his world, from his family, Trinity felt pity stirring in her chest. She knew he was dead, his mind and spirit long gone, but something in her wished she could go to him and hold him, whisper that it was all right and that he would be sent home to sleep in the earth of his home world, rather than kept as a specimen in a lab for all eternity.

The door to the conference room opened, and a young Asian man probably close to Trinity's age walked in. Without looking at her, he said to Brant, "Empathy. Compassion. This is risky."

Blinking, she glanced from the stranger over to Gabriel. "Excuse me?"

Without missing a beat, he said, "Trinity, this is Blake Chu. He's our…well, you could say he's our resident psychic."

What the…. She refocused her attention on Blake. Now that she was looking a little more closely, she realized he was probably a few years older than she, maybe as much as thirty standard. His hair was cut so short it bristled all over his head, and he wore glasses—an affectation, she knew, since everyone these days had corrective surgery to repair minor defects such as myopia.

Didn't your mother ever teach you it was rude to stare? he thought at her, and she jumped. She'd never had anyone directly invade her thoughts like that before. She'd always been the one reading other people, not vice versa.

I don't know…didn't yours ever teach you that it was rude to barge into someone else's brain without permission?

He grinned, then said aloud, "No, she didn't. But then, you're doubly guilty, since you've made a career out of reading people's minds without them knowing it."

"I have not—" she began, then stopped herself. Quarreling with this stranger in front of Brant couldn't be a good idea.

Apparently not, since he smiled thinly and said, "Children, behave." Then his eyes narrowed, and he appeared to study Trinity, his head cocked to one side. "Blake seems to have picked up on something just then.

What were you feeling when you looked at that dead Zhore?"

Her first impulse was to lie, since she guessed that Brant would see any evidence of compassion as a weakness. But with Blake Chu standing there and watching her thoughts, lying was an impossibility. He'd know she was trying to hide something before the words even left her mouth.

"I felt sorry for him."

She'd thought her response would annoy Gabriel, but instead he nodded, appearing pleased. "Excellent."

Blake had the opposite reaction. Scowling, he slanted a look up at the handler. "I don't see how being a weak, romantic fool could possibly be excellent."

Weak and romantic she could handle. But fool? Trinity planted her hands on her hips and opened her mouth to speak, but Brant was too fast for her.

"You'll have to forgive Blake for his candor. He doesn't have much of a filter. Which makes him well-suited to some tasks, but not others." A smile, one that didn't fool Trinity a bit, and he continued, "Which is why we need you, Trinity. You see, one vital piece of information we've discovered is that the Zhore, while not precisely psychic, are a highly empathic race. Someone like Blake could never move amongst them undetected, because his talents lie in a different area. But you—you have powers that are similar to Blake's, and yet you also are highly sensitive. This makes you a perfect candidate."

"Candidate for what?" she asked, her tone guarded. Despite her question, it really wasn't too difficult to look past all the compliments and get to the meat of what he wanted.

He wanted her to be a spy. But that had to be impossible. Even though the Zhore seemed to wear their hooded cloaks at all times, that still didn't mean it would be safe for her, a human, to mingle with them. She'd be sure to be discovered, psychic powers or no.

Gabriel shot her a knowing look, one that told her he could tell she'd already guessed what he wanted. And Blake was smiling slightly and rocking back on his heels, as if in anticipation at watching and sensing her reaction to what was coming next.

Asshole. But at least he wasn't actively intruding on her thoughts at the moment.

"Simple enough, Trinity. We want you to go among the Zhore and observe them. For exactly how long depends on how well you integrate into their society. Using the data we've gathered from the specimen in our possession, we'll perform a series of bio-mods that will make you visually indistinguishable from any other Zhore."

Bio-mods—well, anything beyond correcting vision problems and other congenital issues—were illegal, and had been banned ever since the Yangtze Outbreak in 2127, but Trinity had a feeling Gabriel Brant knew that and didn't care. After all, it wasn't as if the Consortium didn't have a long history of overlooking its own laws whenever the situation called for it. Beyond that, though, her insides seemed to congeal into an icy mush at the thought of having her appearance, her very identity, erased so she could become some alien…thing.

Not a thing, she told herself quietly, not caring if Blake Chu was listening in. *A person. But not human. Not you.*

Her hands curled into fists at her sides, and she asked, "And if I refuse?"

"That's always your prerogative. As it's ours to send you to the MaxSec on Titan and find a nice deep hole for you. Not too deep, though. Not so deep that the guards there couldn't have a little fun. I'm sure they'd enjoy that. It's not every day they get sent a pretty young woman, after all. And it gets lonely out there beyond the rings of Saturn."

She hadn't been expecting anything other than that sort of response, but even so, the cold at her center seemed to intensify. Not much of a choice, was it? Be turned into something other than herself, or become a plaything for the prison's guards. Part of her wanted to believe that wouldn't happen, that even if she was sent to Titan, its personnel would be too professional for that sort of thing.

There was a joke.

Okay, then, she'd have to play Gabriel Brant's game. How he ever expected her to pull off such an insane plan, she had no idea, but she supposed he'd delight in telling her, detail by excruciating detail.

And if the worst happened, and the Zhore discovered she was an impostor?

Seeing Gabriel's self-satisfied smile and the expression of barely concealed glee on Blake Chu's face as they both stared at her, Trinity had a feeling the aliens couldn't do anything worse to her than her own government already had.

"You did not take your sabbatical," Leizha said.

Zhandar hadn't even heard her approach. It had felt good to stand here in this rooftop garden and smell the flowers and the fresh breeze all around him. In that moment, he'd wished he didn't have to be swathed in these robes, that he could let them fall away so the wind and the sun could touch his skin. To do so, however, would be a scandal. No Zhore ever exposed himself so, except in the privacy of his own home, or on his own property, if the grounds were extensive enough that discovery was not an issue. Here in the heart of Torzhaan, his people lived close enough together that such a thing would be unthinkable.

Repressing a sigh, he turned back toward his assistant, who stood a respectful three paces away, a tablet clutched in her gloved hands. "No, I did not," he replied. "I did not think it a good time to be away, not with so many renovations on the schedule."

She didn't nod, but he could feel the approval emanating from her all the same. Approval…and something more. He'd been sensing it for some time now, but had continued to hope that it would go away on its own, once Leizha understood that he was not emotionally ready to let another woman into his life.

Besides, she was not *sayara*. Quick and dedicated, with an almost uncanny ability to sense what each plant wanted and needed to thrive and grow, she would have been an exceptional mate, but his heart could not answer hers, because there was no echo of her soul within him. True, there had been isolated incidents when those of his people had come together even when that sacred bond did not exist between them, but those cases were few, and not widely accepted. The *sayara* connection was necessary for the continuation of their species, because the Zhore could not conceive without it.

And even its existence is no guarantee of success, he thought then, not bothering to keep the bitterness out of his thoughts. If Leizha sensed the emotion, perhaps she would realize that he would never be able to look upon her in the way she wanted.

She did not move, however. Voice soft, she said, "It is true. We seem to be busier than ever. This same time last year, I had thought I might take my leave, go on a retreat for a few months. But the work came in, and I did not feel it would be right to leave you after…." The words died away, as if she had just realized that speaking of Elzhair's death almost a year to the day from when it had happened would not be good form at all.

The silence seemed to pulse between them. And as it stretched, Zhandar realized he must be the one to fill it.

Glancing away from Leizha, at the terraced gardens on the next tower over from where they stood, he said, "It would have been difficult, training a new assistant while maintaining our current pace. And so I thank you for staying. As I am sure the residents of Torzhaan would thank you, if they but knew."

Leizha inclined her head. Then her shoulders seemed to square under her heavy cloak, and she picked up the tablet and brushed a gloved finger across its surface to bring up a new screen. "The *lazhir* on Trezhar Row are blooming early. Would you like me to reroute tomorrow's crew and have them go there, rather than to the repiping project in the Maranzhar District?"

In that moment, he couldn't help but feel grateful that she had retreated to formality, to the business at hand. But perception was not Leizha's problem…only hoping for something that could never come to pass. Although he needed her assistance, he found himself wishing that she had gone on that retreat. Perhaps then she would have met someone who was *sayara,* and she would have been able to leave behind her entirely inappropriate affection for him.

Where it had even come from, he couldn't be sure. They'd worked together for some time while Elzhair was still alive, and there had never been even a hint of impropriety then. But it was one thing to hunger for someone who did not share the soul bond, and quite another to covet another woman's husband. Leizha was far too honorable for anything like that. No, it was probably more that she had hoped, now he was free....

But he would never be free. Elzhair would always be with him, a ghost of what might have been, of happiness lost forever. Grief would be his constant companion.

He could not imagine ever having another.

THREE

As Trinity had feared, her handler was all too happy to go over every detail of the operation with her. They'd been cooped up in this conference room for hours already, with no end in sight.

Well, at least he waited until after you had a good night's sleep and a decent breakfast, she thought. That was something. The suite they'd provided had a very comfortable bed, and the food that had been left outside her door that morning was fresh, hot, and tasty. It was all designed to lull her into a false sense of security, she was sure. That was fine. It would take a lot more than a plate of real eggs, not reconstituted soy, and newly baked scones to make her lower her guard.

The same with the change of clothes and the grooming supplies they'd given her. She'd awoken to a care package of sorts waiting out on the coffee table in the sitting area of her suite. Inside it had been several new outfits, underwear, cosmetics, toiletries…everything she required to feel more or less human again. It would have all been fine and good…if she hadn't known they planned to turn her into something that was very not-human.

"The lab-grown epidermis will be laid directly on top of yours," Gabriel was saying. "It will fuse with your skin."

Repressing a shiver, Trinity asked, "And when I'm done with this mission…what? Do I shed my Zhore epidermis like a snake sheds its skin?"

A cutting look from those icy charcoal eyes, and he replied, "No, it's not that simple, I'm afraid. It will have to be surgically removed."

Of course it will, she thought, holding in a sigh. But she only nodded and hoped that she looked unruffled by that particular revelation, then asked, "How much more will you have to change?"

"The Zhore male we were able examine had very human-looking eyes. Blue. Because your own eyes are in the same blue-green-gray color spectrum, we feel confident that we will not have to alter that part of your appearance."

Well, that was something. Color grafts to change one's eyes were commonplace these days, but Trinity had always felt squeamish at the thought of someone touching her eyes, even for such benign purposes. Luckily, she had perfect vision and so had never required any kind of surgery.

"Your hair is entirely the wrong color, but because it is long and straight, we'll simply dye it rather than graft it with something more suitable."

It took an actual effort of will for Trinity not to reach up and touch a strand of her hair, which now lay loose over her shoulders. She wouldn't say she was exactly vain about it, but she was proud of its length, reaching nearly to her waist, and its warm golden-brown color was something she'd never felt any need to alter. But at least removing black dye from her heavy tresses would be far easier than getting rid of the lab-grown Zhore skin they planned to encase her in.

Assuming you survive long enough to even get back to "normal," she thought, glad that Blake Chu wasn't around to eavesdrop on her thoughts. Apparently there was some way to guard against that sort of mental intrusion, or Gabriel wouldn't have been able to prevent her from looking into his mind. But Blake was the only other psychic Trinity had ever met, and so she'd never had any need to learn how to hide her thoughts from others.

"And false nails, I guess, so mine look like a Zhore's," she said, earning herself another irritated look from Gabriel. He really hated being interrupted.

However, he sounded neutral enough as he replied, "Yes. We've analyzed the fabric content of the garments he wore—there were close-fitting pieces under the robes—and feel confident that we can duplicate those without any problem."

Maybe she'd feel better about all this once she had concealed herself in those robes. At least it wasn't as if Gabriel and his superiors expected her to wander down the streets of Zhoraan with her face completely bare to its populace. If Zhoraan even had streets. Who knew what it was actually like?

Which brought her to her next question. Since Gabriel was already annoyed with her, she thought she might as well go for broke. "It seems as if you have the issue with my physical appearance pretty much figured out. But simply making me look like a Zhore isn't going to make me fit in with Zhore society. What, are you just going to drop me in the middle of nowhere and hope for the best?"

That remark earned her another of his tight-lipped smiles. "Of course not, Trinity. We've been monitoring Zhoraan from a safe distance for many years. They are careful—extremely careful—and we've never been allowed on their planet's surface the way we have on Eridani. Even so, they can't keep everything hidden. We've picked up enough of their speech so that we were able to analyze it, reproduce it. You'll be given sleep conditioning in their language, so that speaking it will be no different from speaking Galactic Standard."

She wondered whether she would think in the Zhore tongue as well, but decided that was one question she wouldn't bother to ask. Most likely, Gabriel Brant didn't have an answer. She'd heard rumors of that sort of sleep training, but it wasn't something that anyone outside the government was able to use. And she had a feeling she would be the first to receive training in the language of the Zhore.

"So I'll look like one of them, talk like one of them," Trinity said slowly. "But who am I to be? How will I fit in with their society?"

"I was hoping you would ask." This whole time, Gabriel had been standing near the window, which looked down over an endless cityscape. Trinity didn't recognize it, but then, she'd never really been outside the western territories, hadn't ventured any farther east than Arizona. That could be Chicago down there, or New York, or the vast megalopolis that had overtaken the Fort Dallas area. One big city looked very much like another now, after the distinctive landmarks of the Normerican continent had fallen one by one to the developers, the improvers.

But now he moved away from the window and moved in her direction, going around her and stopping directly behind her chair. He stood so close that she thought she could almost feel the heat coming from his body, but that, she told herself, even as she sat still and tried not to react, had to be her imagination.

What wasn't her imagination was his hands dropping to her shoulders, fingers squeezing ever so slightly. What exactly he was trying to prove, she didn't know. Almost involuntarily, she reached out with her mind, attempting to read his thoughts, but once again it was like running full-force into a duracrete wall.

"I must feel a little tense," she quipped, hoping she could deflect whatever game he was playing by treating it as if it were nothing.

"No," he said, fingers digging even more deeply into her flesh, "you're remarkably relaxed, all things considered."

Trinity decided that her body must be doing things her brain didn't know anything about, because everything in her wanted to shrink away from Gabriel's touch. But she sat still and replied, "Well, I suppose it must be because of that amazing massage you're giving me."

"Perfect," he murmured. His hands stilled but remained resting on her shoulders. "So my touch doesn't bother you?"

Define "bother," she thought, but only said, "No. Should it?"

He paused for a second or two, then bent down, his breath hot against her neck. His lips grazed her skin. "What about this?"

Her flesh wanted to crawl right off her bones. Was this how it started? Maybe those prison guards on Titan wouldn't be such a bad alternative after all. Willing herself not to react, she replied, "I don't know, Gabriel. I suppose if you're going to push it any further than this, you might want to get us a more comfortable room."

A chuckle. Then his hands lifted from her shoulders and he stepped away. Trinity wouldn't allow herself to sigh in relief, but she could almost sense her body relaxing. Not all the way—that probably wouldn't happen until after she survived this whole ordeal...*if* she survived it—but enough that she didn't feel as if she was about to throw up anymore.

"Now, that would be against regulations. But...." Gabriel paused for so long that Trinity wondered if he was going to push beyond a mere shoulder massage anyway, and what in the world would she do then? To her infinite relief, he lifted his shoulders and moved away from her, going back to the window. "Your reaction was very interesting. You didn't flinch, or pull away. You endured my touch because you'd clearly decided it was something you just had to do, like it or not. Excellent."

She didn't think she liked where this was going. No, wait—she hadn't liked where this was going pretty much from the very beginning. It was just that things seemed to have abruptly taken a right turn toward the outer circle of hell.

"To answer your question," Gabriel went on, gaze fixed on the shimmering spires of glass and steel and composite just beyond the duraglass window, "you will be sent to a city called Torzhaan. It lies in Zhoraan's temperate zone, and is the capital of the planet's most populous district. There, you will be placed in a position with something that is roughly the equivalent of a city planning office, although in Zhore society, that means more focus on the arcosphere—"

"The what?" she interrupted, still too shaken to prevent herself from breaking into his narrative, even though she knew interruptions annoyed him.

But apparently he was still pleased with himself over the whole shoulder-massage incident, since he replied in mild enough tones, "The Zhore are very focused on horticulture, on sustainable living spaces. Even in their cities—which are far less dense than ours, because of their lower population—every rooftop, every balcony, has its own garden. As far as we can tell, the local government has its own agency to oversee those gardens and make sure that they're functioning at full capacity. Anyway, it's in that division where you'll be placed. People seem to come and go more or less at will, taking what they call 'leaves' from time to time as it suits them."

That sounded very odd to Trinity. At least, no one she'd ever known had just walked away from a decent-paying job. They were difficult to get, and living on Gaia was expensive. She asked, "And no one will ask any questions about why I'm suddenly working there, out of the blue?"

"It's always a possibility, but our analysis of the Zhore so far shows them to be a trusting people, not given to suspicion. Maybe something to do with their empathic traits—if they can sense the emotions of those around them, then it's far more difficult to pretend, to dissemble."

To lie. Trinity knotted her fingers together. She supposed that Gabriel Brant and his superiors were relying on her psychic abilities to keep her out of trouble; if the language conditioning did its job, she'd be able to read the Zhores' thoughts easily enough, and could ask for an immediate extraction if her cover was penetrated somehow. And although what she knew about gardening could fit into her bathroom sink, at least working with plants and flowers didn't sound too scary. It could have been worse.

"So I go and work on these arcospheres, or whatever you call them," she said. "And…what? Just spy on everything I see?"

"You, Trinity, will have to do very little, except maintain the façade that you're merely a worker like hundreds of others. You'll have a device implanted that sees everything you see, hears everything you hear. The device will transmit all that data back to our operatives, who will analyze it."

"As easy as that?" she asked. Just being a passive data collector didn't sound too difficult, at least once you got past the whole infiltrating an alien society thing.

Gabriel turned away from the window and watched her for a few seconds. No, he wasn't exactly smiling, but something in that cool regard made the hairs on the back of her neck want to stand right up. "Well, there is one more thing…."

Of course there was. She lifted her chin and matched him stare for stare. "And what might that be?"

"We're very curious as to what the offspring of a human/Zhore pairing would be like, which traits it would inherit from each parent." Now her handler did smile, a lift at the corners of his mouth that was as empty and soulless as the grimace of a shark. "We want you, Trinity, to locate a compatible Zhore male and mate with him, then return to us so we can study the resulting pregnancy and subsequent birth."

Zhandar wasn't sure why Rozhara would request his presence at another counseling session so soon after the last one—it had been less than a week—but he dutifully went to her offices at the third hour of the afternoon after informing Leizha that he would most likely be gone for the rest of the day. She hadn't asked any questions, for which he was grateful. The last thing he wanted to do was admit that his once-weekly counseling appointment no longer appeared to be sufficient in his counselor's eyes. The appointments were something he hadn't bothered to hide from his assistant, although he knew the rest of his staff was so far unaware of his destination when he left every third-day at the eleventh hour of the morning.

When he entered Rozhara's office, he was startled to see someone else there. A man, judging by his height and the breadth of his shoulders. Not quite as tall as Zhandar himself, but tall enough that they would have been able to look into one another's eyes…if either of them would ever be mad enough to indulge such a breach of protocol.

"Zhandar," said Rozhara. "This is Jalzhin. He is with the Ministry of Health Services."

Anxiety bubbled within Zhandar, but he pressed his hands together and bowed, giving the ancient gesture of respect. "Your presence honors me."

"As yours does me," Jalzhin replied.

Custom satisfied, Zhandar crossed his arms and transferred his gaze to Rozhara, whose head was slightly bowed. Although she was too well-mannered to broadcast anything of what she was feeling, he could tell that she was not overly thrilled by the intrusion of this Jalzhin, whatever his reasons might be.

But because she was a forthright person, and not one to hesitate even in uncomfortable situations, she said briskly, "Zhandar, you know I must submit reports to the Ministry as to the progress of my patients. No particulars, of course, nothing that would identify any of you individually. However—"

"However," Jalzhin broke in, "there were enough details in your case that it was not difficult to ascertain who it was that had suffered such a tragedy in the recent past. My condolences."

"My thanks," Zhandar said stiffly. He already didn't like the tenor of this interview, although nothing unpleasant had yet been spoken. Then again, Jalzhin's presence here was enough to send flickers of unease down Zhandar's spine. Agents of the Ministry of Health did not, as a rule, make social calls.

"We find it somewhat troubling that there does not seem to be any particular progress in your case."

"Indeed?"

Despite the ice in Zhandar's tone, Jalzhin appeared unfazed. Voice smooth and unruffled, he went on, "We all understand that one does not recover from such a loss overnight. But it is time that you thought of Zhoraan."

"I…what?" Zhandar swiveled his head toward Rozhara. Now her gloved fingers were knotted together, a sure sign of her distress. In fact, even though she usually was more than capable of blanking away most of her emotions so they would not trouble those around her, or interfere with her sessions, now he could feel the agitation flowing out from her, coupled with an awkwardness at having to be present during this conversation at all.

"You cannot be unaware of the crisis that faces us all."

"Of course I'm not unaware! That is precisely why Elzhair lost her life—attempting in her own way to stave off our ruin. But she is gone, and our child with her. What else do you expect of me?"

Jalzhin did not flinch, even in the face of so embarrassing an outburst. "We expect you to do your duty by Zhoraan. You have shown yourself capable of fathering a child. There are many of your generation who cannot even do that. It is time for you to look past your grief, and try again."

This was impossible. If he had not been here, listening to Jalzhin's outrageously inappropriate suggestions, he would have thought someone was playing a very cruel joke. As it was….

"I believe I have had enough of this conversation," Zhandar said, and began to turn toward the door.

But Jalzhin's voice stopped him. "Perhaps you have, but I have not. I will say the things that must be said, and you will stay and listen to them."

Never in his life had Zhandar been spoken to in such a manner. This was not the way of his people; all was politeness, all was courtesy and grace. At least in conversations among strangers. Other emotions, darker things, could swim beneath the surface in intimate discourse, but never would they be allowed to rise to a point where they could be seen.

Until now, apparently.

Jaw clenched, he slowly shifted back toward the agent of the Ministry. "I doubt very much that I will want to hear what you have to say."

"Perhaps not." Beneath his heavy robes, Jalzhin's shoulders lifted. "But when the very future of our planet is at stake, we cannot afford to maintain the niceties that have served us for so long." He paused, and for the first time Zhandar could sense a hint of uncertainty in the other man's manner. "As soon as our scientists and statisticians began to note the decline in our population, we began to conduct secret research, work that we did not want to share with the general population for fear of creating, if not a panic, then at least an ever-increasing fear that our way of life may be coming to an end."

It is coming to an end, Zhandar thought bitterly. *Even if no one has the courage to admit it.*

He did not speak those words aloud, however. Instead, he asked, "Am I to assume this work has something to do with me?"

"In a manner of speaking." Some of the confidence seemed to have returned to Jalzhin as he continued, "For uncounted millennia, we have relied upon the concept of *sayara* to bring our people together. And for all that time, it served us well. Unlike the other sentient races of the galaxy, we have no acrimony in our marriages. Divorce was an alien concept until we moved into the wider galaxy and witnessed such practices among the Gaians and the Eridanis."

The agent of the Ministry paused then, as if expecting Zhandar to comment. But he had nothing to contribute. He had heard of such things, yes, but he was not a member of the diplomatic corps. He had seen no need to study the alien races of the galaxy in any depth. His life was here on Zhoraan…a life he had expected to share with Elzhair until it was their time to move from this world into the next. It had mattered very little to him that the Gaians or the Eridanis—and, for all he knew, the Stacians as well—could not count on that sort of permanence in their relationships.

Jalzhin seemed to gather himself and plunge ahead, since Zhandar had not spoken, and Rozhara appeared content to be a silent witness to their conversation. Perhaps she had insisted on remaining, rather than allow her counselee to be left alone with a Ministry official.

"But the concept of *sayara* is failing us now. Indeed, it is *sayara* itself that causes some of the problem, for in some cases it seems to circumvent the very act of conception, rather than aid it. Because of that, we can no longer rely solely on the elusiveness of that emotional bond to dictate who we pair with, who we can conceive our children with. We must put it aside and focus on the practical."

This was—it was beyond blasphemy. It was a negation of everything the Zhore held dear. To lie down with a woman who did not share the sayara bond with him? He had heard the Gaians practiced such things, removing completely from the equation of conception any sort of emotional intimacy. He had merely thought it another of their oddities. Certainly he had never considered that he might one day be put in a similar situation.

"And so you expect me to be…what, exactly? A stud who will service as many females as necessary, like a bull rezhar?"

Rozhara winced at the harsh words. Jalzhin, however, did not flinch. But his counselor's voice was calm enough as she said,

"That sounds quite dreadful, Zhandar, and far worse than what Jalzhin actually intends. Please let him speak."

The agent from the Ministry tugged at his robes, making a minute adjustment that wasn't necessary. "I believe the process will not be nearly as painful as you anticipate. As I had begun to tell you, our scientists have been working on what you might refer to as an acceptable alternative."

"'Acceptable alternative'?" Zhandar repeated, not bothering to hide the disdain in his voice. "I wasn't aware there was a way you could find an alternative to the need to have an all-encompassing emotional connection to someone."

Perhaps Jalzhin smiled within his hood. Of course Zhandar couldn't see the other man's face, but something about his stance seemed to alter subtly, as if he was pleased by Zhandar's remark, even though he hadn't intended it to be anything other than sarcastic.

"What you, Zhandar, see as a sort of mystical bond—what all our people see as such a thing—is in reality only a series of chemical reactions within the brain and body. After much study, we were able to successfully replicate those reactions in the laboratory. We now have the means to artificially create the sayara bond."

This was getting worse and worse. So that was all his connection to Elzhair had ever been—chemicals and pheromones, and nothing more? Zhandar refused to believe that. He would not believe that.

"And so you think you will administer this drug to me, and present me with a woman who has taken the same drug, and we will bond immediately and produce many children for Zhoraan?"

"That is rather a callous way to phrase it," Jalzhin replied. "But yes, in so many words."

"And if I refuse?"

Rozhara shook her head, saying, "I know how difficult this must be to hear, Zhandar, how it challenges beliefs you've held all your life. But you must look past your pain. Do you want Zhoraan to dwindle into the dark, to become nothing? We have not sought to make the galaxy ours, not the way the Gaians have, but at the same time, we have a stake in its future. I would like to believe that we make it a better place by being among its citizens. All that will go away—not in our generation, perhaps, or even the one after it. But that day will come if we do not do something. If I were still of an age to bear children, I would be offering myself. But that time is past for me. It is not, however, past for you."

For just the briefest second, right before she tamped it down immediately, Zhandar could feel a pulse of emotion coming from Rozhara—frustration, regret. And laid over all that, annoyance with him, for what she saw as his selfishness. In that moment, he wondered whether she had done a bit more than simply submitting reports about him, and had actually put his name forward as a promising candidate for Jalzhin's insane program.

That suspicion only made anger flare in him, so he pushed it away for now as being unproductive. Instead, he had to ask himself, was he being selfish? He had only thought he was honoring Elzhair's memory by being so steadfast to her. After all, it was very uncommon for those among his people to create a second *sayara* bond, if fate or misfortune took one's first life partner away.

And now Jalzhin was saying that such a bond could be created with a simple shot, or pill, or implant, or whichever delivery system they'd devised to administer their drug. How many subjects had they tested it on? Enough to be certain that it worked, or Jalzhin would never have come here with his ridiculous proposals.

Or perhaps not so ridiculous. Zhoraan faced a grim future. If he, Zhandar, could do something to stave off the darkness, was it not his responsibility to take on the task, no matter how repugnant it might seem to him at the moment?

And he had so very much looked forward to being a father....

Well, there wasn't much of a question after all, was there?

"Very well," he said heavily. "Tell me what I must do."

FOUR

BILE ROSE IN THE BACK OF TRINITY'S THROAT, BUT SHE FORCED herself to swallow. "I've had my shots," she told Gabriel Brant, referring to the quarterly birth control shots every woman on Gaia began to receive as soon as she turned fourteen. True, there were a few precocious types who still managed to find themselves pregnant before then, but the incidence of unplanned conception was still very low.

His smile didn't falter. "They can be neutralized with a series of counter-shots. That will not be a problem."

She'd had a feeling her stratagem wouldn't buy her much, especially since she herself was the result of her mother using those very same counter-shots, but she'd still had to try, just in case. Time for another angle. "And maybe I'm not even fertile."

"Oh, you are," he replied smoothly. "Your latest physical indicated that you were in perfect health, including reproductive."

Of course they'd pulled her medical records. Why had she been expecting anything different? Gabriel and the people he worked for probably knew more about her than she herself did, right down to her scores on the standardized tests she'd taken back in primary school. She'd been a good student. And that was before her powers even began to manifest. No, that hadn't happened until she was twelve. Once she'd understood what was happening to her, she realized she could tap into anyone's mind to get the answers to test questions, to see what their take on the latest essay assignment was... anything at all, really.

But she hadn't. She told herself that she'd done well in school before this strange ability to read minds had developed, and she wasn't going to turn into a cheat. Back then, she hadn't been entirely certain that the whole thing wouldn't simply go away, disappearing as quickly as it had appeared. Relying on this new talent to get ahead in school hadn't seemed very smart.

However, the powers hadn't gone away. They'd turned out to be as much *her* as the color of her eyes or the shape of her mouth. And ever since she'd been wrestling with them—how to use them, whether she should tell anyone besides her mother. At least, for all Acantha Knox's problems, she'd never tried to exploit her daughter's talents, had in fact almost looked frightened and told Trinity that she had to be careful, that she could never reveal that secret to anyone else. And she never had...not until Caleb.

That hadn't gone so well.

Not that this little session was going so great, either. She swallowed again. "So, all right. I get pregnant and have a half-Zhore baby. What then?"

"We'll study it, of course."

Of course. "You won't—you won't *hurt* it?"

The shark smile returned. "Developing maternal instincts, Trinity?"

"I don't know about maternal, but I do know about basic human decency," she retorted. "This child—if I even have it—will be half mine as well."

"Not really. Handing the child over to us will be a condition of your release."

She already disliked him, but in that moment, hatred flared in her, a raging fire of loathing burning in her belly. It would be better to go to Titan than suffer through this. How could it be any worse to be some guard's plaything than it would to be forced to have sex with an alien, bear his child, and have that child taken away to become someone's science experiment?

Without thinking, she pushed herself up out of her seat. She had to get out of here, get away from Gabriel. Never mind that she wasn't sure she'd even be able to open the door of this conference room without his assistance.

She hadn't made it more than two strides before he was beside her, his hand clamping down cruelly on her arm. Despite the pain, she wouldn't allow herself to cry out. She wouldn't give him the satisfaction.

"Do you really think you have any say in all this, Trinity?" he asked. His grip tightened even more, and she couldn't help wincing. How long would it take for those bruises to appear? Not very long, probably.

She didn't respond, but only glared at him. What would be the point in speaking? He knew he held all the cards here, and trying to protest that reality wouldn't change anything.

"You forfeited your rights when you committed a crime," he said. "You belong to us now. Do you understand?"

That was wrong. Even accused criminals had rights. Rights to a fair trial. Rights to contact a sympathetic party, whether friend, family member, or advocate. She'd been given none of those things, because she was no ordinary criminal. She had something the Consortium's intelligence arm wanted. Now she was an asset, something to be ruthlessly exploited.

Her heart was hammering so hard in her chest that she was sure Gabriel must hear it pounding. Not trusting herself to speak, she nodded.

"Say it."

A lump seemed to have formed in her throat, preventing her from speaking. She swallowed, hard. "I understand," she whispered.

"Good," he said. "Now, let's get to work."

There were a depressing number of candidates to bear his child. Most of them quite young, not having yet made a *sayara* match. A few somewhat older, possibly unlucky souls like him, women who had lost their partners through some misfortune.

And then there was Leizha.

He'd blinked in surprise and almost dropped his handheld when her name and image appeared on the screen. Jalzhin had sent him information on all the possible applicants, saying that Zhandar should choose the one who most appealed to him. Apparently, the Ministry had been sending out feelers for some time, searching for young women who were of the proper age and temperament to be suitable.

When Zhandar had asked whether these women knew the identity of the man they might possibly be matched with, Jalzhin had shaken his head. "No. They are given a general description, along with a few particulars of your case. But they do not know your name, or your position."

That had been somewhat reassuring. However, as he gazed at Leizha's image—not that it revealed much, since of course she was hooded—Zhandar began to wonder. True, most of these women could know nothing of who he was. But Leizha had worked with him almost every day for the past two years. She knew of the loss he had suffered. She knew how old he was, where he worked, where he lived. It wouldn't have been that difficult for her to put the pieces together and realize that this man the Ministry was setting forward as a possible future partner was none other than the person she'd been quietly pursuing—in her mind, if nowhere else—for the last few months.

"Perhaps it would be better that way," he mused aloud. Since he was now alone in his apartment, it didn't matter. No one was there to hear him speak, and besides, he sometimes worked through problems this way, voicing them out loud, as if actually hearing them gave them more substance, something he could wrestle with.

Elzhair used to tease him about his habit—"talking to yourself again?"—but she'd always smiled as she'd done so. She understood why the process was important to him.

And now he was utilizing it to possibly choose her successor.

No, not that. Whoever he selected, she wouldn't truly be Elzhair's successor. She would be some strange counterfeit, an impostor, bound to him only because of that insidious drug the Ministry's scientists had devised.

Frowning, he set the handheld down on the tabletop, then rose from his seat and went to stand at the window. Because he was alone, he'd divested himself of his heavy robes and had on only the close-fitting tunic and pants that were customary to wear beneath the billowing hooded cloak. There was no danger of anyone seeing him thus unrobed, however, as the glass of the window was treated so that he could see out, but no one could see in. The sun was setting, sending a brilliant golden glow over Torzhaan, making the tall buildings sparkle and the leaves of the plants in the rooftop gardens turn almost bronze.

It was beautiful, and yet it still awoke an ache within him. He'd often stood with Elzhair thus, watching the sun go down. Most of his kind preferred their widely scattered homesteads in the countryside. Cities were a necessary evil, and part of the reason why so many felt the need to go on retreat after a few years of work in a population center. But he had always loved these towers of glass, which should have been cold and sterile, but weren't, because of the work he and others like him did to make every roof and balcony bloom with life.

"At least I know Leizha," he said. True. They had spent many hours together, overseeing the irrigation systems that fed the city's gardens, choosing the plants that would flourish, conducting seminars on how best to care for these precious living resources. He knew something of how she thought. The sound of her voice was familiar to him.

But to be together in such a way....

"Can I do that?"

He had no answer. Jalzhin had assured him that the drug would topple those barriers, create an attraction where none should have existed. But there could not be any artificial conception beyond that. They had developed the drug, but the scientists had been unsuccessful in fertilizing a female Zhore's egg. There was something missing, something that could only occur during actual intercourse.

To be that intimate with Leizha?

Perhaps it would be easier with a stranger. He had put the mere notion of such physical acts out of his mind for many, many months. That was not to say that he hadn't enjoyed it very much when he was with Elzhair. He'd heard that the Gaians and the Eridanis thought the Zhore odd and cold, in the way they covered every inch of their bodies and never, ever touched one another in public. That was not because they were cold, however. It was the very opposite. Their blood ran hot when with their partners, a heat that could only be quenched in hours of exploration of one another's bodies. Why, one time with Elzhair, they hadn't risen from their bed for nearly an entire day....

Zhandar had to push that thought aside, as even now the memory stirred the need in his body, waking a desire he could do nothing to satisfy. Well, that wasn't precisely true. He knew that all he had to do was make his selection, then send the information on to Jalzhin. And soon after that—very soon, based on the other man's hints—the woman of his choice would be sent to him. A small purple pill, and then he would want her as he'd once wanted Elzhair. Simple as that.

Or perhaps not so simple.

He picked up the handheld and activated the screen. Although it was taboo to reveal one's face, save to one's immediate family and *sayara* partner, and perhaps a few very close friends, Zhandar wished he could see Leizha's features. Perhaps then he'd know whether he was making the right choice. Unlike humans or Eridanis, the Zhore did not base their attractions on physical appearance, but rather spiritual and intellectual compatibility.

Even so, he would have given a lot right then to be able to look into Leizha's eyes.

It had been a long black sleep, one in which uncounted hours passed. When Trinity finally blinked at the darkened room around her, her eyelids felt gummy, lashes pasted together the way they once had been when she'd had a bad fever as a child. Everything seemed to swim around her.

But then there was pressure on her flesh, someone's fingers wrapping around hers. She'd floated in darkness for long that she instinctively latched onto those fingers, clinging to them the way someone drowning might grasp their rescuer's hand.

Gabriel's voice. "How do you feel?"

Realizing it was his fingers she clutched so tightly, she let go at once, then forced her eyes all the way open. She lay in a hospital bed. Tubes ran from a machine placed off to one side and terminated in her left arm.

No, wait…that couldn't be her arm. The skin was black as night and yet shimmered with all the colors of the rainbow at the same time. And when she jerked in shock, staring down at the unfamiliar limb, she could see the scales rippling as her muscles moved beneath that alien skin.

One of those hateful chuckles. "Yes, the operation was a complete success. No rejection of the foreign tissue so far. But the doctors want you to stay in bed for another twenty-four hours. After that, you'll be able to get up."

Even though she hated to display such weakness in front of him, she had to know. Almost of their own accord, her fingers reached up to touch her face, to explore the contours of her cheeks and nose and chin. Yes, that felt like her eyebrows, like her mouth. The bones underneath hadn't changed. It was only the skin that lay on top that was so very, very different.

"I suppose it will take some getting used to," he added. "On the other hand, I think it suits you. It brings out your eyes."

She wanted to scowl at him, but it hurt. That was when she realized she ached all over, as if someone had shoved her in a sack and then kicked her repeatedly. Well, maybe that wasn't too far off the mark. It wasn't every day that you had your entire epidermis replaced.

All right, not exactly replaced. According to Gabriel, she was still underneath there somewhere. She certainly didn't have the strength or the courage to make a tiny little cut in that new skin and find out for herself whether her own human skin lay untouched below it.

Off to her left, a door opened, and a doctor entered the room. At least, Trinity assumed the tired-looking woman was a doctor. She came over and peered at the readouts on the machines, then tapped a few notes on the handheld she fished out of the pocket of her scrubs.

"Everything all right?" Gabriel inquired.

"Healing nicely," the doctor replied. "I understand the need to speak with her, but try not to tire her out too much."

"Of course."

Brisk fingers against her wrist, feeling her pulse, and then the doctor made a final notation before letting herself out again.

"How long?" Trinity finally rasped, the words feeling like sandpaper against her dry throat.

Gabriel didn't reply at first, but instead lifted a blue plastic cup from the bedside table and held it against her lips. "Try some ice chips."

She let them slide over her tongue and then down her throat, cool, soothing. "More," she whispered.

Obliging her, he tipped a few more of the chips into her mouth. She hated feeling like this, like she didn't even have the strength to lift a plastic cup. And she hated even more that it was Gabriel Brant helping her, watching her helplessness and somehow taking a perverse pleasure in it.

Then he said, "Three days."

Three days of her life gone. Three days she'd swum in darkness. She remembered nothing of the surgery, which was probably just as well.

It hadn't all been dark and empty, though. For some reason, she recalled a man's voice, soft, deep, speaking words she'd never heard before, a language of sibilant sounds and rounded vowels, one that seemed to wrap around her and warm her.

"*Zhara sel tranhir?*" Gabriel asked, and she responded automatically,

"*Zhahir en trallen.*" Then her eyes widened. "Was that…?"

"Yes. Zhoraani. We had the sleep conditioning going the entire time you were out."

Trinity blinked. Yes, Gabriel had said that her language training would go on in the background while she swam in unconsciousness, would be implanted in her mind so she would not have to spend rigorous weeks or even months learning the alien tongue, but she hadn't thought it would be this easy. She hadn't even stopped to pick out the words, but had replied as naturally as if she were speaking the Galactic Standard that she'd known all her life. What they'd said was,

You are all right?

I am fine.

Was it possible that this insane plan might actually have a chance of succeeding?

"Your accent is very good," he said. Then he reached down and touched a strand of her hair. It, too, was black as night, startling against the white hospital gown she wore. If she hadn't been so tired, she might have flinched.

"Sleep now," he added. "We can talk again tomorrow, after you've gotten more rest."

Trinity wanted to protest that she'd already slept for days, but for some reason, she couldn't find the energy to speak. Instead, she felt her head sliding back against the pillow, lassitude overcoming all her limbs. Maybe she'd had enough of darkness, but it hadn't yet had its fill of her.

The next morning, she asked for a mirror. Yes, she knew she was changed, altered to become a facsimile of something unutterably alien, but she needed the evidence of her own eyes to tell her it was all real.

"Go ahead," Gabriel told the nurse, who hovered near the door, looking anxious. "She'll need to see sometime."

The nurse nodded and then fled, returning a few minutes later with a small steel-framed mirror approximately ten centimeters square. However, she didn't give it to Trinity, but rather to Gabriel, as if she wanted him to be responsible for any reaction Trinity might have to her altered appearance.

He smiled. "I'll call if I need you."

And of course the nurse went right back out again, closing the door behind her. Trinity still didn't know his exact title, but it was fairly clear that Gabriel's word was law around here.

Gazing down at her, he turned the mirror over and over in his hands. Stray images reflected in its surface and then disappeared—the blinking lights of the machines overseeing her recovery, the muted fixtures overhead, the face of the man who stood next to her bed, with those gleaming charcoal eyes and ironic mouth.

But not once was she able to catch a glimpse of her own reflection.

"Please," she whispered. She knew by doing so she was giving in to his need to see her subordinate to him, but right then being able to see what they had done to her was far more important than playing mind games with Gabriel Brant.

Wordlessly, he handed the mirror to her. She took it from him, her fingers touching the cool surface. Strange how the information transmitted to her brain from her skin didn't seem any different. She'd worried about that, wondered if having the world translated through another race's flesh would change her perception of it. But no, the mirror felt like a mirror, although the hands holding it were so incredibly altered.

A long pause. She was conscious of Gabriel's eyes on her, but she didn't dare glance up at him. Bad enough that he was there at all. She wouldn't give him the satisfaction of seeing the fear in her eyes.

Then she slowly lifted the mirror toward her face.

The eyes were the same, although their blue-green shade now seemed intensified a hundred-fold because of the night-black skin around them. Her lashes were as sooty and black as her hair. And that was her nose, and the high, wide cheekbones. Strangely, her mouth seemed the most different, although as she looked more closely, she realized its shape hadn't been altered, only that it appeared so changed because it was more or less the same color as the rest of her skin, and she was used to wearing deep-toned lip stains that contrasted with her fair complexion.

So…it was her, that reflection, and yet it wasn't. It was Trinity Knox, translated into Zhore.

"Well?" said Gabriel at last.

"It's…different," she managed. A silly response, but she really didn't know what else to say. She wasn't about to confess to relief that she could still see herself in there, if she looked closely enough.

"True." He moved closer to the bed and took the mirror from her. "You're beautiful, Trinity."

She did slant a glance up at him then, sure he was teasing her in the cruelest way. And perhaps he was, but she couldn't tell for sure. He looked serious, the ironic glint gone from his eyes. For once, he wasn't even smiling in that smug way of his.

"I don't know about that," she replied. How shaky her voice sounded. She could only hope he'd attribute that tremor to her continued recovery from the surgery she'd undergone.

"I do." He set the mirror down on the bedside table and turned back toward her. "So how do you feel today?"

"Better, I suppose. I don't hurt as much. My head still aches, though." Which was only the truth. She'd woken up with her temples pounding. Her thoughts had seemed to ring with alien syllables, sounds that she could only translate if she didn't concentrate too hard.

In a way, it had reminded her of being twelve again and having her talent—or curse, depending on how you looked at it—descend on her. At first, she'd thought she was going crazy. The inside of her head had sounded as if someone had turned on every channel in their entertainment unit simultaneously. It was too much, and she'd missed almost three weeks of school, writhing in bed, hands pressed against her ears, until slowly she began to build up the barriers she needed to keep out other people's thoughts. She'd had no one to assist her; it had all been trial and error, pushing at the voices in her head until they finally, mercifully left her alone.

Well, unless she wanted to hear them. She'd learned to focus on a particular person, if she needed to know what they were thinking. It wasn't nearly as much fun or as interesting as she'd thought mind reading might be, once she understood what this particular gift of hers entailed. People's thoughts tended to chase one another, round and round, and as for their opinions of those around them…well, they weren't nearly as charitable or as complimentary as Trinity had hoped. She'd quickly learned to keep them all at bay. It was just easier that way.

She must have been frowning as those unpleasant recollections surfaced, because Gabriel leaned toward her solicitously and asked, "Should I call for the nurse? She can give you something for that."

Trinity was sure they had all sorts of useful drugs on hand. Now that she'd come out safely on the other side of her surgery, however, she didn't feel at all inclined to dull her senses any more than they already had been.

"No, it's fine," she replied, summoning a smile, although the flesh of her face felt strange as the skin on her cheeks stretched. Perhaps Zhore skin wasn't as elastic as human skin. "I'm sure it'll go away soon enough. My headaches generally do."

He seemed satisfied with her reply, since he put aside the discussion of her headache and said, "Good. I was hoping you'd be recovered enough to begin the next phase of your training."

"Which is?" She didn't think she liked the sound of this "training," although she knew there was probably a great deal more preparation she'd have to go through before Gabriel and the people pulling his strings deemed her ready for her infiltration of Zhore society.

"Nothing too strenuous," he told her. Now the smile was back, showing his amusement at her trepidation. "We went back and forth on this, but we decided that it would be better for you to experience as much as you can in this form, so you can get used to it, so it can become you. You'll be training with Blake next. Your power to read minds is very strong, according to him, but your natural defenses aren't as robust as they should be."

Trinity began to bristle, and Gabriel raised a hand.

"I don't mean that as an insult. But besides Blake, have you ever met anyone with your particular talents?"

She shook her head. "No."

"Not surprising. We've calculated that the incidence of true psi powers such as yours is less than one in a hundred million. So it makes sense that you would never have crossed paths with another 'talented' individual, and therefore wouldn't have developed the abilities that would allow you to keep intruders out of your mind."

No arguing there. The way Blake had been able to penetrate her mind had been disturbing, to say the least. True, she'd created her own barriers, but those were intended solely to keep other people's stray thoughts from getting into her brain. Dealing with someone like Blake was completely different.

Since she offered no comment, Gabriel seemed happy to plow ahead. "But living among the Zhore will be very different. They aren't true psychics, but they still can sense emotion, as far as we've been able to tell. So Blake will train you how to keep all that banked down. After all, the last thing we want is for the Zhore to smell fear on you."

No, she supposed not. Precisely how easy it would be to train that fear out of her…or at least block it…she wasn't sure. After all, she'd never counted on being dropped in the middle of an alien planet to spy on its inhabitants…to get closer than she'd ever dreamed to one of them….

A shiver went through her, and all she could do was nod. In that moment, she thought her fear and her worry must be so intense that the Zhore could sense it all the way from their home world here to Gaia.

She didn't think a barrier existed which could conceal terror like that.

FIVE

IN THE END, ZHANDAR DID NOT CONTACT JALZHIN, AGENT OF the Ministry of Health. Instead, he waited until he and Leizha were alone, the other workers in their department out on their various field assignments, making sure the plants and flowers of Torzhaan continued to replenish the air and feed both the stomachs and the souls of the city's inhabitants.

Since he was the supervisor of the department, he had a large private office situated in one corner of the building. Leizha came to him there, trepidation clear in her hesitant steps and the way she cast a glance backward at the empty space behind her. Zhandar had heard that the Gaians liked to put their workers in little boxes to work, but that was not the way here on Zhoraan. He had his office, true, and Leizha, as his assistant, a smaller one, but the rest of the workspace was open, with tables and chairs arranged attractively in the center of the floor, and potted plants all around. Water cascaded down glass waterfalls to either side of the corridor that led to the banks of elevators.

A smaller waterfall flowed down an expanse of beaten copper on the wall behind him. Normally, Zhandar found the sound soothing, but now, as Leizha entered the office, he found the soft burble of the water almost intrusive.

"What is it, Zhandar?" she asked after shutting the door behind her, then taking the chair in front of his desk.

In his mind, he had practiced myriad ways of broaching the subject to her, but now, with his assistant facing him on the other side of his desk of carved zhel, he could only push his handheld across the tabletop, the screen set to her hooded image with her information overlaid on top.

A small sigh escaped her lips, hidden behind the hood that drooped low to conceal her face. "Ah, so it was you."

Was she really going to be that disingenuous? "Are you saying you did not know before this?"

Her gloved fingers twisted around one another. "I had thought...I had guessed." A long pause. "I had hoped."

How could he respond to that revelation? Her voice had sounded calm enough, but he heard the tremor behind it. Although his people were supposed to keep their emotions tightly controlled at all times, he could sense some of her worry, her doubt, seeping out from beneath those barriers. And even farther down, beneath the fear…a sense of relief?

"So you would allow yourself to be part of this experiment?"

The words had come out more harshly than he'd intended, and she seemed to flinch. But then she straightened in her chair. Although he couldn't see her face, he thought she must be staring directly at him.

"Yes, if it meant a chance at having the life I've always wanted. A life with you."

In that moment, he could only marvel at her bravery. He wasn't sure he would have been able to be so forthright if their roles had been reversed. "How long?" he asked simply.

"Longer than you would care to know." Her shoulders lifted. "I knew it was wrong. You were bonded to your wife. I knew I was not *sayara* with you. I did my best to put the attraction aside, to try to meet someone suitable. But no one was *sayara* for me, either. I thought I was doomed to be one of those who live their lives alone, unpartnered. And then after Elzhair…." Leizha let the words trail off, even as Zhandar felt his throat constrict, the loss seeming as fresh now as it had been a year ago. His assistant took a breath, then went on, "Once you were alone, I thought…I hoped…perhaps there would be some way for us to be together, even if we did not share the *sayara* bond. It is not entirely unprecedented, although rare."

"And yet you said nothing to me."

"How could I?" she said simply, but he could feel the embarrassment and the tension flaring out from her. "There seemed to be no end to your grief, and I would not intrude on that. But when the call went out from the Ministry...."

"Yes, about that. How precisely did that work?"

Again she shrugged. "There was a message on my handheld. I suppose they must have been tracking those of us who were of a certain age but who had not yet bonded with a partner. But all that message said was to arrange an appointment with my local branch of the Ministry. It wasn't until I went and spoke with one of its agents in person that I was told what their true mission was."

"And it didn't shock you?" If it had, Leizha seemed to be recovered now. Despite those frazzled emotions leaking past her barriers, her voice was still measured, calm.

"At first. After all, how could anyone manufacture the *sayara* bond? It is one of the things we hold most sacred. But after I spoke with Jalzhin, I understood better how it all might work."

Jalzhin again. Zhandar supposed it wasn't that strange that he should be the one to speak with Leizha. There was a finite number of agents working at the Ministry's offices here in Torzhaan, so the odds dictated there was a good chance he would also be assigned to Leizha. Even so, Zhandar had the distinct impression that more than the hand of fate was at work here.

"And then once you received your own list of possible candidates…."

This time she did look away from him, her hood swiveling toward the window. "It was not so simple as that. We were told we would be the ones being selected, not the other way around. However, Jalzhin did tell me of several of the men who would be approached, described their situations. And when he said that one of them had lost his wife a year earlier, and that he also had a prestigious position here in the city…well, it was not so difficult for me to piece together those details and deduce that the man in question must be you."

As he had thought. The question was, now that they had both been revealed to one another, what next? Should he bow his head to fate, and become part of the Ministry's experiment?

The thing was, he had sensed yearning and need from Leizha, but no real passion. It was possible that she had done a better job of hiding it than her other emotions, but Zhandar wasn't so sure. In all their time working together, Leizha had always impressed him as a remarkably level-headed woman, even more so than one might expect from one of his race. Perhaps she had no true fire at her core, and that was why she had never bonded with anyone else. Her attraction to him could be based on a simple need for companionship, without truly understanding what could attach a man to a woman, make him want to live for her.

Or die for her.

The sound of the waterfall somewhat masked the silence in the room, but it could not erase that uneasy quiet completely. Leizha waited, clearly expecting him to speak next. However, he had no idea what to say. That he would put aside all his misgivings, take Jalzhin's misbegotten drug, and see what happened next? That perhaps the drug would engender the passion she so far seemed to lack?

His entire body and soul quailed at the prospect. He had told Jalzhin he would consider it, and had in fact called Leizha in to speak on the topic so that he might make up his mind once and for all. Now, though, with her sitting there and watching him, Zhandar found his resolve deserting him. He could not do this. He *would* not.

"Thank you for your honesty, Leizha," he said at last. "You have given me much to think on."

He'd meant the words as a dismissal, and she did not overlook that. A brief clap of anger, quickly hidden, and then she got to her feet, saying,

"That is all? After I have told you the truth of my heart, you will send me away as if we had discussed nothing more important than a new order of irrigation tubing?"

That, he felt, was being somewhat melodramatic. Yes, she had spoken somewhat of her feelings, but it was not as if she had flung herself into his arms and told Zhandar of her undying love for him.

Not that he would have wanted such a thing, of course. In fact, he was very grateful for her restraint. Now, though, he thought she had begun to push things a bit too far.

Forcing his tone to remain even, he said, "This is not something I can make a decision on right now. I wanted to know how matters stood with you, and now I do. If you find my hesitation hurtful, I apologize for that. But I hope that you would not expect me to rush into something as important as this without thinking it over carefully first."

He'd expected her to nod and accept his words as the truth they so plainly were. Instead, she stalked to the door and pushed the button to open it. Stopping in the open doorframe, she snapped, "If it was something you truly wanted, then you would not have to stop and think about it, would you?"

With that parting remark, she was gone, the door whooshing to a close behind her. And Zhandar was left staring after her, wondering what he had just done wrong.

"Freaky," was Blake's observation as Trinity took a seat across from him in a small conference room, one outfitted with only a round table and two chairs.

Since Gabriel had guided her here but then left, saying that Blake didn't want the intrusion of someone else's thoughts in these exercises, Trinity knew she had to stick up for herself. Not blinking, she stared at Blake across the polished plastic surface of the table and asked, "Wasn't that sort of the whole point?"

To her surprise, he grinned. "I suppose so. It's just one thing to hear about it in the abstract, and quite another for it to be facing you in reality." He stopped then and peered into her face, so rudely that if it had been anyone else, she would have been tempted to give him the middle finger. That sort of behavior wouldn't fly here, however. Gabriel might not be physically in the room, but you could be damn sure he was watching through a hidden surveillance system.

"And I'm the 'it'?" she inquired icily.

"Maybe." He continued his inspection of her features, then said, "It's just weird because it looks like you under all that. It's almost like it would be easier to process if you looked completely like someone else."

"Well, I don't. This is how it all worked. So are we going to get on with this?"

Since Blake, as Gabriel Brant had pointed out, didn't have much of a filter, he also didn't take offense at the same things that would irritate a regular person. "Sure. It's not that hard, really. You already have some mechanisms in place to keep other people out, so now it's more a matter of redirecting those mechanisms so you can keep your own emotions and reactions hidden from others."

She nodded. Put that way, it didn't seem too complicated. Of course, things that sounded simple in theory were often difficult when actually put into practice.

"Okay, then." He reached out and pinched her arm, hard. Since her flesh was still tender from the procedure that had turned her into a Zhore, it hurt far more than it normally would, and she gasped.

"What the hell?"

"Hurts, right? And I can feel you broadcasting that pain right at me. So tamp it down before the whole world knows about it."

Bastard. She'd never punched anyone in the face, but in that moment she understood why someone would. Gritting her teeth, Trinity blinked back the throbbing ache in her arm, doing her best to shove it behind the same wall she used to keep other people's thoughts from invading her every waking moment.

"Not bad," Blake allowed. "But I can still feel some of it."

All right, so those walls needed to be a little higher. Even though they existed only in her mind, she made a conscious effort to visualize them, twenty meters, no, fifty meters tall, smooth gray duracrete, impregnable to anything short of a pulse cannon attack. Behind that wall, her emotions could rage all they wanted, but they weren't getting past that barrier.

Blake was silent then, brows knitted together. Trinity realized that he was trying to probe the wall she'd built, looking for any sign of weakness. He wouldn't find one, though. She'd spent the last twelve years making sure nothing could get into it from the outside. It circled the hemisphere of her mind, a fortress that should be able to keep out anyone or anything…even Blake Chu.

"Pretty good," he said at last, settling against the back of his chair with a faint sigh. He reached for the pouch of energy drink he'd brought with him and took a long swallow.

Of course no one had thought to give her an energy drink. Not that she really wanted one; she'd always thought they were pretty nasty. But a nice glass of ice water would do well right about now.

She wouldn't ask for one, though. That would be a sign of weakness. She was pretty sure Gabriel and Blake had conspired to make sure she'd be thirsty during this meeting, and therefore not at the top of her game.

Bring it on, boys, she thought, secure in the knowledge that Blake couldn't possibly get through her defenses. *I can suffer for a half-hour or so. It's not going to kill me.*

"Thanks," she replied, her tone tight. "Anything else?"

He didn't reply at first, but only sat there and stared at her through those rimless glasses he wore. At first she'd thought they were only an affectation. Now she realized they served another purpose. With the light reflecting off the lenses, it was difficult to get a good read on the expression in his eyes. She'd always relied on those sorts of observations to assist her in deciphering what other people were thinking, how they were reacting. In many cases, watching someone's shifting expressions could tell her almost as much as their thoughts did. Now, though....

"Yeah," he said. "Not as easy as you thought, huh? And I'm just one guy wearing glasses. How about a planet full of aliens, all of them hooded? No faces to read. No expressions to interpret. And they tamp down their emotions pretty hard, from what Brant told me. So the only way you're going to get anything from them is if you probe. Hard." He rocked back in his chair. "Try it."

"On you?"

"Who else? No one here but us chickens."

She raised an eyebrow, not understanding the reference. But she knew he didn't want her to ask any questions. He wanted her to do what she'd come here for.

In the past, she'd always been careful when dipping into other people's thoughts. It was easy to get lost in the welter of their emotions, of their hopes and fears and the million stray ideas that passed through someone's head at any given moment. She'd only ever gone in to get one particular piece of information, and in her own mind, she'd always thought of the procedure as rather like using a laser scalpel, a beam of targeted light aimed at a very specific point.

Now, though, when she tried to use the scalpel approach, it was clear that it wouldn't work. It was like trying to poke a needle through a surface made of concrete.

She needed a sledgehammer.

And that was how she visualized it—like an enormous hammer she could slam down on the smooth, unyielding surface of Blake's own defenses.

"Ouch!" he exclaimed, then pushed his chair away from hers. "Subtle, Knox. Real subtle."

"Sorry," she said, although she really didn't mean it. Anyway, trying to get into Blake's mind that way hadn't worked at all. It had felt like swinging a mallet into shatterproof glass. Her attack had bounced back, shaking her as well.

"Obviously, that approach isn't going to work." He shifted, moving so he was perched more or less on the edge of his seat. "You try pulling that crap on a Zhore, and they're going to feel it and be on you so fast, you won't even realize what's happening until you're locked up in jail. Or whatever they use for jail, I guess," he added, with a scratch on the side of his nose. "Anyway, the last thing you want is to do something that's going to attract everyone's attention. So try again."

Trinity frowned, doing the exact opposite of Blake and instead settling against the back of her chair. She could tell she wouldn't be able to brute-force this, so she had to figure out something else. The whole trick was to pick up his thoughts in a way that he wouldn't notice. She needed to be as invisible as the air he breathed.

Like air….

All right, maybe not air exactly, but like the finest of mists, something so delicate and unsubstantial that she could drift through the tiny chinks and cracks in his mental armor, openings so small he probably didn't even know they were there. For all she knew, she had the same sort of defects in her own defenses, but Blake hadn't yet figured out how to exploit them. Hopefully, he never would.

Her intention drifted on the air, settling down on the surface of his mind and seeping through, in the same way the spray from the misters in a greenhouse would gently penetrate the earth in which the plants were growing. He was sitting very still, but she didn't see him startle or make any kind of movement at all. There was even a lopsided smile on his mouth, as if he was laughing internally at her ineptitude.

Yes, that was it exactly. He didn't think she would ever be able to master these skills enough to successfully conceal herself in Zhore society, and he was wishing he'd been tapped for this project instead, even if that meant looking as creepy as she did now. And below that was impatience, because he didn't want this all to drag out too long, since he'd just gotten an upgrade on his VR equipment, and the new model he'd programmed as his companion was even hotter than the last, and….

"And you think I'm a loser," she remarked, pulling herself out of his thoughts and thinking she'd like a shower right about then. "At least I sleep with real people."

Blake's eyes widened in shock, and then he scowled. "Yeah, see where that got you. Computer-generated girlfriends are a lot more trustworthy."

Well, Trinity couldn't really argue with that. And even as she lifted her shoulders to give a fatalistic shrug, Blake seemed to pause, realizing at last the actual implications of her comment.

"You got in."

She nodded.

"All the way in. And…I didn't feel it." He jabbed at his glasses with his index finger, pushing them farther up his nose. "How'd you do it?"

"Trade secret."

His frown deepened. "You shouldn't withhold that kind of information. It may be a technique I could use as well."

"I doubt it," she replied. Maybe he was right; maybe she was breaking some unspoken rule by not telling him everything. But unless Gabriel came in and forced her to divulge how she'd managed that infiltration of Blake's thoughts, she wasn't going to say anything. The last thing she wanted was to give him a weapon he might use against her.

"Trinity—"

The door opened then, and Gabriel stepped in. Trinity stiffened at once, thinking for sure he was going to compel her to explain how she'd gotten past Blake's defenses so easily. But he surprised her by saying,

"Well done, Trinity." His gaze shifted over to Blake. "You can't really expect her to give up all her secrets, can you? But then, I suppose you don't have a lot of experience with women who aren't of the virtual kind."

Blake bristled. "Refusing to share information with fellow team members isn't in anyone's best interests."

"Perhaps." Gabriel gave a negligent wave of his hand. "Leave it for now. I'd like to take Trinity to show her something."

She wasn't sure if she liked the sound of that, but she knew she had no real choice. Rising from her chair, she gave Blake a sticky-sweet smile, then went over to meet Gabriel by the doorway. He watched her closely as she walked toward him, and a shiver went through her. Something about that intent stare made her want to turn and run in the opposite direction.

Stop trying to scare yourself, she thought. *He's probably just looking you over to make sure there isn't anything about your walk that's too un-Zhore-like.*

Then again, how would he even know the way a Zhore female might walk? No, there must be recordings of some kind. The Zhore didn't come to Gaia, but there were other worlds and space stations they did visit occasionally, and it must not be that difficult to get surveillance footage from the cameras in those locations so it could be thoroughly analyzed.

She stopped a foot or so away from Gabriel. He looked past her to Blake. "Write up your findings from this session and send them along to me. I'll expect them within the next two hours."

"Sure, boss." There was such a sneer in Blake's voice that she expected Gabriel would call him on it, but he didn't. Instead, he pointed down the corridor toward their left, saying,

"This way, Trinity."

There was nothing for it but to head in the direction he'd indicated. The hallways were empty, but that didn't surprise her. They were always empty whenever she ventured out of her rooms. After two days in recovery, the doctor, whose name Trinity never learned, said she was healed enough to go back to her suite, and so that was where she'd spent the majority of her time, resting, reading, watching whatever vids Gabriel had determined were safe for her.

And now, going wherever he directed her. Was this it? Had he determined she was ready? She prayed that wasn't the case; although each morning she woke up feeling a bit better, and every day became a bit more accustomed to seeing that alien face in the mirror, she knew she was not prepared for the ordeal of being surrounded by Zhore on all sides, with no friends, no support system, nothing but her own desperation and Gabriel's threats to keep her on course.

The corridor ended in a wide door. Gabriel went to the control pad in the wall next to it and lowered his head so the biometric scanner could read his retinal patterns. Then the door slid open, and Trinity gasped.

She'd assumed they were still somewhere in the large building she'd first been brought to, concealed in plain sight within one of Gaia's many metropolises, although she hadn't recognized the actual location at the time. But they stood now in a lounge area that boasted an entire wall of windows, and beyond those windows was no cityscape, nor anything of Gaia at all. Instead, the glory of an unknown nebula blazed out of the darkness, shimmering in shades of purple and red, pearlescent white and palest gold.

"Where—" she began, then stopped. Maybe she really didn't want to know the answer to that question.

It was too late, though. Gabriel had heard that one syllable, and came up beside her, reaching back with one hand to shut the door behind them.

"One of our bases," he said. To her relief, he kept moving, apparently focused on a long bar of burnished steel to one side of the chamber. After stepping behind the bar, he went on, "We thought it best to perform your… procedure…far away from anyplace where the procedure might be discovered. Besides, we are now located a little more than halfway to Zhoraan, which means a shorter trip when it comes time to send you there."

A shorter trip. Trinity exhaled, thanking whoever or whatever might be looking over hapless creatures such as she for that reprieve, however brief it might be. At least she was not about to be immediately bundled onto a shuttle and sent off into the unknown.

"What would you like?" he inquired, rummaging through one of the cupboards under the bar and producing two glasses.

He'd brought her here for a drink? If it had been someone else, she might have said he merely wanted to have an innocuous celebration of her astonishing recovery, but she doubted that Gabriel Brant ever did anything that could be labeled "innocuous."

Warily, she replied, "Are you sure I should be drinking so soon after…well, after?"

Smiling, he brought out a smooth ovoid bottle of some purple liquid and poured a few inches into one of the glasses. "You're doing remarkably well, Trinity. The doctors have given you a clean bill of health. I doubt one drink will do anything to affect your progress."

She still didn't think she agreed with that observation, but she also knew that arguing with him wasn't a very good idea. "I'm not much of a drinker." How could she be, when she had to keep such a tight grip on her mind's defenses at all times? True, she'd never met anyone like herself, up until now, but she'd always lived with the fear that she might run across someone with similar talents and that they'd be able to see into her thoughts. It was better to stay in control, just in case. Since Gabriel was still staring at her expectantly, she added, "What's that you just poured?"

"'That' is Eridani *volshir*. Would you like some?"

"It's a pretty color."

He grinned and shook his head at her response, then poured just a hair less into her glass than he had into his own. When he was done, he lifted it toward her.

It was an invitation she wished she could refuse. However, her feet somehow carried her across the room and over to the bar. At least its not inconsiderable steel bulk was between her and Gabriel Brant as she reached to take the glass from him.

Their fingers never touched, and relief rushed through her. That was something. If he'd wanted to, he could have made sure she had to touch him to retrieve the glass of *volshir*. Whatever that was.

Maybe he really didn't want to touch her. After all, her skin was no longer human, nor the rest of her. Well, the exterior. Inside, she was just as human as she'd ever been. She wouldn't let them change that about her. She had to cling to that, so she wouldn't forget who she really was.

"To exploration," Gabriel said, and again one of those nervous little shivers flickered its way down her spine.

But she had no choice. "To exploration," she echoed, then lifted the glass to her lips and took an experimental little sip.

Sweet, like the fruit ices her mother used to buy her on hot summer days. The similarity ended there, however, because as the liquor trailed down her throat, it seemed to turn to fire, burning its way down, lighting a flame inside her.

Coughing, Trinity set down the glass. The whole time, Gabriel was watching her, an amused tilt to his eyebrows.

"I suppose I should have warned you about that," he said casually, then reached under the bar and brought out a pouch of water. It was cold, and Trinity realized there must be a refrigeration unit tucked under there somewhere.

"You think?" she gasped, then seized the pouch and flicked the tab to open it. After a few swallows of cool water, she thought she might be able to feel sensation in her mouth again. "That tastes like something a Stacian might brew up, not an Eridani."

"Actually, it's distilled, not brewed, but I take your point." Gabriel lifted his own glass and took a measured swallow. He must have had a good deal of practice drinking the stuff, because he didn't even flinch. "Try again."

That was perhaps the last thing she wanted to do, but she knew better than to refuse. She wrapped her fingers around her glass and brought it to her lips, then allowed herself a very small sip.

This one burned, too, but not as badly as the last one. Maybe she'd damaged some nerve endings with that first swallow. And now that it didn't hurt as much, she could feel the heat of the drink moving through her body, seeming to warm her right down to her toes.

"Better?"

She nodded, then sipped again. All right. She could do this.

He moved out from behind the bar. "Come with me to the window."

Again, his words were more of a command than a request. Glass in one hand, she followed him across the room, which she now realized truly was a lounge, with low divans and tables, all designed for viewing the amazing sight of that nebula hanging just outside. All right, not actually just outside. It had to be millions of miles away. Still….

They paused there, an inch of duraglass the only thing separating them from the vacuum. Gabriel stood watching those glowing, shifting colors for a moment, then turned back toward her and plucked the glass from her hand before setting it down on the low table directly behind them.

"What do you think?" he asked.

"It's beautiful," she replied. Of course she'd seen holos of celestial phenomena like this before, but knowing it was real, hanging in space, so close it seemed as if you could touch it…well, that was something entirely different.

"Yes, it is," Gabriel said. He wasn't looking at the nebula, however. He was staring down at her.

She couldn't meet his eyes. That would be disastrous.

"That skin we gave you. It has all those same colors flickering in it. Purple and gold and bottle green and red, shimmering over black." He moved closer, then ran a finger along the skin of her forearm.

Don't flinch. Don't shiver.

Don't react.

He didn't seem upset by her lack of response. No, he only moved closer, so close that his arm was brushing against hers.

Still she didn't move. It took everything she had to stand there and not pull away from him. But if this was a test, some form of psychological torture, then she was going to prove that she could handle anything he flung at her.

Well, almost anything.

With one hand, he reached up and touched her hair, which had one lock lying loose on her left shoulder, the rest falling down her back. Then he bent and pressed his mouth against hers.

She tasted an echo of the *volshir* on his lips, the sweetness and the heat of it. At the same time, she tried to push away. This—whatever "this" was—had gone much too far.

His hands grasped her arms, though, holding her in place as he continued to kiss her. Almost as if she was observing the whole scene from outside herself, she noted coolly that his technique was flawless. Some parts of her body were responding, heat flushing through her, even as her mind was screaming that she had to get away.

And then he did let go, and she staggered back a few paces, gasping and wiping at her mouth.

"Excellent," he said, before she had a chance to demand what the hell he thought he was doing. "We were concerned that perhaps the application of the alien epidermis would have damped or even blocked your sexual response. But it seems that everything is working as it should."

"That—that was a *test?*" she finally spat out.

"Of course," he replied, voice calm. "You couldn't think that I would actually want you as you are now?"

She stared at him, shocked to speechlessness. Nothing she could say seemed sufficient to the occasion, so she only remained as she was, glaring at him as he came closer to her once again, then bent toward her ear and murmured,

"But after this is all over...once we've returned you to your natural appearance...then I think I will want you very much."

SIX

WHETHER OUT OF STUBBORNNESS OR MERELY A DESIRE TO SEE how long the strained relations between them might continue with no resolution, Leizha did not go on leave, or request a transfer, or do any of the things Zhandar hoped she might. They continued to work side by side, acting as if nothing had happened, as if nothing could happen.

And if he had his choice, nothing would.

Several times a week, Jalzhin would send communiques to Zhandar's private account, asking if he had yet made a decision, or passing along a new batch of candidates for him to consider. Not that there was anything much to see. Their interests and ages and educational backgrounds might vary slightly, but otherwise those messages contained only another parade of dark hooded shapes.

Perhaps that was Jalzhin's subtle way of pointing out it truly didn't matter all that much which woman

Zhandar ended up choosing. The drug the Ministry's scientists had concocted would create chemistry where there was none, and once a child was conceived and brought to term, then…what? Jalzhin had never explained that part of the plan very clearly. Would the child be raised by its mother? By Zhandar? By the two of them together, even though they had no true bond to seal them as a couple?

He had a feeling Jalzhin and his superiors didn't much care, as long as the child was healthy and lived to ensure that there truly would be a new generation to carry on their way of life. But would that way of life really continue, when such a child would have been conceived in a way so completely antithetical to the tradition the Zhore had followed for millennia?

It was the end of the day…yet another in a long series of very long days. He knew he would have to make some sort of decision soon. And then everything would change.

Leizha entered his office, tablet in hand. He always left his door open, so that she and the others who worked in their department could come and go as necessary. Even though it was late, he assumed she had come in to get his approval on the modifications to the rooftop garden on the Tranzhir Tower in the Ranizhar District.

But she waved her hand over the controls, and the door closed quietly behind her.

Even though he knew she couldn't see them, Zhandar's eyebrows lifted. "What is it, Leizha?" He might have instigated their last conversation on the topic, but he found himself hoping they would not be going over the same ground again this evening. All he wanted to do was go home. He was tired.

His assistant stood there for a long moment. Then she set the tablet down on his desk and backed away. A long pause, and her hands were reaching up to the clasp of burnished metal at her throat.

No...she wouldn't....

But she did. The clasp was undone, and then she grasped the edges of her hood and pushed it back.

The cloak fell to the ground in a slither of fabric. Underneath, she wore a close-fitting tunic and leggings, neither of which left much to the imagination when it came to divining her true form. Green eyes blazed at him, both triumphant and yet somehow desperate.

"This is what I came here to show you, Zhandar. Look upon me now, and then decide whether you want me or not."

She was beautiful. No question about that. And her body was both slender and lush, curved, entirely female. Zhandar wished then that he was Gaian or Eridani or Stacian, so her physical beauty would be enough, that it wouldn't require an echo in his soul for him to desire her.

But he wasn't, and he didn't want her. He wanted to be able to want her, but that was impossible. At least, not without the intervention of Jalzhin's drugs.

"You are very beautiful, Leizha," he said sadly. "If only that were enough."

Her mouth tightened, and long silky lashes swept over her eyes. Just once, as if she couldn't bear to look at him right then.

Then she bent and picked up her cloak, and shrugged back into it. Shaking fingers fastened the clasp at her throat. Quietly, she said, "I think it is time I went on that retreat after all."

And then she was gone.

They left the space station in a heavily modified Sirocco-class starship. Trinity had only read about the nimble little ships; she certainly had never thought she would ever travel in one. Then again, even the Sirocco's original designers had most likely never imagined that one of their ships, designed for swift and luxurious passage between star systems, would be modified with extra shielding, hidden cannons, the very latest in stealth technology, and a host of other upgrades that Gabriel Brant hadn't bothered to explain in detail.

Gabriel. He sat across the cabin from her now, acting as if nothing had happened between them. Maybe in his mind, it hadn't. That kiss was only a test, after all. She'd done her best to wipe it from her mind, but she couldn't forget what he'd said afterward. The horrifying promise he hadn't even bothered to hide in roundabout words.

Even if by some miracle she managed to survive this insane mission without the Zhore discovering who she really was, he would be waiting for her at the end of it. She would never be free.

She supposed it was foolish to have thought she would be able to reclaim her life once this was all over. Her gift was a prize the Consortium would never willingly relinquish.

They'd fitted her with the proper wardrobe of a Zhore—close-fitting tunic and pants underneath, shining black boots, a heavy hooded cloak that seemed as if it weighed fifty kilos, although she knew part of her discomfort had its source in her own anxiety. She was used to the trim, serviceable clothing worn on Gaia and its colonies. How on earth did the Zhore wear these things day after day without tripping over something? And what about in the summertime? Trinity already felt as if she was stifling in those garments, and she knew the cabin temperature was a perfectly calibrated 22 degrees Celsius.

"Your identity," Gabriel said, giving her a small black handheld. In design, it was not so different from the kind she'd used every day of her adult life, and she raised an eyebrow.

"The Zhore have an interesting approach to technology. They are not great innovators. Most of what they use was given to them by the Eridanis, and then modified as they saw fit. Just as they didn't have subspace travel before the Eridanis supplied them with the tech." Gabriel leaned back in his seat, looking almost lazy, although she knew him well enough by now to realize it was all a pose, and that he was wound almost as tightly as she was. He must have a lot riding on this mission, although of course he had never told her what his personal stake in its success might be.

"Anyway, you already know the basics. Your name is Zhanna. We had already planned to place you in Torzhaan, in the office that manages procurement of the various plant species for their gardens, but our intelligence operatives just contacted us to inform us that the administrator's assistant has left her position, for reasons unknown. So you will be the one replacing her, rather than taking the empty botanist's post as we'd originally intended."

Trinity supposed she should be relieved. After all, even after some intensive training, she knew she was ill-equipped to pretend to be a botanist, especially on an alien world whose plant life was completely foreign to her. But she'd worked as an admin herself, back in Barstow. It would be different, but not horribly so. She'd still have to keep track of appointments, set schedules… fetch her boss the Zhore equivalent of coffee. It shouldn't be quite as nerve-wracking as she feared.

The device she held now would contain everything she needed to know about this "Zhanna." Place of birth, parents, education…a life carefully pieced together based on intelligence the Gaians had been gathering for decades. No, the Zhore had never allowed any aliens to set foot on their planet's surface, but that didn't mean the Consortium—and, she assumed, the Eridani Hegemony and the Stacian Federation—hadn't been collecting data from elsewhere in the system. It wasn't the same as boots on the ground…hence the importance of her current mission…but the government definitely knew a great deal more than the Zhore probably guessed.

Or maybe the aliens did know, and hadn't bothered to put a stop to the information-gathering, simply because making a fuss about it would have let the watchers know that they were in turn being watched. After all, it wasn't as if the Consortium government had been sharing its knowledge freely. She'd learned more about the Zhore in the past few days than she'd known her entire life.

"Who is this administrator?" she asked.

"His name is Zhandar. He's held the post for seven years now. Their year is close to ours—345 days. So he's roughly thirty-four standard."

Almost ten years older than she was. But what was a decade compared to being from two completely different races? Not that this Zhandar was necessarily her target. Even her handlers might have decided it was far too risky to put her in such close proximity to the man she was supposed to seduce.

Gabriel's next words seemed to kill that hope, however. "He lost his wife about a year ago. Death in childbirth."

Trinity shivered, even though a few minutes earlier she'd been thinking she was far too warm. What an archaic way to die. "They don't have good medical facilities?"

"As far as we've been able to ascertain, Zhore medical science is on a par with anything you'd find on Eridani or Gaia. No, her death seems to be tied to the same issues they've been having with fertility in general."

What was there to say but "oh"? That was the only syllable to leave Trinity's mouth. She didn't want to think about this Zhandar's wife dying while trying to give him a child, not when Gabriel expected her to go down to Zhoraan, ingratiate herself with the man...or some Zhore male, if not Zhandar...and get pregnant. What if she suffered the same fate as the wife of the man who was about to become her immediate supervisor... what if there was something wrong with his sperm?

"It's almost always the Zhore women who have the problems," Gabriel remarked then, appearing to note her unease. "We still haven't been able to discover exactly why, although it's not anything directly related to the environment on Zhoraan or anything else you'd be directly exposed to. Anyway, you were checked thoroughly by our doctors. You're fine. And there's no reason to think you won't survive the whole experience. Zhore and humans are roughly the same size. It's not as if we're expecting you to push out some Stacian's child."

Far from reassuring her, his comment only made her shudder. She'd never seen a Stacian in person, of course—that warlike race couldn't come within a parsec of Gaia's solar system—but she'd seen the vids. Stacian males averaged easily two meters tall, and were proportionally broad. She couldn't begin to imagine how painful trying to have a baby with one of them must be.

But Trinity would never allow herself to voice her concerns to Gabriel Brant, of all people. She tucked the handheld he'd given her into a pocket of her cloak, and deliberately hardened her voice. "Anything else?"

"Nothing beyond what we've already gone over. The implant we gave you will record everything and send it back to our operatives on Kelzhar, the planet's second moon. It's a way station for off-worlders, since the Zhore don't allow any 'aliens' on their home world itself. Those agents have already established their cover there as the owners of a café on the moon base. They'll be the ones analyzing the raw data and then sending it on to my division."

The implant had been injected into the base of her skull just the day before. If Trinity ran her fingers over the spot, she could feel a faint lump. But her long hair concealed it, and if this Zhandar or someone else decided to kiss her there, well....

Did the Zhore even kiss? Their sexual practices were the one thing about which Gabriel had absolutely no information to give her. They were humanoid, obviously, and the male Zhore the Consortium's spies had bought from that mercenary clan on Bathsheva had been built like a man, right down to his genitalia. So it had to be some variation on tab A and slot B, but anyone who perused the offerings on the upper bands of the vid channels knew that there could be a bewildering number of variations when it came to those basic positions.

The Zhore, however, did not make entertainment based on their sexual practices. No vids. No books. No still images. Nothing. They seemed to mate for life, but other than that, even Gabriel's spies didn't have any information at all.

Well, they will soon, if you succeed in attracting one of their males, she thought grimly. *That horrible little device embedded in your skull will record the whole damn thing.*

That was the worst of it. This entire mission was a nightmare, but knowing that Gabriel and his team would see her having sex with an alien sent the scenario to a truly transcendent level of awfulness.

Thank God Blake Chu wasn't here. He'd stayed back at the base. Trinity was having a hard enough time keeping a grip on her roiling emotions without having to block them all from Gabriel's pet psychic. But she'd have to block them soon, and keep blocking them. Only a few more hours, and she'd be dropped on Zhoraan to make her way as best she could. At least they seemed to have an excellent public transit system in the cities, so she wouldn't have to manage the controls on an unfamiliar vehicle while navigating an alien road system.

"Any last questions?" Gabriel asked. The nasty smile was back on his lips. She hated it even more now that she knew what those lips felt like pressed up against hers.

"No," she replied, glancing away from him and out the window, although she could see nothing but the stomach-churning non-colors of their passage through subspace. "I know what I have to do."

The Sirocco flew in low, skimming over night-dark forests and lakes that glittered under the light of Zhoraan's two moons, both of them thin crescents. Even though Gabriel had assured her that the little ship's stealth technology could beat any sensors the Zhore had, Trinity couldn't help wondering what would happen if they were detected. Would the Zhore shoot them down?

No, that didn't sound right. They were a planet of pacifists, from what she'd been told. They didn't believe in war, in weapons. Why the Consortium hadn't attempted to overrun Zhoraan, she didn't know for sure, but she had a feeling it was because the Eridanis would be sure to step in if Gaia ever attempted any hostile maneuvers in that direction. And while that race of lavender-skinned aliens might seem too cultured to get its hands dirty in an inter-system conflict, Trinity had her doubts. As, most likely, her government's leaders did as well. They wanted to keep expanding their areas of control, not get locked in a wasteful battle over a planet that, in the Consortium's eyes, probably wasn't worth all that much.

Her destination was a small transit station some twenty kilometers from Torzhaan, her home for the next few weeks, or months…however long it took to achieve the mission objective. From the station she could take a maglev train to the provincial capital, then slip into the apartment Gabriel's people had procured for her. What kind of hacking that had involved, she had no idea, but it was probably along the same lines as giving her a false identity and being able to insert that identity into a new life and a new place of business on this alien world.

The Sirocco dipped lower, heading for a small wood about a kilometer away from the transit station. By now it was getting late in this part of the planet, around twenty-two hundred local time. But there was one last train that was supposed to come through in approximately half an hour.

Trinity had to be on that train.

She reached down and retrieved the bag she had stowed under her seat. It carried two changes of clothing and assorted undergarments. That was all. She'd have to purchase everything else she needed in Torzhaan. Her handheld was already supplied with the credit voucher she would use.

"No money on Zhoraan," Gabriel had told her. He'd worn a faint sneer at the time. On Gaia, money was power. Most likely he didn't know what to make of a world where currency wasn't required, where everyone was taken care of despite what they did or didn't contribute to society.

Trinity hadn't bothered to react to his obvious disdain. And now she was only relieved that she wouldn't have to work with unfamiliar currency as well, could simply wave her handheld over the reader at a shop or restaurant and have everything more or less magically handled.

"Almost there," he murmured. "Get ready."

Nodding, she got up from her seat. The Sirocco wouldn't even stop, but would only come in to hover a meter or so off the ground. The hatch would open, and she'd jump out. No one should be around to see the maneuver, and then she'd go on to the transit station and wait calmly there for the maglev, thoughts shielded and giving no indication that the Zhore now had a stranger in their midst.

Here, she would be the alien.

The bag felt heavy in her hand, even though in reality it contained very little. She walked over to the hatch and grasped the handle embedded in the wall next to it. Gabriel rose from his seat as well, and stood a half-meter or so away from her. Why, she wasn't sure. Maybe he thought she'd lose her nerve at the last minute, and so waited there to give her a final shove off the ship if necessary.

That wouldn't happen, though. She might be terrified, but she wasn't about to let him see it. Not that he could…not with her covered from head to toe in those stifling Zhore robes.

A buzzer sounded, and the hatchway opened. They were just skimming the ground, low bushes and grasses seeming to shimmer in the pastel moonlight. She had no idea who the pilot was, but he had to be a master, to hug the ground like this in a ship designed to travel the spaces between the stars.

"Now!" Gabriel said.

She didn't stop to think. He'd already shown her how to make her jump and then roll with it so she wouldn't sprain an ankle or bruise an arm.

The ground was surprisingly soft. Trinity heard her bag land with a *thump* a few feet away from her, and then she was rolling in the grass, coming to rest within a second or two, her gaze fixed skyward. That was just enough to reveal the Sirocco skimming away, picking up speed as it rose. A few seconds passed, and it had already disappeared into a bank of low-hanging clouds.

She was alone.

For some reason, her legs were shaking. She ignored them and got to her feet anyway, brushing at her robes as she did so. Bits of grass and dirt—both of which appeared eerily similar to their Gaian counterparts—fell away with magical ease. Was the fabric treated somehow, or were the fibers it was woven from somehow impervious to soil and other grime?

That was one thing Gabriel hadn't told her; maybe he didn't know, or maybe he'd simply decided that particular detail wasn't important. Whatever the case, she was glad she wouldn't show up at the transit station looking like someone who'd been rolled by a mugger. Not that there were probably any muggers on Zhoraan.

She went and retrieved her bag, then fished the handheld out of her pocket, using her free hand. A few swipes, and the navigation display popped up, indicating that she should move to her left and then walk approximately .43 kilometers to reach her destination.

All that was written in Zhore characters, of course. But because of the language conditioning she'd been given, her mind processed it as easily as if she'd been reading Galactic Standard.

The night air was cool but not cold, and smelled sweet. Had she ever smelled air like that? She didn't think so. That required acres and acres of green growing things, and there hadn't been much that was green in Barstow. Maybe once, before it became the new capital of the western region after the rising oceans swallowed half the West Coast, but now it was just like any other city, kilometers of pavement and glass and steel, with only a few half-hearted parks here and there to break up the urban sprawl.

Her new boots were surprisingly comfortable, and now she was glad of the warm cloak she wore. Yes, it did drag in the grass a bit, and once or twice got caught on a bush and had to be tugged free. Even with all that, Trinity relaxed into the garment as she walked, glad now of the chance to acclimate herself with no one watching or judging.

In no time, it seemed, she saw the outlines of the transit station appearing through the darkness. All the lamps around it were turned downward, as if to prevent too much stray illumination from traveling upward into the night sky. The building itself had smooth, curved lines, and a dome of pearlescent glass that seemed to glow from within. It was surprisingly beautiful.

Pretty fancy for a transit station, she thought, then shrugged. The Zhore were supposed to be great lovers of beauty, of harmony. Probably they didn't want some squat, functional-looking structure cluttering up the countryside.

As Trinity approached the entrance, the doors slid open. At first she thought the place was deserted, and began to let out a breath of relief. Then she spotted a robed figure sitting quietly on one of the soft-cushioned chairs, and almost stopped short. No, wait—she couldn't act surprised. How was she supposed to act? She couldn't smile, obviously. The Zhore had a formal greeting that Gabriel had taught her—"your presence honors me"—but that seemed a little much for a chance meeting with someone in a train station.

She settled for a quiet nod at the Zhore, and, to her relief, the Zhore nodded back but didn't speak. Trinity walked as calmly as she could to a chair near the door, then lowered herself into it.

Her first encounter with one of the aliens, and it looked as if she'd survived it.

That was only the first hurdle, though. Still, she couldn't help feeling somewhat cheered as the train slid into the station a few minutes later, and the other Zhore got up and followed her quietly into the closest car. Inside, it was furnished in soothing shades of soft gray-blue and tan, and the seat was even more comfortable than the one she'd been sitting on back in the waiting area.

Clearly, the Zhore didn't have to worry about anyone vandalizing their train cars or their public spaces. Trinity gazed out the window and watched the dark landscape flash by. Odd how there could be miles and miles of open country like this. In one of her briefing sessions, Gabriel had told her that the best estimate the Consortium had for the population of Zhoraan was around thirty million. So strange, when the greater Southwest area back on Gaia had twice that many people living there.

No population pressure driving the Zhore out toward the stars. No, they had the exact opposite problem. Trinity shifted uneasily in her seat and thought of the Zhore sitting a few seats away from her. From the alien's height, she'd guessed it must be male, but she couldn't know for certain. And what did he—or she—look like under those robes? Trinity had only seen that one specimen, so she had no idea how much variation there was in the Zhores' features and overall appearance.

She'd never know for certain, of course. Even if she did get close enough to one Zhore male to be intimate with him, she would see only that one. They never revealed their faces to anyone except their immediate families and their bonded mates, and, perhaps, a few very close friends.

Trinity doubted she'd be here long enough to make any friends at all, let alone close ones.

The train ride only took half an hour. After once again consulting the navigation app on her handheld, she got off at the indicated station, then made her way down the street. It was quite late by then, with only a few of the hooded aliens on the sidewalks around her. Well, not sidewalks exactly, not as she knew them, but open areas planted with a low sort of ground cover that was cushiony underfoot. It felt good, especially since she had more than a kilometer to go to reach her destination.

Eventually, the little dot on the app turned green, and she knew she had arrived at the building where Gabriel's team had procured an apartment for her. It was fairly tall for a Zhore structure, maybe thirty stories or more.

Unlike any apartment building she'd ever lived in, there was no external security. She passed through a set of glass doors and into a lobby area with walls of some sort of polished stone and a large reflecting pool in the center, with flowering shrubs growing in planters all around it. After a lifetime of living in dingy flats, Trinity thought the place appeared almost impossibly clean and perfect.

But she knew she couldn't stand there and stare, as much as she might have liked to. Her apartment was on the sixteenth floor, so she selected that button from the control panel inside the glass-walled lift.

It rose smoothly, climbing up an open shaft that had some sort of trailing vines hanging down on all sides, except the one wall where the elevator car was actually attached. Yes, she'd been told that the Zhore were lovers of nature and must have it around them at all times, but until she'd now seen it for herself, she hadn't really comprehended the scope of that love.

The elevator made a soft chiming sound when it reached her floor. Trinity got out and stopped, looking around in some confusion. She'd been expecting the standard hallway with doors to the various apartments opening off it, but there was nothing like that here. Only a small lobby area, with the ubiquitous planters, and a single door in the wall opposite the elevator.

Since she didn't know what else to do, she took her handheld and put it up against the screen on the control panel next to the door. Another soft chime, and the door swung inward.

And then she was in—well, she knew it must be her apartment, since it was the code on her handheld that had opened the door, but the place was so huge it must take up the entire floor. And here she'd thought the Zhore must be packed in the building, since it had so many stories. But no, it was simply that each apartment apparently took up a single floor. There weren't hundreds of the aliens living here, but thirty at the very most.

She realized her mouth had dropped open, and so she shut it. As she moved into the main living area, lights came on overhead, triggered by her presence. Soft lights, nothing intrusive, but enough so she could see the polished stone floor underfoot, the furniture in more gentle shades of sand and beige, the color provided by the flowering vegetation that grew in planters along the walls and in containers on top of the tables. And was that a waterfall cascading down one wall in the dining area?

Yes, it was. All right, really a wall fountain, flowing over what looked like polished slate or the Zhore equivalent. The kitchen had a refrigeration unit and dish sanitizer and convective cooktop. Everything sleek and polished, looking like something from a holo set, too perfect to be real. Actually, the whole place seemed like the sort of apartment where a very important Consortium official might live, not a lowly admin.

Then again, the Zhore didn't seem to consider anyone lowly. In their minds, everyone deserved to live in a place this lovely.

Trinity went from room to room, marveling at everything. The bedroom alone was bigger than the dumpy little apartment she'd called home when she lived in Barstow, and was far more elegant.

In silence, she hung up the few garments she'd brought with her, then went into the dressing area. A large mirror covered one wall, although she had to wonder what the Zhore needed with mirrors, when they hid their faces from each other and wore the same thing day in and day out.

Then she undid the silvery clasp that held her own cloak shut and deliberately set it down on the dressing table. Slowly, she pulled off the robe and hung it from a hook on the wall. For a long time she stood there, surveying her alien face in the mirror. Right then she was bone-tired, after that jarring exit from the spaceship that had brought her here, and all the walking that came afterward. That was one good thing about the Zhore skin that covered her own, though; she couldn't see any shadows under her eyes, any trace of weariness at all, except possibly in the droop of her mouth. It was still so odd to see herself looking this way, to have to consciously search for the contours of the face she remembered, shrouded under that dark, glimmering skin.

At last she let out a breath. "You've survived so far. Now go to bed.

"Tomorrow is the *really* hard part."

SEVEN

ZHANDAR FELT IT FIRST AS A FAINT STIRRING ALONG THE EDGES of his consciousness, like a warm breeze blowing in after a long, cold winter. He'd been playing with garden layouts on his computer, moving the modular sections around, attempting to find a design that would be the most aesthetically pleasing while at the same time providing the maximum oxygen and food production. His mind had been distracted, though, drifting. The past few nights, he hadn't been sleeping very well. It could have simply been that he was driving himself harder and harder these days, staying later here at work, even though there was no true reason for him to do so. Well, there was a reason, even if he didn't care to admit what it actually was.

He was just so very tired of going home to an empty house.

Now, though…something drifted over him, then pulled at him. He felt it, sensing the need, the longing, awaken in him, a heat he'd never thought he'd experience again.

Someone in the building was *sayara*.

His first impulse was to get up and hurry out of his office, to see if he could find this miracle in female form before she disappeared out of his life. But then he realized the sensation was getting stronger.

She was coming toward *him*.

Heart racing, he forced himself to stay seated behind his desk. A moment later, Nizhal, one of the junior designers on his team, paused in the doorway and said, "Zhandar? Your new assistant is here."

He stepped out of the way so that a slight hooded female could move forward. Her voice was low, soft as she spoke. "I am sorry I'm late. I am not yet familiar with the transit here in Torzhaan."

Late? As if he cared for that. It was enough that she was here now. His blood surged in his veins, but he schooled himself to calm. She was here in a professional capacity. Yes, his whole body was singing to him of her compatibility. However, he still didn't know if her soul answered his.

And he did allow himself just the slightest flicker toward her, to see if he could pick up on anything she might be feeling. Her barriers were very good, though. That was desirable—no one wanted a partner who broadcast everything she was feeling—but at the same time he wished he could get just the smallest hint of what her reaction to him was as well. Generally, if one felt the *sayara* pull toward another, then that person was experiencing the same thing…but not always. There were rare occasions when it was not reciprocated.

If that turned out to be the case now, after everything he'd already suffered….

"It is quite all right," he assured her, glad that he sounded calm enough, as if she hadn't just touched him to his very core by her presence. "Zhanna, is it?"

She nodded.

He went on, "While our schedule is quite full right now, nothing on it is particularly pressing. Come, let me show you where you will be working."

Nizhal took that as a sign to melt away, leaving Zhanna standing near the open door. Zhandar got up from his chair and went to join her. This close, her presence was almost unbearable—thrills worked their way down all his nerve endings, and his heart sped up. He wanted to take her by the hand and pull her to him, push down the hood that concealed her face, undo the clasp at her throat.

Control yourself, he thought then, making that inner voice as stern as he possibly could. *The last thing you want is to frighten her.*

Of course, if she was also experiencing a pull toward him, then it would not be fear that she felt.

He could see no sign of any reciprocity from her, however. She followed him in silence to the office next to his, and waited quietly while he pushed the button to open the door. Since she showed no signs of moving, was obviously waiting for him to go in first, he stepped into the office. Voice as casual as he could make it, he said, "Here is your workstation. You'll find the yearly schedules already loaded into your computer, as well as the design libraries and plant catalogues we work with. Do you have much experience with horticulture?"

"Unfortunately, no," she replied. "But I learn quickly."

That response made even more heat ripple through him. He told himself he was being ridiculous, that she was speaking of something else entirely, and yet it was so hard for him to focus on anything except the low, sweet tones of her voice. Did her face match that voice? Her frame, even muffled by the robes, seemed slight, almost fragile. Unlike Elzhair, who had been quite tall, this young woman barely reached his shoulder.

"Excellent," he responded, hoping that he hadn't hesitated too long before replying. "I think you will find the work here quite pleasant. You will need to coordinate my schedule with that of the other divisions involved in our projects—supply, and botanical, and a few others—and set meetings. You'll also be accompanying me to work sites to keep notes and provide your own insights. We're a team here, Zhanna, and I believe everyone on it has something valuable to contribute."

She nodded then, but for the first time he noted some hesitation in her manner, as if she wasn't quite sure of her own value. It bothered Zhandar, and not merely because she was *sayara*. All of his people were taught to believe in their own strengths, and address their weaknesses. Everyone was valuable. Everyone had something to contribute.

"Where were you before this, Zhanna?" he inquired. It had been a polite question, nothing more, but she still seemed to startle, then recover herself, saying,

"Oh, I was born in Morzhaan Province. I actually had no real thought of leaving, but then." She hesitated then. When she went on, her voice was small and still. "I suppose you have heard of the incident in Alizhaar."

Everyone on Zhoraan had heard of it. In that maritime province on the other side of the world, a terrible earthquake and resulting tidal wave had flattened half the small city of Alizhaar.

"I lost my family," Zhanna said. "My parents, but then also most of my relatives on both sides. I survived only because I had gone inland that day, running errands for my mother. Afterward…afterward, there didn't seem to be much reason to stay."

His heart ached for her. Yes, he had lost Elzhair, but he was not entirely alone in this world, even if he often chose to think so. Both his parents were still alive, in their homestead some forty kilometers outside Torzhaan, and his sister Alizha as well. She had been more fortunate than many of her generation, and had a child of her own, a daughter.

But Zhanna…no wonder she questioned her place in the world. She had lost everything, and yet had somehow mustered the strength to start over in a new place.

"I am so very sorry," he said, and her shoulders lifted.

"Thank you. Now, though, I just want to get to work. Keeping busy is the best way to forget, I've found."

How could he argue with that, when he'd been driving himself to exhaustion lately in the hope that if he just worked long enough, hard enough, he might begin to forget the hole in his world, the one that had once been filled with Elzhair?

"Of course," he replied. "Well, if you will go to your computer, we can look at what we have lined up for this week...."

Trinity had known this was going to be difficult. But she hadn't realized exactly how difficult until she stood in the doorway of Zhandar's office and felt the strength of his presence wash over her. It was like nothing she'd ever experienced before...a tide of heat, of warmth, of...she couldn't even explain what she'd felt to herself. Not exactly.

All she knew was that she wanted him. It was a very odd sort of lust, since she hadn't seen his face, knew he was an alien, and it didn't matter. Hearing his voice was enough. Watching the grace of his movements as he rose from his chair and walked toward her, dark robes flowing away from the broad shoulders.

Somehow she'd managed to remain calm and act as if nothing was wrong. Yes, her mission was to be with Zhandar—and her body was telling her right then how much she wanted to fulfill that mission—but above even that, she had to be inconspicuous. Running up to him and pulling him to her approximately thirty seconds after they'd just met didn't exactly qualify as keeping a low profile.

So she'd followed him into her office, listened to his warm, rich voice as he explained what her duties would be. She'd even dutifully recited the details of her back story as laid out by Gabriel Brant when he'd briefed her on her new identity. And Zhandar seemed to accept it.

Then again, why wouldn't he? He wasn't expecting his new assistant to be lying to him, and Trinity was exerting all her effort in keeping those mental walls she'd built as strong and impregnable as they possibly could be. She'd thought it would be hard to merely hide the truth of her identity from him. What she hadn't counted on was having to mask these new and unwanted feelings as well.

But he didn't seem to have noticed anything, and after an awkward few more moments as he showed her where to find certain files on her computer, he mercifully left, saying he'd let her explore a bit, but to ask any questions if she came across something she didn't recognize or understand. Thank God the Zhore had borrowed their technology so heavily from the Eridanis, which meant it was more or less recognizable to her as the sort of thing common throughout the galaxy. Yes, the symbols scrolling across that screen were Zhoraani and not Galactic Standard, but she found if she didn't make a conscious effort at reading the words they formed, and instead allowed them to more or less flow right into her brain, she could get along just fine.

No, it didn't seem as if the technical aspects of her new job were going to give her any real difficulty. The real problem was the man sitting in the office next to hers.

What problem? she asked herself. *This is what you came here for. Give it a few days so you can gracefully ease into it, then do the deed and get out. If he's half as attracted to you as you are to him, then the whole thing is that much easier, isn't it?*

Well, that sounded simple on the surface, but she wasn't sure it would really work that way. For one thing, just because she'd been seized by the kind of attraction that made it hard to think straight didn't mean Zhandar was experiencing the same thing. Was this normal? Was this almost overwhelming compulsion to be with someone what made the Zhore mate for life? And if that was the case, how in the world was she, a human, experiencing it? Trinity couldn't begin to guess, because it wasn't something a human being was ever supposed to experience.

Then again, she possessed abilities that most regular humans didn't. Maybe she was picking up on what Zhandar was feeling for her, and her talents…powers… whatever you wanted to call them…were amplifying his attraction.

She wanted to think that wasn't possible, but there had been that girl on Lathvin IV. Reading between the lines of what Gabriel Brant had told her, Trinity had the impression that a Zhore couldn't reproduce without feeling a special connection, even though human beings weren't technically wired to require perfect compatibility when it came to choosing a mate. That young colonist—Annika Jespers—had possessed some quality that had drawn her Zhore lover to her. Which meant that maybe she, Trinity Knox, possessed the same thing, or at least something that was attracting Zhandar.

Assuming that was even true, and she wasn't making all this up out of her head. Maybe all the stress had scrambled some of her mental wiring.

Laying her hands flat on the desktop, Trinity pulled in a breath, then another. The view out her windows, from up here on the twentieth floor of this building, was really quite astonishing. Yes, Gabriel had explained to her how the Zhore made their cities living things, utilizing practically every inch of usable space for plants and trees, but it wasn't until now, as she looked at all that green, shimmering and waving from every balcony, every rooftop, that she realized what a difference such a practice made. On Gaia, the cities were cold, shades of gray and white and black. Most of the buildings here seemed to be constructed of materials in soft shades of ivory and warm tan and even a sort of burnished rust color. They provided a welcoming backdrop for all that vegetation, which ranged from a green so deep it was almost black to the brightest, freshest chartreuse. And the flowers, too, many of them white and blue and purple, were cool and soothing to the eye.

She had guessed it might be beautiful. She just hadn't realized quite how beautiful.

All that beauty wasn't enough to drive the doubt from her head. Something strange was going on here, even though she couldn't explain what. This sort of sudden, insane attraction was nothing like her. Oh, she'd had her relationships, but she'd either eased into them slowly, never sure how long they would last before seeing into her lovers' minds got to be too much and she had to break things off, or going for the quick and easy lay, not allowing herself to get too involved.

If only she'd been smart enough to do either of those things with Caleb.

Thinking about him was not a good idea. Scowling inside her hood, she went back to the screen that held Zhandar's schedule for the week. It looked as if they were supposed to be headed out to a work site later this afternoon.

Together.

So check your raging hormones at the door, she told herself. *Because whatever else is going on, I doubt the people who live in that particular building would be too thrilled to find you and Zhandar having hot sex in the petunia bed.*

Not that they had petunias on Zhoraan, but still.

It was torture to have Zhanna so close to him within the confines of the air car they were driving to that afternoon's project. Very well, she wasn't so close—safely on the other side of the console that separated the two front seats—but even so, he felt as if he could almost breathe in her presence, feel her heart beating.

She sat quietly, watching the streets of Torzhaan flash by outside. He hadn't asked how long she'd been here, but he guessed it couldn't have been much more than a week or so. Her birth town of Alizhaar was much smaller than Torzhaan, and very different topographically. Here the land rolled in gentle hills, rising gradually to the Sarazhin Mountains to the east of town. At this season, they were bare of snow, although they wore white caps in the winter, even if the city itself rarely saw any real snowfall.

"And how is your office?" he asked, thinking he should make some sort of conversation. True, he and Leizha had often driven in silence, but that had been a quiet born of long acquaintance, of knowing that they did not have to talk if neither one of them was inclined to do so. Here, he felt as if the silence was too thick, filled with a need that was certainly palpable to him, if not to Zhanna.

"Very nice, thank you." She shifted in her seat so she wasn't so obviously staring out the window. "The view is beautiful."

"Yes, Leizha always enjoyed it."

A little pause. Then, "She was your assistant before?"

"For several years, yes."

"And she left to go on retreat?"

There was certainly nothing out of the ordinary about that. It was anyone's prerogative to take their leave, to go where they could meditate and rest and relax. There was always someone to come along and take over their position, to help out so things kept running smoothly. And yet Zhandar found himself tensing. "Yes, she did. She felt it was time."

Another brief silence. "Have you ever gone on retreat?"

"No. Not yet, at any rate," he amended hastily, since he realized it was somewhat strange for someone to have held a single position for as long as he had and not take a single sabbatical.

"I suppose it would be hard to tear yourself away, if you truly loved what you were doing."

It was such an un-Zhore-like statement, in its way. Work was never supposed to be the center of one's world; that importance was reserved for one's mate and children. And yet he did love what he did, making Torzhaan bloom and flower. For too many months, it had been all he had.

But in that moment, Zhandar felt his need for her intensify. They'd only met a few hours earlier, and yet, in a few simple words, she'd shown that she understood him far better than those who'd been in his life for years.

His fingers tightened on the steering wheel. He actually didn't need to drive manually, as the air car was equipped to maneuver itself anywhere within city limits, but he'd come to enjoy steering the vehicle, feeling it respond to his commands. And if he ever did make a mistake, the automatic systems would come back online, ensuring that no one could be harmed by a moment's carelessness.

"I suppose that is true. I hope you'll come to love it as I do."

Her hooded head tilted toward him. For a second or two, he feared that he'd stepped over a line with that statement. It was one thing to express a wish that she would enjoy the work, or find it rewarding. But to love it?

Then she replied, "I think I will. I do love flowers."

He couldn't allow himself to let out a sigh of relief, but he did feel his fingers loosen slightly on the steering wheel. "Well, we also plant decorative grasses, and vegetables, and fruit," he said, his tone teasing.

She chuckled. He loved the sound of her laugh, throaty and warm. The only problem was, he could feel himself responding, his body aching with need for her. He pushed the desire down with every bit of willpower he possessed, at the same time thanking all the spirits of his ancestors for the bulkiness of the robes he wore. There would be no evidence of his arousal that anyone could see, least of all Zhanna.

"It will be interesting to see how it all works when you're building it from the ground up," she said, and now she sounded quite serious. "In general, you're replanting and retrofitting, rather than starting from nothing, correct?"

"Yes," he replied, matching his tone to hers. "But this building is new construction, and so we'll be starting from scratch. It's an interesting process."

She nodded then, and the moment was lost, just as some of the heat began to recede from his body. Zhandar couldn't even regret that; he was too relieved that he hadn't betrayed himself. He knew he could say nothing to Zhanna until he knew for certain that she felt as he did. With Elzhair, it had all happened quickly, but he could already tell that his new assistant was a very different person from his late wife.

Watching Zhandar stride around the bare rooftop, pointing here and there, and sometimes waving expansively with his arms as he explained a particular point of design, Trinity wondered if it was like this for all the Zhore. Did it hit them like a bolt out of the blue, charging them up as they realized the person they faced was the one they were destined to spend the rest of their lives with?

She didn't know. All she had to go on was what Gabriel Brant had told her, and it had been explained to her in purely clinical terms, that the Zhore mated for life, although Gaian scientists didn't yet know exactly why. Maybe her briefing had been so coldly clinical on purpose in order to keep her from forming any foolish romantic notions as to what coupling with a Zhore would be like. He'd already made it pretty clear what he expected of her when she returned.

If she returned.

She shivered. Funny how she could feel so drawn to Zhandar, an alien whose face she hadn't even seen, and yet repelled by Gabriel, who was of her own kind and, she had to reluctantly admit, too handsome for his own good. Had he made all his trainees a conquest, or had he bestowed particular attention on her because of her peculiar talents?

It was an attention she could have done without. And, speaking of attention, she should really be paying more attention to what Zhandar was doing and saying, rather than woolgathering while he worked. Even after being here less than a day, she could tell the Zhore were far more lax about workplace discipline than the Gaians, but even so, she didn't want to make a bad impression.

Stylus in hand and tablet in the other, she approached the spot where Zhandar was engrossed in conversation with the foreperson on the construction crew. She could tell from the height of the other Zhore and her smaller frame that she must be a woman, although she was still taller than Trinity herself.

Not that that took a lot. She'd never been blessed with height. Maybe her diminutive size had something to do with men thinking they could walk all over her.

"…and a water feature there, I think," Zhandar was saying, pointing with one gloved finger toward a sheltered corner where a wall was being built to contain what she thought must be the air-circulation units and other equipment used for climate control in the building.

"That wasn't in the original plans," the construction foreperson said. Her voice was surprisingly clear and sweet, but even so, Trinity could hear the doubt in it.

"True, but now that I've walked the site and seen where the light falls, I think it will be helpful there. And if we open up this area next to it, we can place benches among the planters so that the people living and working here can come up and relax and meditate as it suits them."

It was difficult, listening to them speak but not being able to see their expressions. Zhandar's tone was mild enough, but she could tell that he expected to have his way on this.

The foreperson's barriers weren't as strong as Zhandar's, that was for sure; Trinity could feel annoyance slipping out around the edges, coupled with a faint tinge of worry that the project wouldn't be done on time, and that she would be the one who suffered the consequences, not the high and mighty designer from the planning ministry. It was a very human reaction, and, sensing it, Trinity felt herself relax a little.

Guess they're not quite as different from us as I thought. I suppose they couldn't be, or how would a Gaian girl ever marry herself off to one?

That was probably not what she should be thinking about right now. Thoughts of marriage and children naturally led to thoughts of the necessary prelude to such things, and she'd just barely managed to shove lustful thoughts about Zhandar out of her head as it was.

"What do you think, Zhanna?" he asked then, and she nearly jumped out of her skin.

Her borrowed skin.

"I think it would be beautiful," she said honestly. Fresh water was a precious resource on Gaia, and not something to be wasted heedlessly in waterfalls and fountains purely for decoration's sake. But it was clear to her that they didn't have the same restrictions on Zhoraan, so why not create a little oasis around every corner? She added, "And being in the shade like that, there won't be too much of a problem with evaporation."

"My thoughts exactly." Right then his barriers seemed to slip a little, and she could sense the approval radiating from him. Approval, and....

But then it was as if a wall had come up, and she was cut off from him. Since she was desperately managing her own barriers, she didn't try to probe. It was enough that he liked what she had said, and that she'd supported him.

"Very well," the foreperson said, sounding resigned. "You will put in an addendum that there will be a delay of approximately a week to accommodate the change in design?"

"Of course," Zhandar replied. "I certainly wouldn't expect you to face any kind of repercussions because of my own whims."

If someone else—say, Gabriel, or Blake Chu—had uttered those same words, Trinity would have been looking for the undercurrent of sarcasm in them, as if the foreperson should be to blame for wanting to preserve her own hide. But because it was Zhandar saying them, Trinity knew they were only the truth. He had changed his mind, once he truly walked the site, and he wanted the blame for any delays placed squarely on him.

That was so refreshingly unlike any other man she'd ever known that she felt another surge of warmth toward him. This one, however, was not like the blaze of desire she'd felt when she first met him. This was different. She thought she might like him, or at least she liked what she'd seen of him so far.

And that scared her more than anything else. She could just barely accept that they might have some strange chemistry going on. Gabriel hadn't actually warned her that this might happen, but if she looked at it logically, it did make a strange kind of sense. Her psychic abilities meant her mind wouldn't necessary react the same way to the presence of the empathic Zhore as other humans might. Why Zhandar, of all people, she had no idea. The Zhore themselves obviously didn't have a problem with this kind of instant attraction. Just the opposite, from what she could tell. Empaths couldn't lie, and would know right away they were with their soul mate.

Even so, she wasn't sure she wanted to like Zhandar. It would be so much easier to let her body take over, when the time came, to share passion but not intimacy, and then leave as soon as she knew she was pregnant. That way, there wouldn't be any emotional ties. Liking him shouldn't factor into the equation. But she couldn't be cold and clinical. She knew she would have to hurt him, and that realization pained her more than she wanted to acknowledge.

The foreperson had nodded, and then handed her own tablet and stylus over to Zhandar. He'd been scribbling on it while Trinity was ruminating, and so when he spoke again, she had to force herself not to startle.

"That should be all for now," he said. "Zhanna, could you please make a note as to the change in the schedule so it can be filed with the planning commission?"

"Of course," she replied, using a gloved finger to flick to the page she needed. Then she moved the box containing the project completion information to one week later. Again, the software was unfamiliar, but not so much so that she couldn't manage working in it. Clearly, the people who had written the program had borrowed a good deal from the Eridanis.

Zhandar thanked the foreperson for her time, and then he indicated to Trinity that they should head to the stairwell. At least they were descending this time, and not walking up; the elevators hadn't yet been installed, and it had been a long climb of fifteen stories to get to the roof. She would have said she was in fairly good shape, but she'd certainly never made a climb like that before, especially burdened with heavy robes that had to weigh a good ten kilos.

As she trailed along behind the Zhore, she couldn't help staring at the breadth of the shoulders under his robes, and wondering what his body would look like when he took them off. He seemed very well built, but it was so hard to tell.

And thank God for that, she scolded herself. *Because if you could really see him, you'd probably be in even more trouble than you already are.*

Well, true. The one Zhore she'd seen had been... "handsome" didn't seem precisely the right word...but beautiful, features regular, skin shimmering and oddly lovely. If Zhandar was anything like that under the hooded cloak concealing his face, she'd probably spend all her time staring at him instead of getting any work done.

Right then she didn't want to analyze why she thought that work was so important, considering she'd come here to seduce him...or some other likely Zhore. Playing secretary was only incidental.

And yet, she realized, as she followed Zhandar out to his car, she wanted to do a good job for him. She wanted him to value her, not as someone to be used, but as a part of his team.

How she'd reconcile that longing with her true reason for being here, she had no idea.

EIGHT

"You're sure?" Rozhara asked, not bothering to keep the incredulity out of her voice.

"Of course I'm sure," Zhandar replied. He sat in his counselor's office, on one of the comfortable divans she used for these sessions. "You think I'm unable to tell when a woman is *sayara?*"

"That is not what I meant. It is only…." Her words died away then, as if she was pausing to gather her thoughts. Her gloved fingers tapped the soft material of her chair, and she went on, "I mean no offense, Zhandar, but you can see why this surprises me so much. To have a compatible woman appear almost out of nowhere, just as Jalzhin was pressuring you to make a choice…."

"Believe me, I am just as surprised as you are." That was an understatement. He still kept wondering if he had fallen into a hopeful dream, one where he would be granted everything he desired. That he would want

Zhanna so badly—well, he was still wrestling with that. In the back of his mind, he had hoped that perhaps one day he would be able to allow another woman into his life, but as the same time, he couldn't help experiencing pangs of guilt over the strength of his current need. After Elzhair, he hadn't thought he would ever feel this way again.

Actually, to be honest, he wasn't sure if he had felt this way with her, either. Their bond had been undeniable, and their marriage a beautiful thing, but at the same time, he knew deep down that this pull he felt toward Zhanna was even stronger than what he had experienced with Elzhair. And that seemed like a betrayal of her memory.

Tone harsh, he went on, "I did not look for this. But it came to me—a gift from the universe, it seems—and now I must work with it as best I can."

"Does she know?" Rozhara inquired.

"I don't believe so." The past few days, he'd kept himself even more tightly controlled than usual. It was the only way to maintain his sanity. Otherwise, he would have felt compelled to reach out to Zhanna every time she came into his office with a question or a request, to pull her to him so he could push back her hood and claim her mouth with his. And that would be utter disaster. He could make no overtures until he knew she felt the same way he did.

"And this Zhanna? Do you have any sense that she might reciprocate this bond?"

"I don't know. She is very controlled. She lost her family in the Alizhaar incident, and I am certain she is still working her way through that."

"Oh, that is dreadful," Rozhara murmured, and Zhandar nodded.

"Yes. So she has her own healing to manage, and perhaps she is concerned that she will jeopardize her position here if she says anything to me. Assuming, of course, that she even feels as I do."

Rozhara was silent for a moment, apparently turning over in her mind everything he had just told her. At last she said, her tone quiet but firm, "You should speak to her, Zhandar. It is never good to hold these things inside. If it turns out that she feels the same bond with you, then there is no point in wasting time that you could share with her. And if she does not, then at least you will know that it was not meant to be, and you can proceed with selecting a partner from one of the candidates Jalzhin has proposed to you."

His counselor's words made sense, and yet Zhandar still found himself hesitating. For while it was true that he should not be wasting even a precious second that might be spent with Zhanna as a partner, at the same time, if it turned out that she did not feel as he did, then he would be left with not even the fragile hope he nurtured now.

He left aside Rozhara's comment about moving on to be with one of Jalzhin's candidates. After feeling the *sayara* pull from Zhanna, Zhandar couldn't allow himself to consider such a counterfeit.

"Very well," he said, after a hesitation he didn't bother to hide. "I will speak with her. On my own time, however," he added. This was not something he could do on the spur of a moment. He would need time to gather his thoughts, to think of the best way to approach Zhanna so that she would not feel any sort of pressure or intimidation from him. She was younger than he, starting her life over in a strange town, and had suffered a terrible loss. He did not want to frighten her, or make her think that she could not stay on as his assistant if she did not reciprocate his feelings.

"That is fair," Rozhara said. "Important conversations such as these should not be rushed into."

Zhandar felt as if he were rushing. He had only been working with Zhanna for three days. And while it was considered perfectly normal among his people to form a lifelong attachment after such a short acquaintance, if both of those involved felt the same resonance, something about this entire situation seemed odd, although he couldn't quite put his finger on why.

He'd put that aside for now. Far more important that he resolve this uncertainty, and decide how to proceed from there.

Working long hours was nothing new for Trinity. Lord knows all her previous bosses had abused the system for all it was worth—as an unclassified employee, she had a specific salary deposited in her account each month, and the government had never much cared how many actual hours she'd worked to earn that salary. But putting in extended hours here was a particular kind of torture, just because it meant more time spent around Zhandar. She'd been here for two weeks now, and she couldn't help wondering how long she'd have to maintain her disguise. Although she didn't have direct contact with Gabriel—that would have been too risky—she could almost sense his mounting frustration as the days went by. No doubt he'd expected her to make some sort of move before now, which just showed how little he truly understood about Zhore psychology.

Oddly, she actually enjoyed what she was doing, once she'd relaxed enough to realize that her true identity wouldn't be immediately exposed. Sometimes she liked to pretend that this was truly her life, and not merely a subterfuge she was engaging in because it suited her masters' purposes. She'd never had a supervisor like Zhandar, someone who asked for her opinion because he truly wanted it, and not just because he was condescending to some counterfeit notion of equality. And she liked the work itself. They were doing something to make the world a more beautiful place, not just pushing numbers around.

So when Zhandar had asked her to stay late and work on editing the report he intended to submit to the planning commission the next day, Trinity didn't think anything much of it. In the two weeks that she'd been here on Zhoraan, he'd made similar requests once or twice, always softening the requirement by saying she could come in a little late the next morning, or take a long, leisurely midday meal. Anyway, what difference did it make if she stayed late? It wasn't as if she had anything to go home to. Yes, the apartment she'd been given to live in was more luxurious than she could have imagined, but it was still empty. No boyfriend, no pets, no friends. Maybe she should have attempted to get out and explore more of Zhore culture, but she was keenly aware of the implant that kept recording everything she saw, everything she said and did. She didn't see why she should give Gabriel Brant the satisfaction of learning anything more about Zhoraan than he absolutely had to.

Besides, she figured that the less exposure she had to the Zhore in general, the less chance there was of her making a misstep that would unmask her. At work she could be quiet and take her cues from the people she worked with. She picked up snatches of emotion and thought from them, and none of those coworkers seemed to pay her much attention, except to think of her as quiet and unassuming. At work, she seemed safe enough.

To fill the empty hours when she was at home, Trinity usually turned on the vid. Watching the Zhore version of entertainment was rather educational, since it seemed to consist entirely of documentaries about Zhoraan and its solar system, and none of the more lurid romance or action-adventure shows she was used to. On the other hand, discussions of Zhoraani flora and fauna could go a long way in her book, and she often went to sleep earlier than she'd intended, since there was nothing to keep her awake.

She had to wonder what Gabriel Brant and the rest of his team made of it all. No doubt they were busily cataloguing everything she saw and heard, dull and dry as it might be. But that was all they could track—that damned implant couldn't read her thoughts, thank God. Those were still her own.

While she was woolgathering, the comm on her desk beeped. Here on Zhoraan, comms were audio-only, probably because there was no point in wasting bandwidth on video when everyone you talked to looked more or less the same. Trinity pushed the button, knowing it had to be her supervisor, since everyone else had gone home for the day.

"Did you need something, Zhandar?" In a way, she wished she could call him "sir." It would have put some much-needed distance between them.

"Yes, Zhanna. Could you come into my office, please?"

Since he hadn't been specific about what he wanted, Trinity picked up her tablet and stylus in case he needed her to take some notes. By then, Zhoraan's bluish-white sun had dropped below the horizon, and the lights of the city had come alive. Not too many; the Zhore wanted to interfere as little as possible with the glory of their night sky, so much more vibrant than the one she'd grown up with on Gaia. But it was enough to tell her that the hour was even later than she'd thought.

She stopped in the open doorway of Zhandar's office. He was working, not on his computer, but on the 3-D holo-modeler that showed the work in progress on the new building being constructed. She always enjoyed seeing him play with that particular piece of tech, just because it made a project real in a way that only seeing it displayed on a computer screen did not.

He looked up, then said, "Please come in. And please close the door."

That request made a warning flare through her. He never shut his door. Asking her to do so now meant that he must have something to say that he didn't want overheard.

But everyone had already gone home for the evening.

Tamping down her unease, she did as he requested, brushing her gloved hand over the door controls. It slid shut behind her, something final about the soft hiss it made as it snicked shut.

Zhandar stepped away from the table where he'd been making adjustments to his 3-D model of the roof-top garden. Maybe it was just being alone with him like this, when before there had always been someone around, but he seemed somehow taller, more forbidding. Although Trinity knew better than to actually probe his mind, she couldn't help sending out just the smallest tendril of thought to see if she could pick up any hint of why he'd asked her to come in here.

Nothing. She wasn't the only one good at putting up solid barriers, it seemed. Then she wondered why she should be surprised. Not once in the two weeks she'd been here had she detected anything in him, and she'd had to work damn hard to make sure she was equally opaque.

"This may be awkward," he began. "But it is something that we need to discuss."

Oh, hell. Was this the Zhore way of getting fired? Trinity racked her brains to see if she could come up with anything she'd done wrong over the past few days, something that would have resulted in her being dismissed. But there hadn't been anything. She and Zhandar worked well together, even though the entire time she'd had to pretend that her body wasn't aching for his touch.

Might as well plunge right into it. "Is there something wrong with my work? I know I have made a mistake here and there, but I thought—"

"Oh, no," Zhandar said at once. He took a step toward her and stopped just as quickly, as if he'd intended to draw closer but then thought better of it. "No, that's not it at all."

Relief went through her, but it was only a small trickle, not a flood. There was something else going on here, and she wasn't sure if she wanted to know what that something might be.

"It is only…." He stopped again. Trinity could see how his gloved hands were clenched at his sides, as if he was forcing himself to continue. "You have done very well as my assistant, Zhanna. But the entire time, it has been difficult for me. You see…you see, I feel the *sayara* bond with you. I know it is there…at least on my part. But I have no idea what it is you are feeling."

Torzhaan was not in a seismically active region, and yet it still seemed as if an earthquake had just rocked Trinity to her very core. She had not heard the word "sayara" before, because there was no equivalent in Galactic Standard and it had not been part of her language conditioning, and yet in that moment she knew exactly what it was. The insane attraction toward the man who stood before her, the unique pull of one Zhore for another.

Zhandar was experiencing the draw of *sayara* with her, even though she was human. This whole time she'd been trying to resist the surging tides of her own emotions, and he'd been feeling the very same thing. Or maybe it wasn't exactly the same. She was human, and he was Zhore, and she had no true frame of reference for what those empathic aliens might feel in these situations.

Her mouth was dry. He was just standing there, watching her, although of course he couldn't see her expression. This was her opportunity, the perfect opening her handlers had hoped for. If she didn't seize it, there would be repercussions. Exactly what, she didn't know for sure, but she doubted they would be pleasant. At any rate, that wasn't the most important thing.

Heat was flaring and rippling through her, an aching need that actually made her want to clench her knees together.

God, she wanted him, and she'd never even seen his face.

"I—I've felt it, too," she said at last. "I didn't know if I should say anything, because I was here in a professional capacity. But it has been hard…so hard."

That seemed to be all Zhandar needed to hear. Two swift paces, and he closed the distance between them, even as he reached out to take her gloved hands in his. God, the strength of those fingers. She wanted to yank off the gloves they both wore so she could feel him, skin to skin. All right, it wasn't her skin, not exactly, but it still had nerve endings. It would be enough.

"Zhanna," he said. Her name sounded like a caress on his lips. And again, it wasn't her name, only one she had stolen. But that was all she could have from him. Certainly he'd never be able to call her Trinity. "I had hoped…I had dreamed."

"As had I." She clung to his hands, grateful for even that touch, but wanting more. This was insane. She'd been placed here as a spy, the Consortium's secret weapon. She should be going about this coldly. But none of Gabriel Brant's doctors and psychiatrists and xeno-biologists had considered the possibility that the over-whelming attractions this alien race experienced might work on her, a psychic, just as strongly as they did on any Zhore.

"So...." Zhandar paused for a long moment, her hands still held in his. Then, with excruciating slowness, he gently pulled the glove from her right hand, exposing her bare palm.

Even after two weeks, it was strange to look down and see that gleaming, iridescent skin covering her flesh. That didn't stop her from shivering as Zhandar took her hand and brought it up to his unseen lips, still hidden within his hood.

A shudder went through her. Had there ever been anything more erotic than the touch of his mouth on her upturned palm? His skin was so very warm, awakening the heat that she kept barely coiled within her.

"You are so very beautiful," he whispered.

How could he say that, when he had never even seen her face? But Trinity knew she was judging his words as a human might. He thought her beautiful because of the time they'd spent working together, because of what he thought was her personality. What would his reaction be, she wondered, if he ever discovered that every moment they'd spent together was a lie?

Not all of it, she thought fiercely. *This...him holding my hand, kissing it...that's not a lie. The way I feel about him isn't a lie.*

"What now?" she asked, also in a whisper. "What do we do now? I don't know—" And then she broke off, because she realized she'd almost betrayed herself. Surely a young Zhore woman would know what their next step was.

Luckily, he seemed to misunderstand, saying, "It is difficult, when two people work together, but not unprecedented. We can work through that later. For now, though…."

"For now?" Her voice shook a little, but she didn't think that was necessarily a bad thing. Zhandar didn't have to know it was from relief, rather than a reaction to his kiss on her hand.

Well, maybe it was a little of that.

Although she couldn't see him, she thought he might be smiling within that hood. "For now, I would like to have dinner with you."

One thing Trinity had learned in her time on Zhoraan was that the Zhore did not share the human love of dining in public. She supposed they thought eating too personal an activity to be shared with others. And while the vegetarian aliens did love to cook, they sometimes found themselves too busy to properly attend to the task. Hence, their world's surprisingly bustling food-delivery business.

They went to Zhandar's apartment. Trinity didn't know if this was all a prelude to more physical activities, but she told herself she would follow along and do what was required. Besides, if just the merest brush of his lips against the palm of her hand could arouse that kind of reaction in her, she wouldn't mind finding out what even more intimate contact might feel like.

His place was larger than hers, and located on the top floor of the building it occupied. Penthouse suite, she thought in some amusement. The Zhore might act all egalitarian, but it seemed there were still some strata in their society if you squinted hard enough. Or possibly the apartment was part of his compensation for working so hard at the same job for so long.

Soft lights flicked on as they entered. Here, too, were more of the wall water features, and lush plants in shades of deep green and soft blue in strategically placed planters. The air smelled good, of something faintly sweet and spicy. Trinity didn't know if that was from the carefully cultivated vegetation or something else—the Zhore equivalent of incense—but she liked it.

Zhandar seemed almost hesitant as he led her into the main living area, which was furnished with low, soft couches and a couple of artfully placed ottomans. "Anything in particular you would like?" he asked, pulling his handheld out of a pocket in his robes.

"Surprise me," she replied.

He laughed. The dark, rich sound of it made a delicious shiver go down her spine. "I plan to."

Oh, dear God.

She didn't recognize half of what he ordered as he placed the call, but she had told him to surprise her, after all. So far, most of what she'd eaten here on Zhoraan was surprisingly tasty. She'd been expecting bland, unappetizing dishes for some reason, but the Zhore had a deft hand with their spices, and did such wonderful things with the local mushrooms—all right, fungus—that half the time you couldn't even tell you weren't eating real meat.

He put the handheld away, then stood there, watching her. Then he said, "The next step is up to you."

"The next step?" she echoed, confused. What, did he want her to jump his bones now before the food even came?

Not that that would necessarily be a bad thing, but….

His fingers touched the edge of his hood. "We can wait, if you wish."

Oh. So once a couple had declared that they shared the *sayara* bond, apparently it was time to dispense with the hoods and the cloaks, at least when they were in private together. She would see him.

And he would see her.

What if he didn't like what he saw? What if he no longer thought she was beautiful? Trinity told herself not to worry, that the Zhore were interested in the spirit, not the physical, but that element of their natures had its own dangers. At some point she would have to open up to him. Not all the way, but enough that he could read her emotions. Bonded couples probably didn't hide what they felt from one another. She wouldn't have to worry about Zhandar reading her mind, since he was an empath, not a true psychic, but even her emotional landscape was something of a mine field, let alone what her actual thoughts concealed.

Taking a breath, she said, "Yes, Zhandar...but shouldn't we wait until after the food is delivered?"

He didn't seem too worried about her suggestion that they delay the moment of truth. "Of course. That would be wisest, I think. But in the meantime...."

Turning from her, he went into the kitchen, to the refrigeration unit. "A glass of *zhir*, perhaps?"

Zhir, she recalled, was a mildly alcoholic drink, pale in color. The closest Gaian analogue was a dry white wine. That sounded harmless enough, considering the Zhore beverage had a far lower alcohol content than actual wine. "That sounds lovely."

He pulled a pretty bottle of etched glass from the refrigeration unit, followed by two low, square glasses from one of the cupboards. A precise measure into each glass, and then he was approaching her and handing her one.

"To...the future," he said, raising his own glass slightly.

So the Zhore had their own version of a toast, one very similar to the Gaian custom. Trinity lifted her glass, then drank. The *zhir* was so light it seemed almost to evaporate off her tongue as soon it touched her mouth, rather like champagne but without the bubbles. "To the future," she echoed, and hoped that was a more or less acceptable response.

It seemed to be correct, because Zhandar dipped his head toward her, as if in a nod. "The future was not something I wished to contemplate, until very recently. Thank you for that."

She guessed he was speaking of his late wife. So hard to know exactly what to say, or how to phrase it. Did the Zhore tiptoe around death the way the Gaians tended to, or did the aliens accept it as part of the natural course of life? Even if they did, she could tell that the man who stood before her now had taken his wife's death very hard, maybe because she was certainly far too young to die, except through accident or tragedy.

"I know that feeling," Trinity said quietly. She hated the lies she had to tell him. The story about her parents' and other family members' deaths in the Alizhaar earthquake had been a conveniently plausible one for Gabriel to give her, mainly because it removed the awkward problem of being all alone in a very family-oriented culture, but she still wanted to cringe every time she was forced to mention anything about it. Still, it seemed the correct response to offer now.

Apparently, Zhandar agreed, since he nodded. "I hope I will be able to change that for you."

She couldn't possibly admit to him that she feared the future now more than ever. More lies, more subterfuge, until she could make her escape. He didn't deserve that. She didn't pretend to know everything about him, but the last two weeks she'd spent working with him had told her that he was a good man. He should have someone who truly did love him.

Maybe you do, she thought then. *You certainly want him. You like him. You want to be around him. How is that any different from the other times you fancied yourself in love?*

Basically, it wasn't. And that was an even bigger problem. Because if she loved him...or thought she did...how the hell would she ever be able to carry out Gabriel's plan?

The universe saved her from having to unknot that problem right then, as the door chime sounded. Zhandar set his glass down on the kitchen counter and went to answer the door. A low-slung mech, not much more than a glorified cart, waited just beyond the door.

Zhandar swiped his credit voucher through the mech's card reader. At once, the plastic dome of the little robot opened, revealing a set of covered plates and bowls in various sizes. A quick glance over at Trinity, and Zhandar said, "If you don't mind, Zhanna—"

She hurried over and lifted several of the plates off the mech's tray. Zhandar scooped up the rest, and then the dome closed and the robot whirred away, moving smoothly on a series of small air jets.

"The dining room table?" Trinity asked, and Zhandar replied,

"Yes, if you would."

At least she knew that the Zhore ate their meals in a manner not unlike that of most Gaian cultures, even if the aliens generally chose to only eat with their closest of relatives. She set down the plates, choosing a spot at the head of the table and one immediately to the left. Zhandar followed a few seconds later, then put down the bowls he held. A bit of a bustle while he returned to the kitchen to get eating utensils and napkins that felt like cloth but went into the recycling unit with all the other waste.

Then the table was set, and they were standing there, watching each other.

At last Trinity said, "Should I go first?"

They both knew she wasn't talking about taking a seat at the table.

"No," Zhandar replied. "I was the one to bring it up. So I should take the first step."

It might have been cowardly of her, but Trinity couldn't help feeling a rush of relief. Seeing him first would give her the courage—she hoped—to push her own hood back, to let him see her face. Even if it wasn't really her face.

Slowly, he pulled off one glove, then the other, and laid them both on the table, at the end where no place settings had been set. By now she was used enough to staring at the iridescent black Zhore skin whenever she looked in a mirror that seeing it on Zhandar's hands didn't give her pause. She did like the shape of those hands, though, and the strong, tapering fingers.

The thought of what it would be like, to have those fingers touching her….

Then his hands were lifting, both of them, going to the edge of his hood and grasping it. A subtle pause, one she might not have even noticed if she hadn't been looking for it, and the hood went back.

The first thing she noticed were his eyes. They were gray, but not the hard charcoal color of Gabriel Brant's eyes. Zhandar's were a clear, piercing shade, almost silvery, shocking against the darkness of his skin. The features were strong, high cheekbones and a longish nose, and a wide friendly mouth, although he was not smiling now. No, he was staring at her with an intensity that was almost painful to see—relief that his hood no longer hid his face, but worry that she wouldn't like what she saw.

Oh, she liked it. More than liked. The bones of his face were beautiful, and those glinting eyes, with their fringe of sooty lashes, held hers. Would she be able to look away, even if she tried?

She didn't know for sure. She only knew that it was now her turn.

And so she pushed back her own hood.

NINE

ZHANDAR'S BREATH STRANGLED IN HIS THROAT. PHYSICAL beauty was not something his people counted as highly as beauty of mind and spirit, and yet….

And yet he had hoped that Zhanna would be as physically lovely as her strength and courage and intelligence made her spiritually lovely. A shallow hope, perhaps, but Elzhair had been beautiful, and he'd delighted as much in the curve of her throat and the flash in her eyes as he had in her sense of humor and quickness of thought. It was all those things that had made her Elzhair, and he had never been one to dwell on one quality above another.

But Zhanna…Zhanna was exquisite. His gaze lingered on her mouth, so full, so luscious. Those were the sorts of lips that cried out to be kissed. Her eyes, a brilliant blue-green, seemed shadowed with worry. Although she had always maintained controls so strict that he thought she would make an excellent instructor in the sorts of mental barriers Zhore society required, now he could sense a flicker of unease in her, as if she feared he would look on her and find her somehow lacking.

He knew he must disabuse her of that notion immediately.

Going to her, he took her hands in his and pulled the gloves away. She was slight and delicate, and her hands were no different—fine-boned, fragile, but with a subtle strength underlying them nonetheless. His fingers wrapped around hers, pulled her closer.

A small tremor went through her. That didn't surprise him, as he'd felt the same shiver when they touched for the first time in such a way, naked flesh to naked flesh. And this was only their fingers knotted together.

"You are beautiful," he murmured. "You are perfect."

She began to shake her head. What had happened to her, to make her think she was anything less than perfection? Had she felt the *sayara* bond with someone, only to discover that her feelings were not reciprocated? That could be hurtful, but all his people knew that such things happened from time to time because of a mismatch in biology. It was certainly nothing personal.

He must show her that such was certainly not the case here.

They now stood less than a hand's breadth apart. He bent to her, touched his lips to hers. Oh, the glory of that mouth against his! So soft, so lush, so welcoming. She tasted of *zhir*, and something more, her own delectable flavor.

And then her body was pressed against his, and she was trembling. He wrapped his arms around her, enveloping her in his cloak. But even though she shook, she did not pull her mouth from his, instead allowed him to continue the kiss, to let his tongue touch hers.

Heat was flooding through his body, threatening to consume him. He knew if they didn't stop here, he would lift her up and take her to his bedchamber. As much as he wanted that, he understood these things must be taken more slowly. After all, they had only declared their *sayara* bond to one another an hour earlier. Although it was not unheard of for a couple to follow their instincts and bond in every way soon after such a declaration, neither was it precisely condoned.

Besides, he did not want her to feel rushed. Her heart was pounding so hard he could feel it, like a frightened *razhar* somehow caught indoors and out of its element, wings beating to be free.

He let her go and stepped away, but gently, so she would know he did so out of consideration for her feelings, and not because he didn't wish to continue kissing her.

"Our food will get cold," he said then, and she smiled. Her teeth were pretty, too, even and white.

"Well," she replied, "we can't have that."

It was hard not to stare at him. She wanted to keep staring…and yet she knew with every gaze she sent in his direction, the implant in her brain was capturing the image and sending it back to the station on Zhoraan's moon where Gabriel's operatives would begin the process of analysis.

What would they think of that kiss? Her accelerated heart rate and shaky limbs would have been recorded as well. And Gabriel would realize she certainly hadn't reacted the same way when he'd kissed her.

Save those worries for later. She couldn't allow herself to be too distracted by what Gabriel and his minions might or might not do with the information she was sending back. She was already distracted enough by Zhandar.

He sat next to her at the table, calmly dishing the food he had ordered onto her plate. Or at least, he appeared calm on first inspection. If she looked a little closer, she could see the gleam in those silvery-gray eyes, the way his lips parted every time their gazes met.

Somehow she knew how difficult it had been for him to stop, to not let things go any further. Well, it wasn't that difficult to imagine, actually, because she'd felt the same way. If he'd pressed the issue, she wouldn't have protested. Some sane part of her mind had told her to follow his lead, however, and it seemed that, for now, he was putting off any further intimacy. Maybe the Zhore weren't as quick to jump into bed as the Gaians. Or the Eridanis. She couldn't speak for the Stacians' sexual habits, because she knew next to nothing about them, except that they'd been at almost-war with the Consortium for longer than she'd been alive.

"Is the food to your liking?"

She didn't quite startle, but she did pause, pulling her thoughts back to the here and now. "Very much so. I think you must have a connection with a better delivery service than I do."

He smiled. It was the first time she'd seen him do so, and it was like watching the sun come up. "Perhaps. I can give you their code, although they only cater to a small area. Where is your apartment located?"

Possibly he was asking for reasons other than determining whether his delivery people would come to her building, but Trinity decided to believe otherwise. "It's in the Azharis District."

"Ah, well, that's a bit out of their service area, unfortunately." His eyes glinted, and he added, "I think you will just have to dine here with me more often if you would like continue enjoying their food."

That would have sounded like flirting on just about any planet she'd ever heard of. "Zhandar," she said slowly, her tone teasing, "is that an open invitation?"

Gaze traveling to her lips, he replied, "If you want it to be."

Who would have thought the reserved and elegant Zhore would have this playful, flirtatious side to them? But then she realized she needed to stop thinking of the alien race as a single monolithic block. They couldn't all be alike, any more than she was like Gabriel Brant or Gabriel was like her secondary-school physics instructor, the one who refused hair implants and so was as bald as an egg.

"For mushroom turnovers like this?" she responded. "Of course I want it to be an open invitation."

Zhandar laughed again then, putting down his fork so he could reach over and grasp the bottle of *zhir* and pour her another measure. Not a lot, certainly not enough to make her even close to tipsy, but it seemed clear to Trinity that he wouldn't mind if things got a bit...elevated...this evening.

She didn't think she would mind, either. It would be nice to kiss him again after dinner, maybe snuggle on one of those sofas in the living room. So what if that was the sort of thing her teenaged self might have done, once upon a time? Maybe it was time to let her brain know that every first evening together didn't have to lead to a night in bed.

Yeah, right. None of her other lovers had gotten her anywhere near as excited as Zhandar, and yet she was pretending that she'd be satisfied with a few kisses?

Her body warmed at the thought of what would happen after they were done with kissing, and so she said hastily, "What are we going to tell everyone at work?"

"The truth, of course," he said without any hesitation. "They will be happy for us. We all grieve for those who are alone, and rejoice when anyone finds their soul match."

Of course they would. Unlike the Gaians, it didn't seem as if the Zhore had a petty or jealous bone in their bodies. That probably wasn't completely accurate, but so far, she hadn't come across anyone who wasn't striving for the common good. And of course the good of the planet included as many of its citizens as possible having harmonious and healthy relationships.

"I am glad to hear that," she said. "Only…can we hold off on saying anything, just for a little while?"

For the first time, his expression clouded. "Of course, if that is what you wish."

Damn. She hadn't meant for him to take it that way. "It's not that—I mean, I'm happy, Zhandar. Very happy." *And soon to be happier still.* "But since I am still so new there, I thought it might be…I don't know…easier if we waited just a little bit."

At once he seemed to relax, saying, "Ah, I had not thought of it that way. You have been so completely in my thoughts for the last few weeks that I had almost forgotten how recently it was that you came to Torzhaan and your current position. We can wait to say anything, and I promise I will be very circumspect when we are in the office together."

"Thank you," she said simply. With Zhandar, she knew no further comment would be required. He understood what she needed. More to the point, he would allow her to have it, with no argument, because he cared about her.

I don't deserve that kind of consideration, she thought then, and was glad that her Zhore skin couldn't flame with embarrassment the way her own fair Gaian complexion would have in a similar situation. It was horrible that she had to lie to him like this. Maybe she knew their connection wasn't a lie—not all of it, anyway—but the cold truth was that she'd been sent here to gather what information she could about Zhoraan and its inhabitants, and no amount of lust or love or whatever she wanted to call it would change that fact.

With a ruthlessness born of long practice, she pushed those thoughts away, making sure none of her unease and worry and self-loathing could rise far enough to the surface that Zhandar might be able to detect it. Instead, she smiled at him, and ate her dinner, and told herself she would do what had to be done.

Whatever that might be.

They did kiss again, after the dinner plates had been cleared away and the last of the *zhir* poured into their glasses. And once again Trinity felt her body flaring with heat, with need. But Zhandar stopped it there. How he found the willpower to do so, she wasn't sure. Wherever he got the strength, however, it was enough for him to pull gently away from her, then lead her to the elevator so they could descend to the parking garage, where he'd left his car. No question of using Torzhaan's excellent transit system to get her home; she could tell Zhandar wanted to stay close to her for as long as possible.

He did not go with her up to her apartment. Respecting her desire to keep their relationship concealed for the moment, he drove into her building's garage, then waited as she made her way to the lifts. One last glimpse of his hooded face watching her from the interior of his car, and then the elevator doors closed in front of her.

No sooner had a sad little sigh escaped her lips than she realized she was not alone in the elevator. Another hooded Zhore stood there in the corner. Trinity didn't often see any of her neighbors—her schedule seemed to be quite different from theirs—and so she tilted her head at the stranger, a common greeting among the Zhore, acknowledging his presence but not bothering him with unwanted conversation.

He did not incline his head in return, however. While she was still registering that particular act of rudeness, he moved toward her with lightning speed. One hand grabbed her arm, while the other came up to her neck. A sudden sharp, piercing pain, and then darkness as black as her cloak enveloped her.

"She's waking up," an unfamiliar male voice said, speaking in Galactic Standard.

"Good," another voice replied, one she recognized all too well, unfortunately.

Gabriel Brant.

Trinity sat up, placing one hand against her head as she did so in a vain attempt to quell the pounding in her temples. A few blinks, and she saw that she was sitting on a hospital bed in a small room with blank gray walls. After the lush plants and natural materials of the Zhore buildings she'd been frequenting lately, the sterile chamber around her looked alien, forbidding.

Or maybe that was just because of the way Gabriel and the two men with him were looking at her. Like something under a microscope.

"What the hell, Gabriel?" she said then, glad that at least she sounded only ordinarily irritated, and not frightened or worried, which was how she actually felt.

"I might ask you the same thing."

She glared at him, then flicked her glance toward the other two men in the room. She knew she'd never seen either of them before. They looked to be in their late thirties or early forties, nondescript, one of them even a little chubby. Their expressions were unreadable.

"Where am I?" This place was as unfamiliar as the two men who accompanied Gabriel. Trinity couldn't begin to figure out why she was here at all. Had something happened to compromise her mission? Were they pulling her out early?

Her relief at the thought of such a prospect was outweighed by the despair that immediately followed. If she was being removed from Zhoraan, that meant she'd probably never see Zhandar again. And that was something she couldn't bear.

"On Kelzhar."

Of course. Zhoraan's second moon. The satellite where off-worlders were allowed to build shops and cafés on the moon's base, thus providing perfect cover for the operatives who'd been put there to monitor and analyze the transmissions from her implant. Those were the two men she didn't recognize.

"What am I doing here? Has something gone wrong with my implant?"

"Yes. The transmissions were becoming garbled, so we had to replace it."

Well, that explained something of why she was here. She wouldn't let herself dare to hope that her last few exchanges with Zhandar hadn't been transmitted at all, but she could see why an equipment malfunction might have forced Gabriel to haul her up here for a replacement.

There seemed to be something else, though, something that made her hackles go up. She couldn't explain why, since she couldn't read anything of what her handler what was thinking. All she knew was that she desperately wished she was back down on Zhoraan.

Gabriel paused, then flicked a glance over one shoulder at his two operatives. "Leave us."

Not even a "please." But that was how things worked in the Consortium's shadow ops. No room for common courtesy there. No need, Trinity supposed. Everyone was used to doing as they were told.

Well, that was one thing she had in common with the two men who'd just left the room.

Once they were gone, Gabriel's attention returned to her. For a long, long moment, he said nothing, but only sat there on the hard metal chair that had been placed next to her hospital bed. She realized then that her heavy hooded cloak had been removed and lay draped across the foot of the bed, although she still had on the close-fitting tunic and slim pants she wore underneath. Thank God for that.

Then Gabriel stood and came over to her. One hand reached out and grasped her by the chin, hard. Trinity winced, but otherwise did not move. It didn't take a psychic to know that she'd done something that angered him. Then again, while his controls were usually very good, right then he seemed upset enough that some of his rage had begun to slip out around the edges.

Not rage, she realized then, her entire body seeming to clench.

Jealousy.

"We were getting some very interesting readings from you, Trinity," he said. He let go of her chin, but only so he could grasp her by the arm. "Spikes in your blood pressure, heart rate…changes in your body temperature readings. But only when you let this Zhandar kiss you. Would you like to explain yourself?"

"There's nothing to explain," she said calmly. In a way, she knew that acting as if his anger was of no great importance would only infuriate him more, but right then, she didn't care. "Wasn't that my mission, to be with, if not Zhandar, some other suitable Zhore male? It turns out that he and I are compatible, though, in the way that the Zhore on Lathvin that you told me about is with his human partner. I was surprised by that, but I

knew what I had to do. So I don't know what you're getting so upset about."

Those anthracite-gray eyes—so different from
Zhandar's shimmering silver—narrowed. "Yes, you were
given a mission. But—"

"But what?" she broke in, pulling her arm from his
grasp. To her relief, he didn't try to grab hold of her
again, but just waited there, hands now clenched into
fists. "I wasn't supposed to enjoy it?"

Right then, she could feel the anger radiating from
him. Alone like this with her, he didn't seem to care
whether he was blocking it or not. "How could you
enjoy it, with that alien?"

Because he's a good man, she thought. *Because my
body sings when he touches me.*

That sort of response probably wouldn't play very
well with Gabriel Brant, however. She knotted her fingers in her lap, still vaguely mesmerized by the play
of light along the tiny, delicate scales of her surgically
applied skin. "An alien who's an empath, remember? I
can block a little from him, but not too much, because
otherwise he'll wonder why he's not sensing responses
in me that he would have felt from any other Zhore
female with whom he had a connection. You can't lie
about those sorts of things, Gabriel. I have to allow
myself to respond to him, because otherwise he'll know
something's wrong. He might begin to guess. And that
would get us all in a world of trouble, wouldn't it?"

While logical, her reply clearly just irritated Brant that much more. Mouth clenched almost as tightly as his fists, he stepped away from her, as if he needed to put some space between them so he could gather his thoughts. At length he said, "I don't like it."

"Yeah, I know." Who would have thought Gabriel Brant would act like some jealous boyfriend, sulking because some other male paid attention to his girlfriend at a bar or club?

The thing was, he wasn't her boyfriend, though. He was the person assigned to handle her, to make sure she carried out the impossible mission the Consortium had seen fit to give her. Somewhere along the line, though, it seemed as if he'd gotten his wires crossed, and now he apparently viewed her as his property. The government wouldn't care about that, not if it got the information it wanted, along with a little half-breed its scientists could study. Once she was done on Zhoraan, she would be Gabriel's.

And although it had seemed at first that he was indifferent to the notion of her having to be intimate with a Zhore, now it looked as if he'd changed his tune. She'd dared to enjoy kissing Zhandar.

Trinity hated what she knew she had to do next, but she didn't see any way around it. Allowing herself a quick breath for courage, she crossed over to where Gabriel stood and laid a hand on his arm.

"It's not as if I really want to do it," she told him. "It's more like...I can let my instincts take over when

I have to. And that's all it is. Instinct. Automatic body functions. You can't think that I'm consciously enjoying myself, can you?"

His eyes scanned her face. Her expressions were still her own, more or less, but they looked so very different now. Because of that, she had no idea what he actually saw in her features.

Whatever it was must have convinced him, however, because in the next moment he was bending down and slamming his mouth on hers, forcing his tongue inside. Trinity forced herself to keep from gagging, and instead pressed her body against his, wrapped her arms around him. And as much as she wanted to shut her eyes so she wouldn't be confronted by the visual evidence of who she was kissing, she knew that would be a mistake.

So she gazed up at him, lids somewhat droopy, as if with desire, but not enough to completely veil her eyes. It seemed to work, because his arms tightened around her as he attempted to claim her with his mouth.

And, thank God, her heart was beating quickly, and her breathing was speeding up, but with tension, not desire. The two goons monitoring all her readings wouldn't be able to tell the difference, though, and that was the important thing. Gabriel could never learn that she was faking all this.

At last he released her, although his eyes never left her face. "You enjoyed that?"

"Of course I did."

A long pause. Then the door opened, and Blake Chu stepped in.

Trinity's mouth went dry. That whole time, she'd been keeping her barriers up—it was just easier to maintain them at all times, rather than raise and lower them at her whim—but had it been enough? Or had Blake somehow managed to see through the lies she'd been telling Gabriel?

Gabriel glanced over his shoulder at Blake. "Well?"

Blake's thin shoulders lifted. "I didn't get anything from her. She must be blocking herself all the time now."

Damn straight. And thank God for that. Fixing what she hoped was a look of innocence on her face, she said, "Was I? I guess I've just been so focused on making sure the Zhore can't get anything out of me that I didn't stop to think about it." Then she lifted an eyebrow and sent a searching glance of her own in Blake's direction. "I thought you'd stayed back at the base."

"I did, but then Gabriel called for me to help out here." Blake smiled, but the eyes behind his glasses remained cold. "Who else could go down there and stab a needle in you to knock you out? I'm the only one who could have kept the Zhore from figuring out the person Gabriel sent wasn't one of them."

She supposed she should have thought of that. "How'd you get me away? It's not like you could have zapped me out of there like on one of those shows set in the future with matter transporters and all that other crap."

Gabriel and Blake exchanged a glance. Then Gabriel replied, "He took you up to the roof of your building, where a shielded craft was waiting for you. We're now able to mimic their transponder codes. They didn't notice anything out of the ordinary. And that's how we'll return you…when we're done with you."

That wasn't really what she wanted to hear. Then again, as angry as he was, Gabriel still needed her to complete the mission. They didn't have anyone else. And whatever his personal feelings on the matter might be, he certainly wasn't about to defy his own superiors to keep her out of the clutches of an alien male. So she knew he wouldn't hurt her, or force himself on her. Not when the entire goal was to get her knocked up by a Zhore.

Despite those reassurances, Trinity wasn't about to let her guard down. "Haven't I done everything you've asked? I'm playing a part. That's all." She almost added, *You need to trust me,* but she knew that wasn't going to happen. She doubted Gabriel Brant trusted anyone. Maybe not even himself.

He gave the slightest tilt of his head toward the door, but that seemed to be enough for Blake. He sent Trinity a last speculative glance, then sidled out. After the door closed again, the little room was deathly quiet. She didn't dare say anything. Now it was Gabriel's turn. He'd have to decide whether he believed what she'd been telling him, or not.

The seconds ticked by. She stood very still, hands at her sides. Then he took a step toward her. Another. They were only a few inches apart. He was very tall. Not quite as tall as Zhandar, but enough that she felt her own lack of height even more keenly.

Gabriel bent toward her, pushed her heavy black-dyed hair away from her ear. His breath came hot as he whispered, "Don't enjoy it. I'll be able to tell."

Then he stepped away. All she could do was remain standing there, until Blake returned to take her back to Zhoraan.

TEN

I<small>T SHOULD HAVE BEEN TORTURE, HAVING</small> Z<small>HANNA THERE EVERY</small> day, and yet not being able to touch her, or even tell the people they worked with how their relationship had changed. And yet, strangely, it wasn't. Perhaps that was simply because they had their stolen hours after work, when she would come to his apartment and they would eat and talk, and lie in each other's arms—still clothed, still only kissing—until the hour grew late enough that he knew he must return her to her home.

Of course he wanted her to stay, but he told himself he must be patient. They would have the rest of their lives to share, and it had only been ten days since they revealed their feelings to one another. There was time.

At any rate, work was keeping them both busy. Zhanna proved over and over what a valuable companion she was, not only in the private times they shared, but also in keeping track of his numerous projects and appointments. Young she might be, but it was clear she had a good deal of experience in this type of work.

And if she seemed reticent to discuss her own past, while at the same time encouraging him to speak of his own family, Zhandar couldn't blame her too much for that. Her losses must still be very fresh, very painful, and if it soothed her to hear about his sister and the child she'd been blessed with, or his parents and their homestead some fifty kilometers outside Torzhaan, Zhandar found himself happy to oblige. He wanted to take her to meet them, but because he and Zhanna had not yet formalized their bond, he decided it would be better to wait. They would have time enough in the future.

Jalzhin had not bothered to contact him again. Rozhara must have passed the word along, and Zhandar was grateful to her for that. But when he'd suggested that he did not need to attend any of their sessions any longer, she told him sternly, "I am pleased that you have found someone who is *sayara*, Zhandar. But that does not mean you've left all the pain of the past behind. You cannot place all your hope for healing on this woman you have only just met."

He'd wanted to protest that he'd done no such thing, but he knew that Rozhara had a point. Besides, if he humored her with one or two more meetings, and she saw how well he was doing, then she would be able to make her own decision regarding his mental health, and would let him alone. He valued his counselor's input and the advice she had given him over the past year, but he believed he had no more need of her guidance.

Zhanna came into his office as he was working with the 3-D modeler, making minute adjustments to the placements of the planters in the rooftop garden he was designing. This was the part of his work he loved the most. The retrofitting and the remodeling were also important, but it was when he had the ability to design a garden from the beginning that he felt his talents were being put to the best use.

Although it was late, and they were the only ones left on this floor, she still shut the door behind her. He looked up, surprised, as she moved toward him, then paused on the other side of the pedestal with the 3-D model of the garden.

"I have been thinking," she began.

"You have?" he asked, the words slightly teasing.

But she didn't rise to the bait. Running a gloved finger along one edge of the pedestal, she went on, "We have a weekend ahead of us."

"Yes," he allowed. That was true enough. Three days to reenergize. Perhaps it was time to take her out to the country. They had explored so many of the city's parks, its museums and galleries. No reason why they couldn't begin to go farther afield. This part of the world was still new to Zhanna, and he would enjoy sharing its beauties with her.

Her barriers dropped. Just a little, but it was like getting a taste of *irzhir* honey, thick with desire, with need.

"I thought that perhaps we could spend the weekend indoors this time."

All notions of taking her exploring dropped instantly away. Or rather, he wanted very much to explore with her…they would just be explorations of a very different nature.

"I think that would be possible," he managed, although his heart was already beating more quickly at the thought of three days with her. Three days of sharing, of making love, of making the final commitment to one another.

"Good," she murmured. "Would you mind if I went home and put together a few things? Then I'll come to you at your apartment."

"No, of course not," he said. "Whatever you would like."

"Oh, I'll let you know what I like," she replied, her voice low and husky with desire. She went to the door and paused there, hand hovering near the controls. "Don't work too late."

And then she had let herself out, and Zhandar had to remind himself to breathe.

Was this a mistake? Trinity had wrapped so many lies around herself, around this world she'd created, that she couldn't begin to figure out what her best course of action was anymore. The true thing, the right thing, would be to tell Zhandar who she really was and why she was really here, but she was too much of a coward for that. Better to do as she was told, get this over with, and then slip away. Yes, that would cause him pain, but the longer she dragged things out, the worse it would get.

Besides, she hated the way he was so open and honest with her, how every little thing he told her about his family, about his past, was being catalogued and discussed and dissected by those two voyeurs up on the second moon, the men assigned to pore over the transmissions sent by her implant. Zhandar certainly didn't deserve that. If she pushed things along, then she could leave him before he laid bare any more of his life.

And she could go crawling back to Gabriel, and let him use her as he wished. After what she'd done to Zhandar, it would be no more than she deserved.

Now, though, to prepare for this weekend with him. Because their clothing was so utilitarian, the Zhore had no need of fancy lingerie. She couldn't go shopping for a silky little piece of nothing to tempt her lover with. When the time came, it would be just the two of them, with no teases or games between them. Skin to skin. Flesh to flesh. Soul to soul.

She shivered, and went to pack the practicalities of a weekend visit. Changes of underwear, that deceptively simple loincloth wrap that both sexes on Zhoraan seemed to wear. Breast supports, not that unlike Gaian bras, but softer and more comfortable. Lotion and a sonic tooth-scrubber and mouth rinse. No cosmetics, because such a thing didn't exist on this world. That was one thing she did miss. Yes, applying makeup could be time-consuming, but she'd always found something soothing about it as well, something almost zen in selecting the colors and using the brushes and applicators she'd collected over the years.

What had happened to all her things, anyway? The clothing and toiletries she'd been given at the Consortium base had all been new. She'd left behind an apartment in Barstow, a place that held everything she'd accumulated in her life so far—clothes, a few pieces of furniture, jewelry and electronics and shoes. Had the apartment been emptied, everything given away? Destroyed?

She supposed Gabriel would know, but she'd never ask him what had happened to it. That would let him know that she cared, and caring about something would give a man like him leverage against her.

Once everything was packed and placed in a small duffle-type bag she'd purchased a week or so ago, knowing this day would soon come, she took a look around her apartment. There was no reason to think she wouldn't be coming back here after the weekend was over, but a little shiver went over her anyway.

Don't freak yourself out, she scolded herself. *You're a psychic, but you're not* that *kind of psychic.*

True enough. Her talent had always involved reading thoughts. She definitely didn't pretend to be able to see the future. If she really had possessed that kind of ability, she wouldn't have gotten herself mixed up with Caleb Prescott, and none of this would have ever happened.

Would that have been better, to never have known Zhandar at all?

She didn't want to answer that question.

Then it was time to go, letting the door shut behind her, riding down in the lifts. She used her handheld to call for an automated taxi, since the light rail let out a few blocks from Zhandar's apartment, and she didn't want to walk that far carrying this duffle with her. That would broadcast her intentions a little too clearly.

On the taxi ride to his place, she stared out the window but didn't really focus on anything. By now, these streets were familiar enough to her—the wide walkways of close-cropped ground cover, so springy and friendly under your feet, the black-clothed figures that moved serenely along, as if no one was ever in a hurry. The plants and flowers growing everywhere. Torzhaan was alive in a way no city she'd ever lived in before had been.

She wished she didn't have to leave.

The taxi stopped in front of Zhandar's building. Trinity quickly swiped her credit voucher through the reader and then got out. At least by now dusk was upon them, and the duffle she carried might not be quite so obvious.

Trying not to look too hurried, she made her way to the building's entrance, then over to the lifts. She did let out a little sigh of relief when the elevator door closed behind her. No one else had gotten in, and so she had this small space of time to compose her thoughts.

Because she knew this would be her greatest challenge yet. So far she thought she had done a fairly good job of keeping her thoughts hidden, only allowing the smallest drifts of emotion to get through, just enough to let Zhandar know that his feelings were reciprocated. But having to maintain that control while he was making love to her?

Actually, if she had the choice to keep everything tamped down, that would be easier. Now, though, she'd have to open herself enough that he would think she was truly sharing with him, while at the same time maintaining strong enough barriers that her true intentions, her true state of mind, wouldn't slip through.

All while letting an alien touch her, make love to her.

Not an alien, she thought then. *Zhandar.*

Sometime over the past month he'd shifted from the alien she was supposed to seduce to the man she loved, and she didn't quite know what to do about that. Nothing, she supposed. It was a pleasant fantasy to think she could somehow find a way to stay here, to be with him, but she knew that was impossible. About the most she could hope for was that he'd never discover the truth.

Enough of that. The elevator doors were opening, and she stepped out, chin held high, even though no one could really see her. But for some reason it felt better to be striding forward confidently, acting as if this had all been her idea, instead of some diabolical plan foisted upon her by her masters.

She pressed the chime next to Zhandar's door. He must have been close by, since it opened almost immediately. Then she was inside, and he was taking her bag from her.

"You see?" he said, a laugh in his voice, even though she couldn't see his expression. "I didn't work too late."

"I'm glad I gave you a reason to come home."

"Oh, yes." He set down the duffle, then reached up with both hands to push her hood away from her face. There was something formal, almost ceremonial, about the gesture, and Trinity forced herself to stand quietly and let him do so. It wasn't that they hadn't spent their private time together uncloaked…more that she knew this time, taking off their hooded robes was only the first step.

He bent and kissed her. Ah, that was better. With his lips spreading sweet fire throughout her veins, it was a lot easier to focus only on him, rather than worry about the future. And when the kiss was done, she pushed his hood back as well so she could see his silver-gray eyes staring down at her intently.

"I have a bottle of *zhir* waiting for us, and some light refreshments. But if you're hungrier than that, I could get something else."

"That sounds wonderful," she replied, then smiled up at him in what she hoped was an appropriately wicked way. "That is, I am hungry…but not for food, precisely."

His eyes gleamed. "I can understand that. But a little bite to start might be a good idea, if we want to keep our energy up."

"I can see the wisdom of that."

Zhandar picked up her duffle again and led her into the living room. After guiding her to one of the couches, he disappeared down the corridor for a moment—to deposit her bag in his bedchamber, she guessed. She did note the tray of pretty little delicacies on the low table in front of the sofa: artfully cut fruit on sweet, thin wafers; a variety of cheeses; thin curls of a local vegetable called *arzha,* topped with savory cream. And the bottle of *zhir,* this one of beautiful glass swirled with shades of blue and green. It must have been a special vintage, since she'd learned that the fancier the bottle, the rarer the liquor inside.

All this, for her.

She stomped on the guilt that reared its head in that moment. The risk that Zhandar could detect the burst of emotion was simply too great, and she couldn't have this end before they even got started.

He came back into the room, and Trinity made herself smile at him. By then she was in control. She had to pray she'd be able to stay that way, no matter what happened.

"This all looks lovely," she told him. "However did you have time to put this together?"

As he settled himself on the couch next to her, he replied, "Well, I might have called the local food delivery shop as soon as you left the office."

"Ah, and here I thought you'd come home and worked away in the kitchen." Her first impulse had been to say "slaved away," but the Zhore had no concept of slavery. Luckily, her language conditioning quickly stepped in and course-corrected.

"I decided my energies might be better spent on other things," Zhandar said, leaning over so he could pick up the bottle of *zhir* and pour a measure into one of the two glasses that had been waiting on the table.

"Wise decision."

He poured for himself as well, then handed her a glass. She took it from him. They both still wore their gloves, even though their faces were now revealed. Trinity supposed those gloves would come off soon enough, along with everything else.

A little shiver worked its way through her, but because her body was still shrouded by the robes she wore, she didn't think Zhandar had noticed. At least, she hoped he hadn't.

"To weekends," she said, and he smiled and raised his glass.

"To weekends together."

They touched glasses, but gently, and then they drank. The *zhir* was a mild intoxicant, nothing more, and so Trinity knew she couldn't rely on it to blur the edges all that much. No, she'd have to do this while in full possession of all her faculties.

"You are nervous," Zhandar said.

Damn. And here she'd thought she had things more or less under control. Well, probably the best thing to do would be to admit to some of the truth, just not all. "A little," she replied. "After all, this is not your first time. But it is mine."

He nodded in understanding. "I will be gentle."

Did she want that? Not really. She knew the effect his kisses had on her, and if she was going to do this, she wanted the same wild heat and abandon in their lovemaking.

"Don't be gentle," she said fiercely. "I don't want you to hold back, Zhandar."

His eyes widened, and then he plucked the glass she held from her fingers. In the next breath, his arms were around her, his mouth on hers, and she tasted him as he pressed her down into the soft cushions. This was the first time she'd ever felt him like this, his weight on her. Even the heavy robes he wore couldn't quite conceal the physical evidence of his arousal, pressing into her thigh, so very close....

But there were probably about ten layers of clothing separating them, and she knew it wouldn't be quite that easy. Her fingers were at the clasp at his throat, undoing it, then tugging at the thick fabric so she could slide it off his broad shoulders.

The cloak seemed to get caught at his elbows, though, and he pulled away from her, eyes glinting. "I fear we are not quite in the best position to get rid of all these clothes."

His fingers plucked at her own robes, and she nodded. "I also hadn't quite imagined this happening on a couch."

That seemed to be all the encouragement he needed, because in the next second his arms were going around her again, only this time to lift her from the sofa and carry her from the living room.

Although she'd been at his apartment many times over the past few weeks, she'd never ventured all that far into it, seeing only the public spaces—the living and dining areas, the kitchen, the restroom reserved for guest use. Now he carried her into his bedchamber, nearly as large as the living room, decorated in the cool hues the Zhore loved so much, blue and green and a pale taupe. It had something of the feeling of stepping into a small wood, since delicate trees lined the walls, and in front of those trees a narrow band of water trickled its way over a bed of smooth gray stones.

"It's beautiful," she breathed.

"Then it is a fitting setting for you, Zhanna, as you deserve to be in a space as lovely as you are." While he spoke, he set her down—but only so he could undo the clasp of her robes and push them to the ground, then finish shrugging out of his own hooded cloak.

They had both been here before—the outer shrouds of their robes gone, facing one another in the close-fitting tunic and pants the Zhore wore underneath. Now, though, Trinity realized they were about to go much further than that. She would have nothing left to hide behind.

Her tunic fastened down the front with a line of pressure tabs. Zhandar undid them one by one, each of them coming loose with a tiny *pop* before he moved on to the next. And then the tunic was open, and he slid it down her arms, then tossed it onto the low chest of pale carved wood that had been placed at the foot of the bed.

The air felt cool against her bare skin. No, she wasn't completely unclothed. Not yet. The chest support still covered her breasts, and she still wore her pants and boots. But even this was more than she had imagined—his eyes on her, taking in the contours of her body. Neither of them seemed to breathe in that moment.

Her hands moved of their own accord, mirroring Zhandar's actions of just a minute earlier. Undoing the tabs on his tunic one by one, then pulling the fabric away from his body and tossing it on top of her own discarded shirt.

She'd known from the breadth of his shoulders that he was not a slight man, but even so, she wasn't prepared for the heavy muscles of his arms and chest, nor the way the light seemed to ripple over his skin, all those tiny scales shimmering and bringing the shape of his body into higher relief, rather than obscuring it. Tentatively, she reached out and ran her fingers down his chest, from his collarbone to the tiny nipples, black on black, that topped his pectorals.

He let out a sound that was half sigh, half groan. In response, she moved her fingers lower, finding the fastener for his trousers.

"Wait," he said, and she looked up at him in surprise. They'd come this far, and now he wanted her to wait?

That wasn't the true reason for his protest, however. He bent and yanked off one boot, then the other. Seeing his intention, Trinity did the same. And then there was nothing stopping them from removing the other's trousers and adding them to the growing pile of clothing on the carved wood chest.

Now they wore only their undergarments. Zhandar's might have hid his groin, but that loincloth thing he had on certainly wasn't enough to conceal his erection. She reached for the fastener on one side, but again he stopped her.

"Come to the bed," he said.

All right, she wouldn't argue with that. Silently, she allowed him to lead her to the bed. He kissed her, his tongue touching hers, sweet and sharp with the taste of *zhir*. And as a new wave of desire rushed over her, she felt him reach behind and undo the clasp of the breast support she still wore. She gasped, even as he bent to take a nipple into his mouth.

Oh, God, it might have been wild honey running through her veins, rather than ordinary blood. That was how she felt right then, as if all the sweetness and fire in the universe had somehow concentrated itself in her body. In that moment, she didn't care that someone might be watching, didn't care that it wasn't her skin Zhandar touched, but something grown in a lab so she could be placed here as a counterfeit, a spy. No, all she wanted was his touch, his mouth, the heat of his body next to hers.

Her fingers yanked at the tabs holding his loincloth closed. It fell away, and her hand moved lower, found him, took him into her fingers, feeling his girth, the heavy strength of him. He was bigger than she'd imagined, and if she'd truly been the virgin she was pretending to be, his size might have frightened her a little. Now, though, she could only shiver at the thought of him inside her, filling her in a way no one else ever had.

He groaned, and she gasped as she felt the vibrations from his deep voice seem to travel through her, penetrating her even before they actually truly touched. And then, as if he couldn't hold himself back any longer, he tore the loincloth she wore away from her body and flung it to the floor. The next thing she knew, they were falling to the bed, the two of them pressed together as if attempting to meld their separate bodies into one.

His fingers moved up her thigh, then sank into her. She gasped, then began to rock with him, little whimpers escaping her throat as he stroked her. God, how did he know to touch her like that, to find the exact spot that sent shudders of ecstasy moving through her?

Empath, she realized, with one of the last scraps of rational thought left to her. *He senses what pleases you most, and focuses there.*

Of course.

But she didn't dare lose all control. No, even as her body was bucking and spasming against him, Trinity couldn't let go all the way. She couldn't allow a single thought to bubble up about concealing her identity from him, or worrying about how Gabriel must be watching her with Zhandar and growing increasingly incensed, since she knew she was gasping and screaming like a madwoman, and looking the very opposite of someone who wasn't supposed to be enjoying all this.

As the ripples from the climax began to finally fade away, she shifted, kissing her way down Zhandar's body, her lips feeling the soft ripples of his scaled skin against her. And then she was taking him in her mouth, tasting the sweet musk of him, caressing him with her tongue. A groan went through him, so deep it seemed to reverberate throughout his entire body.

She could make him come, she knew. It wouldn't take much. But her purpose in being here wasn't to get him to climax that way. She had a mission she was supposed to accomplish.

His breathing accelerated, and she pulled away, shifting so she was lying next to him. His eyes opened, and then he nodded as he seemed to grasp what she wanted next.

"Are you sure?" he whispered.

Trinity nodded. "More sure than I've been of anything else."

And that wasn't even a lie. She knew what she had to do…but at the same time, she wanted it. No matter what happened afterward. Right now, she wanted to share this with him.

He pulled in a breath, and then he was over her, pushing between her legs. She could feel him touch her. Yes, he was big, but she was ready. So very ready.

Would he guess that she wasn't a virgin? Or was her interior geometry just different enough from a female Zhore's that he wouldn't notice? It wasn't the sort of thing any of the Consortium scientists or doctors had even mentioned. Maybe they just didn't realize that the Zhore stayed virgins until they bonded with their partners. At any rate, it wasn't anything she could change now.

Just a pause. A heartbeat, then another. And then he was pushing his way inside, filling her, just as she'd hoped, her core seeming to pulse around him, feeling not just his size, but that delicious delicately scaled skin caressing her, awakening nerve endings she hadn't even known she possessed until this moment.

They began to rock together, slowly, then faster and faster. Her nails were digging into his shoulders, but she doubted he even noticed. Everything was in this connection between them—she could feel his love and his desire flowing out and encircling them both, pulling them that much closer together. And she allowed something to escape—just a little, just a pulse of her own need, her affection for him. Anything more, and she knew she ran the risk of him detecting far more than she wanted him to.

That seemed to be enough, though. His arms tightened around her, even as she felt him drive deeper, then release, the wild ecstasy pouring from him catching her up as well, swirling around her while her own orgasm exploded through her, along every vein, every nerve ending, every cell in her body. All she could do was hang onto him, riding it out, knowing that she didn't dare do anything else until that wave of pleasure finally ebbed, leaving her gasping in his arms.

Neither of them spoke. He only held her tightly against him, his mouth against her hair, both their chests heaving for breath. Trinity wished it could always be like this—bodies pressed together, his love for her such a palpable thing that she thought she might be able to reach out and touch it, feel it flow over her fingers like a ribbon of sun-warmed silk.

But even in that moment of perfect harmony, she knew this bliss couldn't last.

ELEVEN

THE MOST NATURAL THING WOULD HAVE BEEN FOR ZHANNA TO move into his residence. After all, they had no need of separate apartments, now that they had shared themselves fully. But when he asked her, she'd only shaken her head and told him,

"Not yet, Zhandar."

He hadn't insisted, although her refusal troubled him greatly. She seemed happy enough to let matters remain as they were between them, even as the days and then weeks began to pass. And because she came to his apartment nearly every night, only slipping out in the early morning hours so she could go home and prepare herself for work, he told himself that their current arrangement was almost the same as living together.

Almost.

The Gaians, he had heard, had quite elaborate wedding rituals, with special clothing and music and flowers, and the Eridanis celebrated their matches by spending at least a month traveling to new places so the married couple could form new memories together. They were not quite as formal here on Zhoraan, of course. The physical communion he and Zhanna had shared was quite enough to prove their intention of spending the rest of their lives together. But it was as if, even though she had taken that very large step, she could not quite steel herself to make the final one of truly living with him as his wife.

He tried to reassure himself that she was only reluctant because they had not yet made a formal announcement at their work. From a few head tilts and awkward pauses, Zhandar had guessed that Nizhal, one of the other designers in the office, had realized something not entirely professional was being shared between his supervisor and the director's new assistant, but of course Nizhal was far too well-mannered to actually say anything to either of them.

And because Zhanna lived in the same city—only one district over from his—and because she came to him every night, Zhandar had not suffered the torture of being truly separated from her. She knew as well as he did that once two Zhore had made their soul bond, an actual separation of any real distance or time would result in their demise. It was only when that soul bond was broken by death that one of his people could survive the loss of their mate.

Not that they would particularly want to. Most who lost their partners did not live long afterward, but then, deaths such as Elzhair's were rare. Old age claimed most of Zhandar's people, not the sort of untimely tragedy that had taken his late wife's life.

Now Zhanna came into his office, but because the door was open and the third hour of the afternoon not yet past, he knew they would share no confidences. Too many people around.

"Brezhanne just contacted me," Zhanna informed him. "All the beds have been laid down, and the piping for the drip system installed. They will need you to come inspect the site and let them know if all is in order so that they can begin bringing in the plants and soil."

Her voice was brisk, businesslike. He expected no less, of course, but at the same time he wished he could hear the soft, throaty tone it took on when they were alone together.

"Let her know that we will be there within the hour."

Zhanna inclined her head and headed back to her office. It would be something, this small excursion of theirs. At least they would be alone in his car, and he might be able to take her hand, lay his hand on her knee. Perhaps even steal a kiss, if the opportunity presented itself. Some might say he was torturing himself with these small intimacies, but better to have that tiny taste of her rather than nothing at all.

Nothing, he thought then, and wanted to shake his head at himself, at this need that seemed to have overcome all his common sense. *Only nothing for these few hours while we remain at work. Once you are home, you will have all of her.*

Again, and again. It seemed he would never tire of tasting her, and she certainly showed no sign of wanting to slow things down. Indeed, he got the distinct impression that she would have been happy making love all night, if it weren't that they had to get up and go to the office, and behave as if nothing untoward was happening between them.

It wasn't untoward, though. Their being together was the most natural thing in the world, and he wondered how long she would allow matters to stand as they were.

And how long he would be willing to wait.

Zhandar was getting edgy, that much Trinity could tell, but living with him as his wife was something she couldn't allow herself to do. Bad enough that every moment they spent together was being recorded by that damned implant inside her head. If she was with him day and night, then he would have absolutely no privacy at all. And while she didn't like using work as the excuse to maintain separate residences, at least it was an excuse that he seemed to accept...for the moment, anyway.

Usually she enjoyed going on these field trips with him. Today, though, she worried that he would use the privacy of his car to talk to her about their current living arrangements, or lack thereof.

Her concerns were confirmed when he said, not even a moment after they left the garage under their office building, "It has been nearly a month since we first sealed our bond."

Trinity didn't reply at once. The now-familiar streets were passing by outside, but in that moment they suddenly seemed alien once again, hostile. But she knew that was only her own emotions coloring what she saw.

After a long pause, she replied, "And it has been a wonderful month."

She couldn't see his face, but she somehow knew that his mouth tightened behind the low-hanging hood. "Yes, it has…but it could have been even more wonderful. Zhanna, no one will think we have acted in a precipitate manner for sharing one roof after all this time."

All this time. Among the commitment-phobic men she'd dated, a month was just barely enough time to be given a spot in a drawer for a few spare pairs of underwear. But Zhandar wasn't like anyone else she'd ever known. And it was true among the Zhore that, once they committed to one another, there were no lengthy engagements, no real courtship periods. They knew they were meant for one another, and so they began to live together. Simple.

Only in her case, things were far from simple. She already knew that leaving would hurt him immeasurably, but at the same time, she stubbornly hoped avoiding that final step would lessen the hurt, if only a little. Living apart, she could pretend that she wasn't truly his wife, even though Zhore society would view their relationship very differently.

"Perhaps we can talk about this tonight," she said. "I don't see any point in having an argument right before we meet with the foreperson at the construction site."

Anger flared out from him, but just as quickly he pushed it back. It was a banked fire, though, one that could come roaring to life again at any moment. "Were we having an argument?" he asked, voice tight.

She turned away from him to stare out the window. "Not yet."

They remained coolly silent for the rest of the ride to the new building. Once they arrived, they stayed quiet during the elevator ride up to the rooftop. Luckily, the foreperson didn't seem to notice anything amiss about the way Zhandar and his assistant acted toward one another, and Trinity thanked God for that. He conducted his inspection with grave courtesy, thanked the foreperson for her patience with his changes, and praised her for the finished product.

"Yes, we are ready for the final step," Zhandar told her. "I'll give the order for the soil and plants to be delivered. They will be here tomorrow morning, if that suits you."

"It suits me very well," she said. "For after this project, I will go on retreat for a while. It is time for me to rest, I think. But I will be happy, knowing that we brought life to this place."

"And I, and my colleagues, will be happy as well." He clasped his hands together and bowed over them, and the foreperson did the same. Standing off to one side, Trinity wondered if she should make the same gesture of respect, but then decided against it, since she hadn't actually been part of the conversation.

He was polite enough as he made a few requests of her, such as asking her to confirm the time of delivery for the soil the next morning, but there was a notable lack of warmth in his voice. She told herself not to worry, that he was merely being formal in front of the foreperson, but she still felt a faint thread of unease working its way down her spine, chilling her despite the mild day.

When they were back in the car and headed toward their office, he said, "Perhaps it would be better if you stayed at your apartment this evening."

"Really?" she replied. "You are asking that of me?"

"Yes," he said tersely, "I am asking that of you."

She lifted her shoulders, not caring whether she looked or sounded properly Zhore in that moment. "Suit yourself."

The rest of the afternoon felt like pure torture, but she managed to get through it somehow. And she left with the rest of her coworkers, rather than lingering in her office, pretending to be busy with some project or another. On the way out, Nizhal gave her the Zhore equivalent of the side-eye—that is, his hood tilted somewhat quizzically in her direction, although he didn't speak—but that was the extent of anyone's reaction to her leaving on time for once.

Which was just as well. Right then she was profoundly grateful for the empathic aliens' reticence about prying into anyone else's affairs. It took her last ounce of energy to take the light rail home, then make her way to her apartment. Why she felt so tired, she wasn't sure. True, being at odds with Zhandar did little to help her outlook on life, but she'd been draggy and listless for the past couple of days.

Probably the return of the monthly trouble, she told herself as she shut the door behind her. *You're not used to having to deal with it, and it should be due any day now.*

Well, that made sense. Once women in the Consortium started getting their shots, their periods were light or, in Trinity's case, basically nonexistent. But who knew how those counter-shots Gabriel's doctors had given her were messing with her system.

Every time she came home, she was on edge, wondering if she was going to find Blake Chu waiting for her in the elevator to whisk her away so she could be on the receiving end of another round of browbeating. She sort of doubted that Gabriel was all that happy to see the way she lost herself in Zhandar's arms night after night.

Who knew that faking *not* enjoying yourself in bed would be so damn difficult?

But she hadn't heard from her handlers, which meant that either Gabriel had found the inner strength to not go all alpha male on her, or that someone even farther up the food chain had told him he needed to back off. Whatever the reason for his hands-off approach lately, she was glad for it. Having to walk a tightrope with Zhandar all the time was hard enough.

And that exchange earlier today…she knew he was tired of her holding him at arm's length, but at the same time, she'd never thought he would go so far as to request some time away from her. That was such an un-Zhore-like response to the situation that she knew she must have upset him greatly.

The trouble was, she had no idea what else she could have done.

Sighing, she pulled off her heavy cloak and tossed it over the arm of a chair. If she was going to order in any food later, she'd have to put it back on, but for now it felt good to be free of that continual weight on her shoulders. She still wondered how the Zhore could put up with those damn things day in and day out, but maybe it wasn't as much of a problem when you'd been doing it since childhood.

It was strange to be here and know that she wouldn't be going over to Zhandar's apartment tonight. Occasionally she would come home first to gather a few things, but now, to be wandering around aimlessly, not sure what to do next….

Maybe a nice hot bath. She'd never been much of a bath person—it was a luxury her water allotment back on Gaia really hadn't allowed—but the bathtub in this apartment was luxurious, carved stone with plants all around it, and no one on Zhoraan seemed to be terribly concerned about water consumption.

The sound of the water filling the tub was soothing enough. On a whim, she'd bought some scented bath oil a few weeks back, but this was the first time she'd used it. She opened the cabinet to retrieve it, and then her gaze fell on the box that contained spare tubes of shampoo.

Well, that was what the box said, anyway. What it actually contained were a series of small innocuous-looking plastic tabs.

If you put one of those tabs on your tongue and it turned purple, it meant you were pregnant.

Trinity had used a couple of them the first few times she and Zhandar were intimate. Due diligence and all that. But the tabs had remained stubbornly white, and she'd decided she only needed to check once a week. The last time had been a week ago, and still nothing. Maybe humans and Zhore weren't quite as cross-fertile as she'd been led to believe.

Still, she knew she should be checking. Her hand hovered over the box, and she hesitated. She'd been feeling so very tired lately....

She really didn't want to complete the thought, just as she didn't want to pick up one of the tabs and set it on her tongue. Because once she knew, there would be no turning back. She'd see it, and Gabriel would see it, and the next thing she knew, an extraction team would be there, taking her away.

And she couldn't bear that. Especially not today, when she and Zhandar had parted on such bad terms.

But if the people watching the feed saw her start to pick up one of the tabs, and not go through with the test....

That would be much, much worse.

Before she could lose her nerve and stop herself, she popped open the box and extracted one of the pieces of white plastic, then set it on her tongue. Thirty seconds to wait, and then she would know. It felt hard and foreign in her mouth, and she wanted to spit it out, even though it had no actual taste. She kept it there, however, because she knew that was what she had to do.

The plastic tingled on her tongue, letting her know that the thirty seconds were up. Using her thumb and forefinger, she pulled out the little tab.

Bright purple.

Her stomach lurched, and the piece of plastic fell from her fingers onto the stone countertop with a faint *clink.*

No, she thought. *No.*

Problem was, she could think that all she wanted, but it wouldn't change the fact that she was now carrying Zhandar's child.

Pressing her hands on the counter, she stared into the mirror, into the alien face that had somehow become hers over the past month, even though she knew it wasn't her, not really. "All right, Gabriel," she said distinctly. "It looks like you got what you wanted. So you can send your lackeys to come get me."

Then she had to turn away from the mirror, because tears had begun to sting her eyes. She tried to blink hard so they would disappear, but that didn't work. Angrily, she reached up to wipe away the moisture that had begun to trickle down her cheeks. The last thing she wanted was to be a big weeping mess when Blake or Gabriel or whoever it was showed up to take her away.

The door chime sounded, and she startled, thinking that they'd gotten here already. No, that was ridiculous. Even Gabriel Brant didn't move that fast. Besides, she doubted he would do anything so polite as ring the door chime.

Mystified, she hurried out to the front room, grabbing her cloak along the way so she could shrug into it and thereby satisfy convention by not shocking whoever was waiting outside her door. But even before she opened it, she realized who stood there. She could feel him, warm and comforting, but at the same time worried and contrite, blaming himself for his harsh words earlier that afternoon.

"Zhanna?" came Zhandar's voice. "What is the matter?"

Oh, hell. In her agony, she'd probably been broadcasting all over the place, her barriers shattered to rubble by the news she'd just received. "Nothing, Zhandar," she said through the door, hoping she sounded relatively normal.

"Let me in," he replied.

It was not a request, she could tell. Anyway, it wasn't as if she could just leave him standing out there in the foyer. At least if he was inside her apartment, they'd be someplace private.

She pressed her palm against the door's controls, and it slid open. Zhandar stood immediately outside. As always, his face was concealed, but she could feel the agitation roiling the air around him, as if he was moving within his own personal thundercloud.

He came inside, and she shut the door behind him. Almost at once he pushed back his hood. His features were strained with worry, and he came to her in the very next second and took her hands.

"My love, I couldn't stay away a moment longer. I had no right to speak to you that way. I—"

And then he paused, his hands tightening on hers. Trinity flinched, worried that somehow he would be able to tell from her very touch what she carried within her. He couldn't know about that. He just couldn't. Bad enough that she should leave, but if she took with her the child he'd been longing for....

It would kill him.

She wanted to wrench her hands away. Instead, she withdrew her fingers from his grasp as gently as she could, using the pretext that she wanted to reach up and push back her own hood. He let her go, but with obvious reluctance.

Her hands were shaking. In a nervous gesture, she peeled off her gloves and tossed them onto the sofa. Damn. Maybe it would have been better to keep them on. Trinity knew she couldn't do anything about that now, so she continued the pretext of wanting to remove the garments that concealed her face and body from him. It was hard to undo the clasp that held the cloak shut, what with the way her fingers were trembling, but somehow she managed it.

"You upset me," she said, not quite looking at Zhandar.

"I could tell that. It is why I came here." He paused then, keen silver-gray eyes searching her face. "But… there is more, isn't there?"

"No," she replied. Of course it was a lie, but she couldn't tell him the truth as to why she was truly so upset. But if he went into the dressing area of her restroom, saw the discarded plastic tab on the counter….

No, he wouldn't know what that was, most likely. It was Consortium technology, not Zhore. Still, it would look very out of place, and she might have to try explaining it away.

Zhore couldn't flush, but something about his expression appeared to darken. "Why are you lying to me?"

Oh, shit. Oh, shit. Clamp it down, Trinity.

Walls. High walls of duracrete. Unbreakable. Unassailable.

But they had shared a bond, the two of them. Trinity tried to push him away, but his emotions—his mind—seemed to hammer at hers, seeking a way in, wanting to know what it was that troubled her so much she would lie to him.

Zhore didn't lie.

His black brows drew together, and he reached out and took her by the wrist. Not roughly, but so she knew she wouldn't be able to pull away. He was too strong for her. She'd worried all along that might turn out to be the case.

"Who are you?" he demanded. Then, as she didn't reply, his grip tightened. Waves of dismay seemed to ripple out from him. "*What* are you?"

It was over. Somehow he'd been able to see inside her mind. Somehow he'd gotten past the defenses she'd worked so hard to build. She could have asked why, but she knew the answer.

Because she loved him. And the more she loved him, the more she hated herself. Eventually, it had to spill out, no matter what she did to hide how she felt.

"My name is Trinity Knox," she said sadly. "I'm a Gaian."

TWELVE

For a long moment, all Zhandar could do was stare at her. Then, slowly, he let go of her wrist. She rubbed it, but absently, as if it didn't matter much whether or not he'd hurt her.

At last he found his voice. "But you look—but we—" He had to stop himself there. They had shared so many intimacies, he and this woman who stood before him. She was *sayara*. He knew that, knew it as well as he knew the color of the sky, the number of moons that circled Zhoraan. But…how could she be *sayara,* and Gaian?

"I know," she said quietly.

He couldn't stop studying her face, attempting to see something in its contours, its shape, that would reveal her as an alien. If the clues were there, however, he couldn't see them. That made some sense. The Gaians wouldn't have sent her if she could be that easily detected.

"Why?" he asked at last.

For the first time, she glanced away from him. Gaze apparently fixed on a blooming shrub in the planter off to her side, she said, "I'd rather tell you that someplace safer."

"Safer?" he asked, looking around her apartment in some confusion. Surely they were private enough here. Or was she saying she'd rather have this conversation in his own home, a place where they'd spent so many happy hours together?

A sad smile pulled at her mouth, but at the same time, he could sense fear slipping out past her barriers. Not fear of him, though. But who?

She said, voice too calm, "On second thought, it's probably better if you call the authorities and have me arrested."

He hadn't really known what to do. The Zhore had no need of a police force the way some worlds did. There were probably agents in his government who would be of help, men and women more accustomed to Gaians and their unscrupulous practices, but he knew no one like that.

So, unable to think of a better alternative, he had contacted Jalzhin, from the Ministry of Health Services. In a very short time, a large transport vehicle showed up outside Zhanna's—Trinity's, he corrected himself— apartment building, and she was whisked away.

Now Zhandar stood with Jalzhin and a man from the government who had only identified himself as Nalzhir.

That in itself was not strange; unlike the Gaians and the Eridanis, his people did not use surnames. In general, though, when introduced, they would state something of where they came from, or the current position they held, simply to provide some context. But this Nalzhir had omitted that particular detail, which told Zhandar that his was the sort of occupation the government didn't want discussed openly.

The three of them were standing in a sort of observation room that overlooked the chamber where Trinity now sat opposite the woman who had been assigned to interrogate her. While the interrogator was still cloaked and hooded, Trinity had not been allowed any such concessions to propriety. She wore a slim-fitting tunic and pants, but her face and head were uncovered, her black hair spilling over her shoulders.

No, not *her* black hair. Nalzhir had shown him, based on her DNA readings, what Trinity truly looked like. Hair a warm brown with deep gold streaks in it, skin fair, almost delicately pink and white, like the blossoms of the *charazh*. Only her eyes were the same, the brilliant blue-green, like the changing waters of the sea.

Alien, and yet…still beautiful. The contours of the features he'd come to love were still there, only with a different wrapper, so to speak. And then he'd hated himself for thinking that, because she had lied to him. She'd been sent here by her government to use him and steal what secrets she could.

His jaw hardened. "What has she told you?"

"Not much," Nalzhir allowed. "Unlike the Gaians, we do not engage in forcible interrogations. All she's said so far is that she never meant to hurt anyone."

"Too late for that," Zhandar muttered.

"Alizhair—our questioner—pointed that out to Ms. Knox. But that didn't seem to do much to persuade her to be more forthcoming. She keeps saying that she wants to talk to you before she says anything to us."

"Then I will talk to her."

Nalzhir's hooded head shook. "I'm afraid that's not possible. At least, not yet." He paused then, and although of course Zhandar could not see the other man's face, he sensed a ripple of unease coming from him, quickly masked. "There is something else, though."

How there could possibly be anything beyond the betrayal he'd already suffered, Zhandar didn't know. His gloved hands, hidden within the folds of his robes, clenched. "Tell me."

"We performed a nonintrusive physical examination, just to make sure she had not brought any Gaian illnesses or microbes with her."

"Did she?" Zhandar asked in alarm, thinking back to the many times he had been intimate with the Gaian woman. But no, surely if she had been ill in any way, he would have shown his own symptoms long before now.

"No," Nalzhir replied. "She is free from disease, as far as we are able to ascertain. Only…."

The government agent—or whatever he was—had very good control, but Zhandar was still able to detect the faintest tinge of unease slipping past his barrier. "Only what?"

"Only it appears that she is with child."

The world tilted, but then Zhandar told himself that there must have been some mistake. Either that, or…. He said, tone dripping with disdain, "The Gaians stooped to sending a pregnant woman on an underhanded mission such as this one?"

"I fear you misunderstand me. She is in the very early stages of pregnancy. It had to have occurred after she arrived her. The child is yours, Zhandar."

There was nothing to hold on to, not a chair, not a frame around the window that looked down on the interrogation room where Trinity sat. Zhandar could only keep himself as still as he could while those impossible words beat inside his brain.

The child is yours, Zhandar.

"How is that possible?" he asked then. "For she is not—that is, she is Gaian." It was just barely comprehensible to him that he could share the *sayara* bond with a woman who was not of his race. But for two entirely different species to be able to interbreed?

A long pause. Nalzhir shifted away from him, his gaze fixed on the young woman who sat at the table beyond the glass, who showed no sign of discomfort at having her face and form revealed to near-strangers. But of course she wouldn't, because a Gaian did not share the customs and strictures of the Zhore.

At last the agent said, "It is not something we have made public. The first instance was not so long ago. A little more than a year. A colonist's daughter and a man of our people named Sarzhin. She had a son, a healthy son. It was a miracle on all levels."

His thoughts were darting here and there so quickly that Zhandar wasn't sure which one he should latch onto first. "This Gaian girl and this Sarzhin. They were—they were *sayara?*"

"Yes."

That a Gaian—a race he had always viewed, when he thought of them at all, as grasping, unscrupulous, and lacking the refinement of mind that was so much a part of his own culture—could be *sayara* was just barely within the bounds of plausibility. But then, he'd felt it with Trinity, even though at the time he'd thought her one of his own people. So he knew it wasn't entirely impossible, even if the logical side of his mind kept trying to tell him there must have been some kind of mistake.

Then he latched on to something else Nalzhir had told him. "You just said 'the first instance.' There have been others?"

"Only one. She is actually here on Zhoraan, with her spouse. Lirzhan, a former ambassador."

"So that is how they met? Because he had gone out into the galaxy?"

"In a manner of speaking." A brief pause, and Nalzhir continued, "She is a month away from giving birth, but so far the pregnancy has been unremarkable. Well, other than it being a pregnancy that resulted from the joining of a Gaian and a Zhore."

It was too much. Zhandar forced in a breath, made himself stare down at Trinity. Of course it was far too soon to see any visible signs of pregnancy in her, but his breath caught at the idea anyway.

"I want to speak with her," he said.

"As I said, that is not possible at the moment."

"Why not? She's asking to talk with me. Perhaps I can have better luck with her."

Nalzhir hesitated. Another one of those uneasy pulses. "Later. The doctors have determined that it would be best to restore her to herself first."

The words took a few seconds to filter into Zhandar's brain. As comprehension dawned, he growled, "You would perform that kind of surgery on her when she is with child?"

"It is for the best. I told you that she is free from disease, but that does not mean she is entirely healthy. From what we can tell, her body is beginning to reject its alien skin. Best to rid her of it, return her to her normal state. It will not be an invasive procedure, so it should not affect the child at all."

Zhandar turned back toward the window, then placed his gloved hands on it. Trinity shifted in her seat and looked up toward him, although he assumed the glass was the sort that would not allow her to see through it. But her reaction told him that she knew he was there. He hadn't thought a Gaian would possess such psychic sensitivity, but clearly Trinity had talents beyond those of a normal human.

He was still angry with her...but at the same time, he didn't want to see her come to any harm. And if the barbaric surgery her masters had inflicted on her was now actively causing her to become ill, then better for his own people to heal her.

And after that...well, he would just have to see.

Once again, Trinity awoke from darkness, but this time she didn't hurt as much. Or rather, she felt sore and tingly all over, as if she'd stayed out in the sun too long, but it wasn't the kind of deep muscle ache she'd experienced upon awakening from the surgery that had turned her into a Zhore.

She glanced down, and saw that the hair falling over one shoulder was warm brown, not black. The gold highlights had even been restored. And when her gaze shifted to her arm, emerging from the short sleeve of the pale blue shift-like gown she wore, she saw that her skin was no longer the mesmerizing shifting black of the Zhore, but her normal pale ivory.

"You're back with us."

The last thing she'd expected to see was Zhandar sitting at her side, waiting for her to wake up. How could he seem so calm, so controlled, when she'd used him so badly?

But she wouldn't think about that now. For one thing, she simply didn't have the energy. "I suppose I am," she said, then lifted her right hand and flexed her fingers, watching the light from overhead pick out the faintest traceries of the bluish veins beneath her fair skin. She realized then that they were still speaking the Zhore language, which by now felt like second nature to her. Her alien disguise had been removed, but what about that hideous implant, the one that had spied on everything she said and did?

Her fingers reached up toward the back of her neck. The tiny bump there was gone, and the flesh left behind tender to the touch. So they'd found it, thank God. Trinity would have loved to see Gabriel Brant's expression when he discovered that not only did he have no way of retrieving her, not with her in the hands of the authorities on this alien world, but that he'd also just lost his only means of seeing what was happening to her.

Did Zhandar know about that implant? Or had the doctors who'd removed it decided that it was better not to tell him that his every interaction with her over the past few months had been recorded?

She decided she'd leave that aside for later. That was some very dangerous ground. Instead, she asked, "How...?" And then she let the question break off, because she knew that what she really wanted to ask was *why*.

He seemed to understand. "You were in the early stages of rejection."

Well, that would explain the tiredness, the vague sensations of nausea and the low-grade headaches. The borrowed Zhore skin had probably been poisoning her from the outside in. Not sure what she should say, she picked up a strand of her hair and held it between her thumb and forefinger, inspecting it as if it was the most important thing in the world right then. "They did a great job with the color."

"I'll pass that on." She caught an unlikely twinge of amusement from him, one that faded abruptly. "How do you feel otherwise?"

"All right. A little tired." His question made her pause and take more detailed inventory. Yes, she did feel somewhat taut and sensitive, but she assumed that sensation would pass as she continued to heal. But her head didn't ache, and she could already tell that if she just rested a bit more, she should be back to her old self fairly quickly.

Her old self. There was a joke.

"Do you feel well enough to talk?"

Physically, yes. But emotionally…? She didn't know. Zhandar deserved the truth from her now, though, since all she'd handed him before were lies. Anyway, she'd told the interrogator the day before that she wouldn't say anything to anyone until she talked to Zhandar first.

Well, here he was.

Trinity shifted in her bed, reflecting it was more comfortable than the one provided for her back on the Consortium base. The room itself here was also vastly more comfortable; there were no water features, but plants hung from sconces on the walls, and everything had been painted a soft, dreamy blue. And Zhandar himself....

He had his barriers up. She supposed she could have expected nothing less. What she hated was that hood, the way it drooped low to hide his face. She needed to see him, to see his expression as she tried to explain to him why she'd done what she'd done. Why she'd been forced into it.

The hood didn't surprise her, though. They were in a hospital room, but it could still be considered a public place. And for all she knew, even though the Zhore were not ordinarily a surveillance-happy race, they had cameras hidden around the room, recording everything she and Zhandar did and said. She couldn't blame them for that. The Zhore might have given her a very comfortable place where she could recuperate, but she was still a prisoner of sorts. She'd been caught spying.

Even with all that, she had to ask. "Zhandar...."

"Yes?"

"I'll tell you everything you need to know. I swear it. But I need to see you. Please."

No response at first. Then he moved in his chair, shifting so he faced her directly. His hands went up to push back his hood. "Better?"

She loved the bones of his face, the sculpted curve of his lips. It didn't matter that he was an alien. He was still so very beautiful. Inside and out. "Yes, much better."

"You don't care that I am…not like you."

A bitter laugh forced its way past her lips. "Zhandar, I am *very* glad that you're nothing like me."

He shook his head, then deliberately peeled off one glove, followed by the other. Fingers now bare, he rested his hand on top of hers. The shields were still up, but she could feel something more now—a hint of sadness, and then worry for her. Well, that was a start. At least she wasn't sensing deep pulsing waves of hatred and anger.

No, she didn't think she needed to worry about that. Zhandar was capable of anger, true, but his soul didn't possess the capacity to hate.

"Tell me," he said quietly. "Why would you allow your own people to mutilate you in such a way?"

"'Mutilate'?" Trinity repeated, startled. "Why would you call it mutilation, when I was made to look like one of your own kind?"

"Because it was not you. Yes, you were beautiful as Zhanna, but you are far more beautiful as Trinity Knox. Because that is who you truly are."

She hadn't allowed herself to think about whether he would find her attractive as a human. What did it matter, when her lies had destroyed any chance of a future with him? Besides, now that she had been caught, she was sure the Zhore government would ship her back to Gaia just as soon as they were done getting any useful information out of her. And no way of knowing how much this incident would set back Consortium/Zhore relations, which had never exactly been what one would call cordial.

For some reason, her throat felt very tight. "Water?" she managed.

If Zhandar had noted her reaction, he showed no sign of it. Giving her a nod, he rose gracefully from his seat and went over to a small table set up against the wall, where a pitcher of bluish plastic and several tumblers sat. He poured some water into one of them, then returned to his chair and handed her the cup.

"Thank you." She sipped the water, relishing the cool, faintly mineral taste of it on her tongue. Why did even the water taste better here on Zhoraan?

But she knew she couldn't delay much more, not with Zhandar sitting there and watching her, clearly waiting for her to go on. After taking a few more sips of water, she didn't hand the tumbler back to him, but rather sat there with her hands cradled around it. As much as she'd loved the touch of his fingers against hers a few moments earlier, she knew she needed to stay focused as she recounted her story.

Funny how she hadn't even hesitated about doing so. He deserved the truth from her, and Gabriel and Blake and the rest of the people who'd done this to her could all go straight to hell.

"I'm not a spy," Trinity began. "That is," she added, when Zhandar's eyebrows began to lift, "I'm not a *professional* spy. I was tapped to do this because of my— well, I guess you could call them gifts. Talents."

"Your psychic abilities."

"Yes." She'd never liked to think of them that way, because that had always made her feel like even more of a freak. But all she felt was a gentle pulse of concern from Zhandar, so she went on, "The Consortium government was obviously feeling threatened by these human/Zhore pairings that were occurring, so—"

"All two of them?" he broke in, sounding amused. "Yes, I can see why that would be quite a threat."

Put that way, it did seem rather ridiculous. But the Consortium took any threat to its hegemony seriously, especially now, when it was still having to field probing questions about its handling of the situation in China. Having the descendants of the toxic Cloud's survivors demanding answers was not something the government wanted to waste its time on. And it wasn't just that isolated group, either. Even the Eridanis, ostensibly allies of Gaia, did not seem overly thrilled by the revelation that the Consortium's agents had been methodically harvesting the bodies of the dead rather than giving them the respectful burials everyone had thought they were receiving.

"Bad enough in their eyes that there are all those human/Eridani pairings," she replied. "Even though they've been going on for generations, the government doesn't make it easy on the people involved. In most cases, they end up emigrating to Eridani space. But the Zhore?" She shrugged. "You're an unknown quantity. The Consortium hates that. So of course you're a threat."

"And so they sent you here." Zhandar's gaze sharpened, and he inquired, "How is it that they were able to be so exact in their reproduction of Zhore biology? We have never submitted to any kind of study by your people."

That was something she really didn't want to explain, but Trinity knew it would be unfair to withhold the truth. At least if she told Zhandar about the corpse of the dead Zhore her government had used for a study specimen, then he could pass the word on to his own government officials, and perhaps then they'd be able to piece together who the dead man had been. His family deserved closure if nothing else.

"There was a—a man of your people killed on Bathsheva. The Bathshevans sold the body to the Consortium."

A wince, and Zhandar shut his eyes for a second. Trinity could feel the shock and sorrow flood from him before he shut his barriers down once again.

"I'm sorry," she said in a small voice.

His fists clenched on his knees. "It was none of your doing, so there is no need to apologize. But it seems your government has even more to answer for than I had originally thought."

You have no idea. She ran her thumb up and down the smooth plastic of the tumbler she held, not wanting to look directly at him.

A heavy silence fell. The chair creaked as Zhandar shifted on it. Then he said, "This still does not adequately explain why you were involved. Yes, you have talents that the Consortium would wish to exploit, but why couldn't you have said no? Surely a citizen of your government still has certain rights, do they not?"

"Generally, yes, although the Consortium is all too willing to play fast and loose with those rights if it suits them. But I—" She stopped there, not sure how she should proceed.

"But you?" Zhandar probed.

It seemed so shameful to admit it to him, when he was everything that was good and honorable, and she… wasn't. However, she'd vowed that she wouldn't lie to him anymore, and that meant giving him the complete truth. What he chose to do with it after that was up to him.

"I—I don't have those same rights, because I'm a criminal."

"A *what?*" He sat up straight and stared at her, consternation thrumming in the air between them. Apparently that revelation had shocked him enough that he wasn't quite able to hold everything back. Then he shook his head. "I refuse to believe that."

She let out a breath, then said, "Believe what you want, Zhandar. It's the truth. Oh, a petty criminal. I could justify what I did, say it was a victimless crime, that I did it because I thought it would provide a better future for me and the man I thought loved me, but the truth is, I could have said no. But I didn't."

His gaze didn't waver. She could feel him reaching out to her, and she let her barriers down a little more. Not that she expected him to be able to read her thoughts, but enough so he could feel the truth in her, the desire to leave all her lies behind.

"So…what happened to him, this man you say you were in love with?"

Those words were spoken carefully, calmly, with very little inflection. That didn't matter; Trinity could still feel the hurt flowing out from him. It was clear that he thought she'd used him.

Well, she had. The thing was, she'd also fallen in love with him somewhere along the way.

But she definitely didn't want him to think she was pining for some man she'd left behind on Gaia. Lifting her chin, she looked Zhandar directly in the eyes. "He took the money we'd embezzled and headed off-world, but not before pointing the finger at me in an attempt to deflect attention from himself."

"He did that? A man who had professed to love you?"

She nodded, then added, her tone brittle, "Well, he wasn't the first man to lie to a woman to get what he wanted, and I doubt he'll be the last. We Gaians aren't quite as noble as you Zhore when it comes to that sort of thing. But since the authorities had a bead on where he was headed, I'm sure he's been caught and locked up by now. Not that that does me much good."

Zhandar still looked a little shell-shocked. "But if you have the power to read the thoughts of others, why—"

"Why didn't I discover what he was planning? There are a few people I can't read. I don't know why. Something different about the way their brains are wired, I suppose. Caleb was one of those people. At the time, I thought that was a good thing, because then I couldn't see things in his thoughts that I didn't want to see. But obviously that didn't work out so well for me in the end."

Another silence then, as Zhandar appeared to think over what she had just told him. Then he said, "And so, because you had a talent the Consortium wanted to exploit, you were drafted for this mission, rather than…." He paused delicately then, watching her to see how she would respond.

"Rather than being sent to the MaxSec on Titan," Trinity said matter-of-factly. Noting his look of confusion, she began to explain, "Maximum-security…." But then the sentence trailed off as she paused, realizing that her language conditioning had failed her because there was no true analogue for "prison" in the Zhoraani tongue. "Prison, jail," she fumbled, lapsing into Galactic Standard and hoping that he spoke it. On Gaia, everyone had to learn GS in addition to Anglic. Some others also learned the semi-dead languages of their native regions, but she'd never much seen the point in that.

"Ah, I see," Zhandar responded, also switching to Galactic Standard. His brows drew together, and he asked, "Would it be easier for you to converse in this language? I did not think of that earlier."

Neither had she, because the conditioning made it so simple to speak the Zhore tongue that she really didn't have to stop and think about it. "No, it's fine if we stick with Zhoraani," she said, using that same language in her response.

He looked somewhat relieved by her reply. His GS was good, but she could tell from the way he paused here and there that he had to work to recall the vocabulary. There wasn't any point in putting him through that when it wasn't necessary.

"Anyway," she continued, "yes, basically, I could go to Titan or I could come here. Women don't fare too well there, as you can imagine." *Or maybe you can't,* she thought. There was no such thing as rape on Zhoraan. "They're mistreated in a sexual way," she added in an attempt to clarify her statement.

From the way he frowned, she could tell he didn't really understand what she was trying to say, and she didn't want to have to explain herself further. But then he appeared to put that matter aside for the moment. Head tilting slightly to one side, he seemed to study her. The frown remained, however.

At length he said, "And…what happened between the two of us?"

Her hand almost slipped down to her belly, still flat and revealing nothing, but Trinity forced herself not to move. "I—I won't lie to you, Zhandar. I was sent here partly so that I could be intimate with a Zhore man and conceive his child. They—the people who were managing me—wanted to be able to study one of these hybrid children for themselves."

Zhandar's face might have been carved from stone. "I see."

"No, but you don't see!" she burst out. He'd retreated from her in that moment, his barriers fully back in place. "That was what they intended, and I did as I was told, but I—I *wanted* to. I met you, and I felt it, this *sayara*, or whatever you want to call it. I didn't go to you coldly, Zhandar. I wanted you. You would have felt it if I hadn't. Tell me that you wouldn't."

His silver-gray eyes glinted into hers. They might as well have been lasers, boring into her, but she didn't look away. He needed to see that she was telling the truth.

Then his body seemed to relax slightly, and he nodded. "Yes. I would have known if this—this attraction was not shared. But you felt it, and you did conceive a child."

So he knew. She wasn't sure whether anyone had told him. For some reason, that realization made her a little sad. She would have liked to have been able to tell him herself.

But then his tone roughened as he went on, "And what would you have done, if I had not discovered you then?"

"My—my handlers would have known I was pregnant because of the test I took. So they would have sent someone to extract me, and then I would have been gone."

"Just like that?"

No, not just like that, she thought. *I would have died inside at the thought of leaving you. But I couldn't have stopped them.*

"And do you understand what your leaving like that would have done to me?" he asked then, jaw tight, eyes glittering.

His anger was to be expected, but it still frightened her. She didn't know how she should respond. And just a minute or two earlier, he had seemed on the verge of forgiving her.

Afraid to speak, she only shook her head.

"Because you are *human,*" he said, giving the word an unpleasant emphasis, "you may not understand the ramifications of such an abandonment. When two people bond in *sayara,* they are meant to be joined until death. If one of them leaves the other, except for short periods that are agreed upon in advance, the one left behind dies. It is not merely the simple matter of a broken heart."

Her eyes widened, and her entire body seemed to go cold as she digested what he had just told her. There might have been something she could have said in response to that horrible revelation, some sort of plea protesting her ignorance, letting him know that she had no idea what such an abandonment would mean for one of his people, but she could only sit there, mute, the words strangling in her throat.

Somehow she was able to force out a single syllable. "*No.*" He had to know that she had no idea such a thing was possible.

As she was fighting to find the words to convince him of that, he pushed himself to his feet and stood there for a moment, gazing down at her.

"Think on what I have just told you, and on what your loyalty to your Gaian masters might have cost my family."

After that, he swept out, slapping the controls to the door as he left. Trinity stared at it as it shut, her heart slamming against her ribcage.

And then at last the tears came.

THIRTEEN

"She couldn't have known that," Nalzhir said reasonably.

The two of them sat in a conference room in the medical center where Trinity was being monitored for any signs of post-operative distress. Zhandar had wanted to go directly home so he could attempt to put together the shattered pieces of his heart and mind, but the government agent had said he wanted to discuss Trinity's revelations first.

For of course the entire conversation they had shared in her hospital room had been recorded. Zhandar wasn't sure why he should be surprised by that, but the realization still irritated him. It smacked just a bit too much of what the men who were manipulating Trinity might have done.

"So I am supposed to be content with that?" he snapped.

"I would not go so far as to say that. I will say that she seemed genuinely contrite. And quite forthcoming."

Yes, she hadn't hesitated before unburdening himself. Through it all, he'd done his best to listen, to understand. On some level, perhaps he did, even though the machinations of the Consortium's agents made his stomach twist. To do that to one of your own, to expect her to coldly give herself to someone she considered an alien....

Not that she appeared to have actually thought of him that way. It was true; her desire hadn't been false. She'd wanted him in the same way he wanted her. Because, as much as he hated to admit it, they were *sayara*, just as the unknown Sarzhin was with his colonist's daughter, or Ambassador Lirzhan was with his own Gaian bride.

And because of that bond, Zhandar knew he couldn't thrust Trinity out of his life. In a way, it would have been so much better if he could have turned his back on her and let his government do what it willed with its captured spy.

That is, it would have been better if he hadn't known there was no way he could cut her out of his life in that manner.

It had been jarring at first, seeing her sleeping there with her human appearance fully restored. Unlike the other two Zhore men who had entered into the *sayara* bond with a Gaian, he had never even been around a human before. He'd seen no reason to go off-world; Zhoraan's beauties were enough for him. But there was something about Trinity, about the smooth paleness of her skin, the lustrousness of her hair, that held his eye despite its alien nature.

Or perhaps it had been because of it.

And when he'd looked closer, he realized he still could see echoes of "Zhanna" in her—the high, wide cheekbones, the full pout of her mouth. A different shell, perhaps, but the same person underneath.

"So she is being cooperative," Zhandar said heavily. "But what will become of her after you have gotten every piece of useful information out of her?"

A ripple of displeasure emanated from the other man before he suppressed it. "We are certainly not forcibly interrogating her, Zhandar, which is more than I can say for the Consortium's government, had the situation been reversed. She is freely telling us what she knows, and after that, we will ask her what she wants to do next. We are not in the habit of keeping prisoners. Besides, there is the matter of the child."

The matter of the child. Yes, that was not something they could simply dismiss. Not the child he'd so desperately wanted, even if the way the universe had seen fit to give it to him was nothing he could have possibly imagined.

"These children," he said, not bothering to hide the anxious rasp of his voice. "Can they even be considered Zhore?" After all, who knew what the result of mixing the two species would even be....

A tablet had been lying on the tabletop near Nalzhir's elbow. He retrieved it, then made a few quick movements with his finger across its surface before handing the tablet over to Zhandar. "See for yourself."

He took it, scanning the flat image on the screen. It showed a smiling young woman with a hooded Zhore standing beside her. She was pretty in a fresh, young sort of way, if not as beautiful as he thought Trinity. In her arms was a bundle of white blankets, and in that bundle, his shimmering black skin contrasting with the white fabric, was a baby boy, probably no more than three or four standard months old.

"He is Zhore," Nalzhir said quietly. "In appearance, at any rate. We sent a team of doctors to Lathvin IV to do some minor tests, nothing invasive. There are subtle differences in his DNA, which is only to be expected when you have two races mix like this. But the child is healthy, and it is clear that his Zhore heritage is the dominant element in his appearance."

Zhandar stared down at the image. A healthy boy. A healthy Zhore boy—one of his people, to all intents and purposes. No wonder the Gaians were nervous about the ramifications of such pairings. "And the Consortium knows of this as well?"

"We have to believe that they do—not because Annika and Sarzhin are not circumspect, but because the girl's family, particularly her sister, are not as good at keeping secrets as they should be. But we've made it clear through the necessary channels that the two of them and their child are to be left alone."

A request that would have to be honored, at least openly. But if the agents of Gaia's government decided to make a play at getting their hands on a hybrid child of their own…well, he supposed they'd thought it would work out quite well, as long as no one discovered what they were plotting.

"We think it best that Ms. Knox stays here, for obvious reasons," Nalzhir continued. "We hope that you can find yourself able to take her into your care."

"Indeed?" On the most basic level, it made some sense. The two of them were *sayara*. They could not spend any great amount of time at any great distance from one another, or Zhandar would suffer the consequences. And then there was the child.

Even so, he didn't know if he could manage that. Yes, Trinity was contrite, and cooperative. But her helpfulness now couldn't simply erase everything she'd done wrong over the past month. He wanted her…possibly he even still loved her…but he was very angry with her.

"Not necessarily in your apartment," Nalzhir said smoothly. "We can make arrangements to have her move into the one directly below yours. And she will have people watching over her. For obvious reasons, she cannot be allowed to return to her work with you. But at least that way you will be near enough each other that it will not jeopardize your bond."

That could work…perhaps. It was entirely possible that having her that close, and yet not truly being with her, would be more of a torture than anything else. At the same time, it would be better than sharing an apartment with her, and infinitely better than having her sent back to Gaia. But no, Nalzhir and those he worked for would never do something like that, for they would be handing down Zhandar's death sentence.

All the same, he couldn't help asking, "And what of Trinity's Gaian masters? Are you going to communicate with them at all?"

"That has not been decided yet. For now, it's enough that they know we have discovered her, and have interrupted their surveillance activities." The agent shook his head, and didn't bother to conceal the disgust he was currently experiencing. "For them to think there was nothing wrong in using a young woman in such a way, to have her every word and action recorded…it is beyond anything any of us could have imagined. Yes, of course we know the Gaians have their spies, but they've never been so bold as to attempt to infiltrate the sanctity of our home world."

The sanctity of my private life, Zhandar thought then. *Every intimate moment I shared with Trinity, transmitted so they could analyze it, study it….*

He shuddered.

Nalzhir said, "Yes, it is a terrible thing. And unfortunately, there is very little we can do about it, except be glad that you did discover Trinity's identity, and that we were able to remove the implant. No doubt the Gaians are poring over all the data, rubbing their hands with glee at having so much information about those secretive Zhore."

The agent's voice held a sort of weary disdain, but at least Zhandar couldn't detect any anger or irritation directed at him directly. His people knew that he had done nothing wrong. The bond with Trinity had been real, even if nothing else in their relationship had been, and so there would be no recriminations, no questions as to why he hadn't detected her alien nature sooner than he had.

Since Zhandar didn't quite know how to respond, he remained silent.

Nalzhir apparently took that as his cue to continue. "I suppose we were naïve to think that we could keep ourselves hidden from the Gaians forever. They are far too acquisitive a race, and unscrupulous. It is an unfortunate combination." He hesitated then, his hood tilted toward Zhandar. "And yet you formed this bond with her, saw nothing untoward in her behavior or her reactions."

The agent's tone was so mild that Zhandar couldn't exactly construe it as accusatory, and yet....

"There was nothing," he said. "Oh, perhaps once or twice she hesitated at odd times, or responded to a question or a situation in a manner I thought somewhat unusual, but I put that down to her being from Alizhaar, a place whose customs are not precisely the same as ours here in Torzhaan. I suppose it was her psychic gifts that allowed her to function so well among us. Even if she could not precisely read our minds, she could pick up emotions we thought were safely hidden."

Nalzhir inclined his head in agreement. "That part is rather extraordinary. We had heard rumors that Gaians existed who possessed these sorts of talents, but certainly none of our people have come across them, and no doubt the Consortium wishes to keep them hidden so it can utilize them as it sees fit. Their abilities do seem to differ greatly from ours."

"Yes. Trinity apparently can read thoughts themselves, although she admitted that her talent did not function the same with everyone, and that there were a few people she could not read at all."

"Once she is fully recovered, we would like to conduct some tests with her."

At that comment, Zhandar couldn't keep himself from recoiling slightly in alarm. "What kind of tests?"

"Nothing invasive, I assure you. Only a small battery to determine how strong her gifts are, and whether they are concentrated in certain areas. It would not be strenuous—she would only sit in a chair, just as you are doing now, and speak with several counselors and scientists."

That didn't sound quite as bad as he'd feared. Even so, he had to say, "But you will wait until she feels she is ready."

A chuckle emerged from Nalzhir's hood. "Zhandar, for a man who is furious with his partner, you are being quite protective."

"She is not my partner," Zhandar replied stiffly.

"Perhaps not. But she is still *sayara*."

They let her out of the medical center after three days. To tell the truth, she'd been ready to leave after the first full day, but the physicians there wanted to continue monitoring her, just to be sure she didn't develop any infections from the procedures to remove the Zhore skin or to remove the implant.

That damn implant. She wished they'd given it to her so she could have ground it under the heel of her boot. But of course the Zhore wouldn't be that wasteful. They would have taken it to a lab to be studied.

At least it was out of her head.

The whole time she'd been "recovering" in the medical center, she'd been wondering what they planned to do with her. Build a special prison, just for their captured Gaian spy? Or simply put her under house arrest?

That appeared to be exactly what they intended. A Zhore agent had come to speak with her, a man named Nalzhir, and he had told her that she would be living in the apartment directly beneath Zhandar's.

"For you have made the *sayara* bond," the government man told her. "So you must remain close by. An agent named Rinzha has been assigned to you. She will stay in your apartment with you and see that you come to no harm."

What harm could I possibly come to on Zhoraan? Trinity wondered then. In the next instant, however, she realized that her watchdog, this Rinzha person, was probably there more to keep any Zhore from being shocked by the presence of a Gaian among them than because the government feared for Trinity's safety.

She hadn't dared to ask whether the Gaians themselves—and Gabriel Brant in particular—had been notified of her capture. Of course he would have known, would have seen everything that happened to her until she was put under sedation and the implant removed. But the Zhore still should have contacted the Gaian government. That was supposed to be the protocol. Or so she'd heard. Then again, the Consortium wasn't known for following rules, even its own, so she doubted the Zhore were too worried about following the conventions in this particular instance.

On the one hand, she'd love to see Gabriel fuming at his current impotence, of knowing that she was in Zhore hands and that there wasn't a goddamn thing he could do about it. On the other...well, even on a good day, Gabriel wasn't the sort of person she would ever trust, and if he was feeling particularly desperate....

Well, she'd have to hope that whoever had reined him in last time, after he'd had her brought to his hideout on the second moon, was also riding herd on him this go-round. With any luck, the Consortium would have decided to wash its hands of her, and had abandoned her to her fate.

Which was, she realized upon inspecting her new home, not so bad. Zhandar's absence hurt, like a physical ache. She hadn't been expecting that. After all, she'd always picked herself up and dusted herself off in the past whenever a relationship went sour.

That was different, though. She hadn't loved those men. Not really.

The agent assigned her, Rinzha, was quiet and unobtrusive. Trinity's new apartment was larger than the one she'd previously been living in, and so there were three bedrooms, one for her, one for Rinzha, and one probably intended as an office or study. It had an entertainment unit, but Trinity doubted she'd use it all that often. Zhoraan's tame offerings had already begun to pall even before she'd been placed under house arrest.

It should have been comfortable, if somewhat confining. They did allow her to go out on the balcony, as long as she wore her robes and made sure that no one could see her face. So there was sun, and fresh air, and flowers and an herb garden off to one side where she could putter around.

The problem was that she could sense when Zhandar came and went. She couldn't even say which was worse— knowing he was there, just a floor above her, and not being able to speak with him, or the times when he was gone at work, when the absence of his presence felt like a great gaping hole in her existence.

She'd been here a week now, and not once had he come to see her. Maybe that shouldn't have been a surprise, but it was. He'd been angry—she hadn't even realized that one of the placid Zhore could get that angry—and yet she'd nursed the hope that he would move past that and at least speak with her. But no. They were living close by one another merely so the physical aspects of the *sayara* bond couldn't be broken, but it seemed he had no desire to do anything beyond that.

No one had mentioned the baby, either. Well, the doctors and the psychiatrists had run a battery of tests and declared her to be in good health, and had gone off to collate the answers she'd given them about her psychic abilities, but other than that, nothing. On Gaia, the first thing a doctor always asked when a woman had a positive pregnancy test was, "Are you going to keep it?" Considering Gaia's chronic over-population problems, Trinity thought that made some sense, although the practice had always seemed pretty cold-blooded to her.

But Zhore had the opposite issue. There was no question as to whether she would be having this child. What happened to it afterward, though....

I suppose they'll take it and give it to Zhandar, she thought drearily. *Then he can have the family he always wanted, and I...well, I'll probably stay in this apartment until I drop dead of old age.*

Maybe it would have been better to be locked up in MaxSec. At least then she wouldn't have known what it was like to be loved by Zhandar, only to have it all taken away.

She'd been standing on the balcony, lost in these dark ruminations. Her mood didn't fit the day, which was sunny and bright, with delicate clouds chasing one another across the sky. But she couldn't seem to shake it, no matter what.

Rinzha came out into the balcony garden, pausing a few feet away. The wind caught at her hood, but of course the heavy fabric stayed stubbornly in place. "You have a visitor. Nalzhir, of the Alien Relations Bureau."

So that was who he worked for. Trinity had no idea the Zhore even had enough relations with other races to require a bureau to handle those affairs, but apparently they did. She couldn't think what Nalzhir might want. Then again, his visit would at least help a little to break up the monotony of her day.

She nodded at Rinzha and went inside, then pulled off the heavy hooded cloak she wore. That was one good thing about having her identity revealed; she only had to wear the damn thing when she went outside.

Nalzhir was waiting for her in the living room area. Upon seeing him, Rinzha bowed at the waist, hands clasped together, and then disappeared into her room. Trinity still hadn't quite figured out what the Zhore woman's exact role was—guard, protector, nursemaid? Obviously, though, she thought Trinity was safe enough in Nalzhir's company, and wouldn't do anything as rude as intrude on their meeting.

"Hello, Nalzhir," Trinity said as she approached him. "I wasn't expecting company, but if you'd like some water, or some honey tea—"

"Thank you, but I require nothing," he replied, sounding positively brusque for a Zhore. Then he gestured toward one of the sofas. "If you would please sit down?"

That should have been her line, but Trinity didn't protest. She went to the couch he'd indicated and settled herself on it. His gaze seemed to track her, but she couldn't tell for sure. And a little probe toward his thoughts didn't help, either. He was very locked down.

"How are you faring here?" he asked.

"Um…fine," she replied. No, she wasn't fine, but she doubted he'd asked because he wanted the truth from her. It was just a polite formality that had to be observed.

"Good." He paused for a second or two, as if gathering his thoughts. Then he said, "We have had a communiqué from the diplomatic branch of your government."

"Oh?" Trinity attempted to sound neutral, but she wasn't sure how successful she had been. All along she'd been hoping that the Consortium had decided to wash its hands of her. If they were contacting the Zhore, however, that wouldn't appear to be the case.

"Yes. They are demanding your immediate return."

Of course they were. Nothing like going on the offensive when you were, in fact, the offending party. "And your response?"

"We have given them none as yet, save to say that we will take the matter under advisement. They are claiming that we are holding one of their citizens unlawfully. And because you were never officially an employee of the Consortium government, or had any kind of standing with them other than as an ordinary citizen, we don't have much evidence to show that you were here as a spy."

She hated that word. They'd been speaking in Zhoraani, but Nalzhir had used the Galactic Standard term, since once again it was a concept utterly foreign to the Zhore. She didn't bother to protest, however. It was exactly why she'd come here—to spy on the alien race.

And become pregnant by one of them.

"That's a little disingenuous of them, don't you think?" she inquired. "I mean, your people don't even allow outsiders on the planet's surface. The only reason I'd be down here would be to spy."

He didn't answer right away. His head cocked to one side, as if he was considering her from within the depths of his hood. "You don't appear to have a very favorable opinion of your government, Ms. Knox."

"No, I don't. I'm not sure why that surprises you."

"Oh, I am not surprised. Except, perhaps, by your honesty."

"Well, that's what I told Zhandar. No more lies."

At least, to no one besides herself.

Nalzhir clasped his gloved hands on his knees. "That is admirable of you, Ms. Knox. And thank you. Then we can speak frankly. The last thing that my people want is an open confrontation. In all honesty, we cannot afford it. Yes, the Eridanis would most likely support our cause, but—"

"Wait a minute," Trinity cut in. "You're not trying to tell me that the Consortium might go to war over this? Over one person?"

"Most likely not, but we cannot entirely discount the threat they represent, either. At the very least, it would give them more bargaining power to represent themselves as the injured party here, which you and I both know they are most definitely not."

"That's for damn sure," she murmured.

"There is more, I am afraid. The diplomatic corps representative in this sector, one Gabriel Brant, is demanding to speak with you in person. He—"

"Gabriel?" Trinity repeated, startled.

"You know this man?"

"He's my handler," she said. "Or my manager, or whatever you want to call him. But he's definitely not a diplomat. He's an operative for a black ops branch of the government."

Again, all in Galactic Standard. The Zhore language couldn't frame those sorts of concepts.

Nalzhir seemed to recognize where the conversation had gone, because when he spoke again, it was in the same language. Smoothly and expertly, with far more command than Zhandar had. That made sense; Nalzhir worked for a bureau whose mission was to reach out to and communicate with alien races.

"I fear that he is representing himself as a diplomat—with the backing of your government, I am sure. It makes sense, as I had never heard of him prior to this. All my previous dealings had been with a woman named Nandita Singh. But even if this Mr. Brant is not who he says he is, we can't risk an escalation by accusing him of being something he is not."

No, of course not. Relations between the various galactic governments were like a very complicated game of chess, one played in dimensions far beyond a flat board. She didn't envy the people like Nalzhir whose work involved negotiating that particular mine field.

"And if I don't talk to him?"

Nalzhir didn't answer at first, but instead seemed to shift so he could look past Trinity and out into the bright sunlit garden on the balcony. "I fear that would not be wise. You see, we should attempt to seem cooperative in the beginning, even if we all know that we have no intention of handing you over to them."

Trinity could feel herself relax at those words. Not that she particularly wanted to be locked up in this apartment for the rest of her life, but that prospect was still infinitely preferable to being wrapped up in a bow and sent back to Gabriel Brant and his cohorts.

"Ah," said Nalzhir. "So you truly don't wish to return to your home world. I wasn't sure."

Trinity sighed. "I must have been broadcasting that pretty loudly."

"Loudly enough." He paused, then went on, "This becomes more difficult because, while you are a citizen of the Consortium, you are carrying the child of a Zhore. Galactic law—the law that the Galactic Council agreed on decades ago—states that such a child is automatically granted dual citizenship. And because the child you carry is a citizen of this world as well as yours, it limits what the Consortium can or cannot compel you to do."

That notion hadn't even occurred to her. Then again, while it sounded fine and good to follow the dictates of such a law, she knew her own government couldn't care less about such niceties. Still, it must give her a little bit of protection. A little was better than none of all. She swallowed, then asked, "Where would I have to speak with him?"

"In the Bureau's office on Kelzhar. That is still technically Zhore territory, although we do lease out space in the settlement to off-world interests. The presence of off-worlders there is common, and so such a meeting should not draw any particular attention."

Yes, she knew that moon, the place where Gabriel had dragged her to threaten her in person. "There's a café, run by two Gaians named Franklin Watts and Dale Luna. They're some of Brant's operatives."

Nalzhir shifted on the couch, although Trinity couldn't tell whether or not her words had surprised him. Even after being here on Zhoraan for almost two months, she was still trying to get used to reading people's reactions by their subtle body movements, rather than the far easier means of examining their expressions or the waves of emotions most of them didn't even know they were transmitting. But the Zhores' feelings were just as concealed as their faces, so she didn't even have that fallback.

He said, "We've long had our suspicions about those two, although so far we have not been able to find anything concrete enough to support an active investigation. So thank you for that intelligence. In fact, I think it might be helpful for all of us if you could make a record of everything this Gabriel Brant has told you, and everything you have seen while in his company."

Clearly, Nalzhir thought Trinity was firmly on the Zhore side. She hadn't really stopped to think about it. The one thing she knew was that she most definitely didn't want to side with the Gaians, not after what they'd done to her. So where did that leave her?

On her own side, apparently. She was okay with that. After everything she'd already been through in her life, she was sort of used to it.

But because Nalzhir had resources she didn't, and because she would have liked nothing more than to see Gabriel Brant cash in all his bad karma points, she just nodded and said, "Of course. I'll do whatever I can to help."

FOURTEEN

Of course no one asked why "Zhanna" had not returned to work in the office. It was not the Zhore way to poke and pry. Zhandar had no doubt that speculation was running rampant behind his back, but he couldn't do much about that. He could have lied and said his erstwhile assistant had gone on retreat, but that was not the Zhore way, either. So he was left to come in to work each day and take care of the tasks that needed attending to, and to say very little to any of his staff, save for when he absolutely had to.

As excruciating as the situation might be, it was a veritable relaxation chamber compared to going home each night and knowing that Trinity was so close by, and yet might as well be on one of Zhoraan's moons for all that he could reach out and touch her. That was his own doing, not hers; from time to time, he could sense echoes of her hurt, of her need, but he could not find it within himself to forgive her. He understood why she had done what she had done, at least in the beginning. However, he couldn't see why she hadn't told him the truth once she realized what she felt for him. Fear of reprisal from her masters might have factored into it, but he thought there was more to it than that. It was as if she'd feared that he would reject her, or....

"Hello, Zhandar."

Leizha's voice.

He startled at the sound of it, then reached out to touch one of the controls for his 3-D modeling device, trying to make it seem as if that little unexpected jump had been nothing more than him moving to touch the screen. Foolish, really. Leizha would see right through a stratagem like that. She knew him too well.

"Good afternoon, Leizha," he replied formally. "Did you enjoy your retreat?"

"Very much so. But I was told that your new assistant had to leave, and so—"

And so of course you came back, trying to see if I would be more amenable to your proposition this time. Zhandar had no way of knowing how much Leizha had actually heard, but he knew he would have to walk softly here and try not to give her any more information than was strictly necessary.

"Yes, I fear she was too homesick for the province where she was born, and so decided to return."

That was the first lie he had ever told. He wondered if he had learned something of the practice from Trinity.

"Ah, that is unfortunate." Leizha paused then, watching as he fiddled with his model of a retrofit of the gardens at the municipal art museum, only a few blocks away, adding a waterfall here and moving a planter there. "I wished to know if you had found a replacement for her yet?"

"No," he said shortly. "I assume you've come here because you wish to take up your position again?"

"It makes the most sense, does it not? You would not have to train someone new, and I have learned some… perspective…during my time away."

Did that mean she'd given up her pursuit of him? That would make working with her much easier, if still a little awkward. After all, he knew what she looked like without the robes, had participated in an intimacy that usually only bonded partners and close family members shared. But he could put that aside if he had to. Indeed, it was difficult to recall any particular details of her appearance. When he tried, he only saw Trinity—that is, Trinity in her guise as Zhanna. Even that memory was beginning to be erased now, overwritten by images of the human Trinity, with her lustrous golden-brown hair and creamy skin.

"So what do you think?"

How easy it was for him to drift off into thoughts of Trinity. He really should be putting her out of his mind. Well, not completely, since she was carrying his child, and sooner rather than later they'd have to work out some sort of arrangement, but…. He blinked, bringing himself back to the here and now. Leizha stood there, staring at him, a faint aura of impatience surrounding her.

"I think that would work out very well," he told her. "In fact, I have an appointment to go look at a new site in less than an hour. Can you accompany me, or would you rather begin in the morning?"

"I can come with you," she replied quickly. Perhaps a little too quickly.

But he had made his decision, and he would have to abide by it. The work was too much for him to manage without an assistant, and yet he hadn't found the will or the energy to find someone to replace Trinity. That Leizha should show up like this, giving him an easy solution to his predicament, meant he would no longer have to worry about juggling two people's workloads.

And if Leizha wasn't willing to let things go, attempted to renew her suit....

Well, he'd worry about it when the time came. He had quite enough to occupy him now, including the ongoing problem of Trinity Knox.

"Should we tell Zhandar what we're doing?" Trinity asked. The streets of Torzhaan flowed past as a Zhore man whose name she hadn't been given drove her and Nalzhir toward the outskirts of town. Apparently, they were headed to a government shuttle pad, where they would take a ship to the second moon and the meeting with Gabriel Brant.

"I saw no reason to worry him unnecessarily," Nalzhir replied. "We will be up and back within the space of a few hours, and you will be returned to your apartment before he even gets home."

She supposed that made sense. After all, if Zhandar really cared about her or what she was doing, he would have attempted to make contact sometime within the last week. Instead, she'd been left severely alone.

So much for this sayara *bond that they keep going on about,* she thought wearily. Everything outside the car window was green and growing and vibrant, and she wondered how much Zhandar had been involved in planning it. Not the whole city, surely—he was too young to have done all of this—but he pushed himself hard, a lot harder than some self-proclaimed workaholics she'd known back on Gaia.

And she could mock *sayara* all she wanted, but deep down she knew she was in denial. She ached for Zhandar every night when she lay down in her lonely bed. Once or twice she'd even considered trying to creep out under Rinzha's nose, then slip onto the balcony and shimmy herself up one of the trellises to Zhandar's apartment.

It might have worked...or she could have broken her neck. In the end, she'd decided that she couldn't take that kind of risk, not when she was carrying his child.

But the ache never went away. She feared it never would.

"If you think that's best," she told Nalzhir, and turned once again to look out the window. Really, she just wanted this over with. The thought of facing Gabriel Brant had her stomach twisted in knots. She couldn't even blame that on being pregnant, because so far she hadn't suffered any kind of symptoms. It was awfully early yet, though.

Nalzhir seemed to sense that she didn't feel inclined to talk, so they rode in silence the rest of the way to the shuttle pad. It was really more like a private space port, with ten landing pads and a low building that seemed to house some offices and a small waiting room. Once they got out of the car, he guided her toward a small, sleek shuttle waiting on one of those pads, then indicated that she should take any seat she liked. She sat in the middle of the cabin, near one of the windows, while he settled himself directly across the aisle. A few minutes after that, the ship began to vibrate slightly, and she realized the atmospheric engines had just been turned on.

It was a short flight, not quite a half-hour. The moon base was unfamiliar to her, since she'd been knocked out before being brought here the last time. But Trinity still recognized the graceful curves and arches of Zhore architecture, even in this airless environment.

The shuttle landed in an open bay and connected its hatch to a corridor that led somewhere into the bowels of the base. A private corridor, it seemed; she and Nalzhir were the only ones traversing it at the moment, although she was under the impression that the base was actually a fairly busy hub. Because she had left her apartment and gone out in public, she once again wore the heavy hooded robes. They were a thin disguise, though, and she knew it. Under those robes and the gloves, she was all too recognizably human.

Nalzhir guided her down another corridor. Almost at once, a group of five more Zhore joined them, tall, silent, in the ubiquitous hooded cloaks. Since her companion didn't appear surprised by their presence, Trinity guessed that he'd been in communication with them somehow and had instructed them to meet up here, out of sight. Although she would have felt a bit better if even one of them had spoken, she was still glad of their presence. As they'd walked, she'd begun to get the sinking feeling that Nalzhir intended to meet with Gabriel with absolutely no backup, which she thought was an extraordinarily bad idea. But it looked like they were going to have some kind of muscle after all, even though she couldn't tell whether the guards were armed or not. They could be hiding anything short of a poleax under those robes.

At last they reached a door, where they emerged from the cramped hallway into a sort of small open plaza, where plants grew around a graceful little fountain in the center. It was hard to believe they were on a moon base, rather than somewhere back in Torzhaan. But then Trinity looked up and saw the domed ceiling high overhead, its smooth metal surface showing plainly that they were most definitely not back planet-side. Still, she appreciated that the Zhore had brought their love of growing things even here to this barren moon.

"This way," Nalzhir murmured, pointing to a door in a one-level building on the opposite side of the courtyard.

Two of the guards moved ahead of them so they could be the first inside, while the others brought up the rear. Trinity clenched her gloved hands inside the dangling sleeves of her robes and wished she'd had the courage to tell the Bureau agent no when he'd asked her to come on this insane mission. No, actually, that would have been the cowardly thing. They were all playing at roles here, Gabriel Brant most of all, but she'd already done enough wrong. She wouldn't compound her past sins by refusing to help out where she could.

They moved along yet another hallway, although this one had been painted a soft taupe color, and abstract paintings hung on the walls. It felt like the kind of temporary office space that high-ranking executives might lease when they needed to conduct business somewhere away from their home base. And then they were going into a conference room, and Gabriel Brant was standing there, Blake Chu at his side. Both of them wore high-collared business suits and looked the very epitome of Gaian style. Well, Gabriel did, anyway. Blake still sported his ridiculous glasses and brush haircut, giving him the appearance of a nerdy computer hacker forced to dress up for a relative's wedding.

The brief amusement that thought caused disappeared rapidly, though, because Trinity could feel Gabriel Brant's charcoal-colored eyes boring into her, as if attempting to see through the thick hood that obscured her face. She forced herself to stand quietly as Nalzhir moved past the guards and spoke.

"We are here, as you requested."

"And I see you brought your basketball team with you."

Nalzhir's head cocked to one side. "I fear I don't recognize the reference, Mr. Brant. But yes, we are within our rights to have an escort. That will not hinder our talks, will it?"

A negligent wave of the hand. "No, of course not. Do sit down." He gestured toward a conference table off to one side, set up with four chairs around it.

Trinity didn't much like the look of that. No matter how they arranged themselves, that meant she'd have to be sitting across from or next to either Gabriel or Blake. She knew better than to protest, though, and so she waited quietly while Gabriel sat at the head of the table and Nalzhir at the foot. Holding back a sigh, she settled herself in the chair to Nalzhir's right.

Once that was done, a mousy-looking woman came into the conference room with water for everyone, pouring an equal amount in each glass before retiring to the sitting area on the other side of the space. There, she picked up a tablet and appeared engrossed in whatever she was reading on its screen.

Trinity didn't know if the woman was pretending to be Gabriel's secretary or assistant, or whether she been rented along with the meeting space where they had gathered. She supposed it didn't really matter. What mattered was that he sat only a few feet away from her, close enough to reach out and grab her by the arm. Not that he would do anything so overtly threatening. She didn't know what he was plotting, but she doubted it was anything that simple.

"So, Mr. Brant," Nalzhir began. "We are here on your request. As you can see, Ms. Knox is quite well, and here by her own choosing. Certainly nothing that should cause a diplomatic incident."

Gabriel lifted his glass of water and took a long drink. Pure theater, of course. Trinity wished she could grab that glass of water and throw it in his face. Then again, she doubted even that would mess up his hair. He had enough pomade in there for three or four men.

Then he said, "Well, I'd like to believe that, Nalzhir, except that I really can't see that Ms. Knox is well. In fact, I can't even say for sure whether that *is* Ms. Knox under all those robes."

"If you're suggesting—"

"What I'm suggesting is that Ms. Knox isn't a Zhore, so there's no reason for her to be wandering around here dressed like a mad monk, is there?"

She should have known he would force the issue. Nalzhir hadn't told her whether he'd informed Brant that she'd been restored to her normal appearance, but that wasn't why she hesitated now. Although she'd cursed the robes more than once for being bulky and heavy and in the way whenever she stopped thinking about how to manage them, they also offered protection. She didn't much like the thought of being exposed to Gabriel's gaze. But she also knew he'd continue to press the issue, so there was no point in protesting.

"No, I suppose there isn't, Mr. Brant," she said, then reached up and pushed back the hood, letting it drop to her shoulders so her hair could fall free.

A small pause. Then he said, "Ah."

That was it. "Ah." His eyes caught hers for a second, and she felt a chill go down her back. And then he was looking away, returning his attention to Nalzhir. "Yes, she does appear to be in perfect health. As for being here of her own volition…well, I suppose we can let her tell us about that."

Voice cool, she said, "I'm here because I wanted to make it very clear that I am not being held against my will on Zhoraan. Therefore, there is no reason for the Consortium to interfere with my affairs. I believe that Consortium citizens still have the right to travel about the galaxy as they choose, don't they?"

"Of course they do," he said smoothly. "That is, regular upstanding, law-abiding citizens of the Consortium. But you, Ms. Knox, aren't either of those things, are you? It seems there's an outstanding warrant for your arrest. Magda, could you show Ms. Knox?"

In response to his request, the mousy-looking woman got up from the sofa and came over to the conference table. She held up her tablet so that everyone could see what currently occupied the screen—the booking image of Trinity, with the word "wanted" flashing in Galactic Standard underneath.

Son of a bitch....

In the seat to her left, Nalzhir didn't so much as twitch. "Well, that is unfortunate, but I do believe the Consortium's laws guarantee that a person is innocent until proven guilty, do they not?"

"Yes," Brant replied without blinking.

"So has Ms. Knox been convicted of any crimes?"

"No, but neither is a person accused of anything greater than a misdemeanor allowed to leave the Gaian system without permission. Her identification would have been annotated to show that, if she had in fact requested and received that permission." He turned toward her, eyes glinting. "Perhaps you could show us your identification, Ms. Knox, so we can get all this cleared up."

God damn him. He was enjoying this far too much, and she knew she didn't dare react either outwardly or inwardly, since Blake Chu had her fixed with his own impassive stare from behind those ridiculous glasses of his. The second she'd seen him, she'd clamped down her barriers as tightly as she could, but if they kept pushing her....

"I don't have any identification," she said. "It was... misplaced."

"Indeed? How unfortunate. You should have contacted the embassy here on the base as soon as you realized it was missing. As to that, I must confess that I am a little curious as to what you were doing on Zhoraan at all, a world that allows no one who is not a Zhore to set foot on its surface."

Of course he knew exactly what Trinity was doing there. And who she was doing it with. This was all part of the charade, but damned if she could figure out what the hell his endgame was. Maybe he was just trying to see if he could provoke her or Nalzhir into the sort of outburst that would reveal more information than either of them wanted to let slip.

"She was occupied with personal business," Nalzhir said, his tone mild. "As for the rest, no one here knew anything of it. Was that why you requested her presence at this meeting, Mr. Brant? So you could take her into custody? I'm afraid I cannot agree to that."

"And why not? She is not a citizen of your world. Not to be rude, but you have very little say as to where she goes or what she does."

The Zhore did shift in his seat them. Just a fraction, but enough that Trinity knew he was being backed into a corner. If the Zhore were capable of lying, then he could have said any one of a number of things. She doubted he would mention the child unless there were no other options left to them, because doing so would reveal that they'd known all along what Gabriel had been up to. Right now they were all playing the innocent, trying to see who would make the first misstep.

Fine, then. Since Nalzhir couldn't lie, she'd step in and do the deed. It wasn't as if she hadn't been lying to herself and almost everyone around her ever since she was a young girl.

She crossed her arms and looked Gabriel directly in the face. "I requested diplomatic immunity."

That did take him aback; at least, a muscle twitched in his cheek, although he didn't show much more reaction than that. "I beg your pardon? On what grounds?"

"The charges against me were trumped up. The real criminal made me his scapegoat. So I thought I should come someplace where the Consortium couldn't possibly track me down."

A glint entered his eyes, and a corner of his mouth lifted so briefly that Trinity wasn't sure she wasn't imagining things. But no…he had tight controls, but every once in a while he let something leak out. Whether that was on purpose or not didn't really matter. Right now, that little flash told her something.

He was actually amused by her playacting. He wasn't going to call her on it. No, he seemed as if he would be content to watch her keep spinning yarns, just to see what happened. Which meant he was definitely plotting something. He wouldn't let things get this out of hand if he didn't have some sort of endgame in mind.

Leaning forward slightly, he said, "Well, that certainly was very…resourceful of you, Ms. Knox. Most of the time when criminals flee Gaia, they go someplace where they can blend into the population, like Iradia. Not much chance of your blending into the population on Zhoraan, is there?"

"I don't know," she retorted. "These robes can hide a lot."

Nalzhir's hood had been swiveling back and forth between the two of them, as if he was bemused by the entire conversation and didn't quite know how to interject himself into it. "Mr. Brant," he said, "because of Ms. Knox's particular gifts, we decided we could bend policy a bit."

"Gifts?" Gabriel repeated. "What gifts?"

"It's all in my file," Trinity said distinctly. "Unless that part has been redacted. It's possible you don't have the clearance to read it."

Across the table from her, Blake grinned briefly, then turned sober again as soon as he realized his superior was beginning to frown.

Both her remark and Blake's reaction to it had clearly annoyed Gabriel; the amused glint disappeared from his eyes, and his mouth pursed slightly. "I assure you, Ms. Knox, I have sufficient clearances to read your entire file. If you're referring to those so-called psychic talents of yours, I'm afraid I don't believe that particular fairytale. You're a gifted…well, let's just call it a 'storyteller' and leave it at that."

"I don't think that is necessary—" Nalzhir began.

But Gabriel rolled right over his words, saying, "I believe I've heard enough. While you might think you're doing the compassionate thing, Nalzhir, the truth of the matter is that Ms. Knox here is a fugitive and a known criminal. She's not the sort of person you want on

Zhoraan, even if you were to, shall we say, open your-selves to more interaction with aliens."

The leer in his voice was more than apparent to Trinity, and she guessed it was to Nalzhir as well, because he sat up a little straighter. A wave of irritation seemed to emanate from him, then subsided.

Don't feel too bad, Nalzhir, Trinity thought. *Gabriel has that effect on everyone.*

"No," he went on, "I really think it best that you allow Ms. Knox to come with us. In the future, you might want to be a bit more selective about the sorts of people you allow down on your planet."

Nalzhir planted his hands on the tabletop and rose to his full height, which was an inch or so taller than Gabriel. "I fear we are at an impasse, then. For we cannot give her up, not when she has been offered sanctuary among us."

That wasn't even a lie. Because the Zhore *had* offered to shelter her from her Consortium handlers, even if she hadn't precisely requested asylum.

"You know," Gabriel replied, "I was afraid you were going to say that." His gaze flicked over toward Magda, the assistant. She still stood a pace or two behind Trinity, tablet clutched in her hands. Incongruously, Trinity noticed that the woman was wearing nail lacquer in a very unflattering shade of dark gray.

"Magda, I think it's time," he said, and she nodded, then tapped something on her screen.

It seemed as if the air circulator switched into over-drive, hissing through the vents. Gabriel calmly reached into his pocket and pulled out a clear plastic mask, fitting it over his nose and mouth. Blake did the same, while Magda pulled a mask from her own pocket and slapped it on.

That all happened within the space of a second. Trinity realized exactly what was going on, and began to push herself away from the table. But then it was as if her muscles had rebelled and refused to do anything her brain was telling them to do. Her knees buckled. Next to her, Nalzhir slumped in his seat.

And then she was falling, hitting the carpeted floor as darkness began to swirl around her. The last thing she remembered was Gabriel staring down at her, a smile of triumph on his lips, as her world went black.

FIFTEEN

ZHANDAR WAS FEELING—WELL, NOT RELIEVED, PRECISELY, BUT somewhat heartened that he had passed an entire afternoon working with Leizha, and nothing untoward had happened. She had just bade him good evening and gone out when his desk comm buzzed.

He glanced at the code, but it wasn't one he recognized. No matter. He often received calls from people in other departments, or managers of buildings who wanted to retain his services. In the cities, all the buildings were owned by the government and leased out, since most people did not wish to spend their entire lives trapped in places of stone and steel, despite all the work that was done to make them as green and growing as possible. But those buildings must still be maintained and managed, and it was the people tasked with that responsibility who generally reached out to him.

"Zhandar," he said.

The female voice that came over the comm was unfamiliar to him. "Zhandar, my name is Rinzha. You have never met me, but I was assigned to watch over Ms. Knox."

"Is something wrong?" he asked, tone sharpening despite himself. Why was it that the very thought of Trinity could send his pulse racing, even when it arose from something as innocuous as a stranger uttering her name?

A pause. "Unfortunately, yes. I am with Agent Nalzhir at the Irizhan Medical Center. Could you please come over at your earliest convenience?"

That was the same medical center where Trinity had undergone the procedure to turn her back to her human self. "What has happened to Nalzhir? Is Trinity with him?"

"Zhandar, it would be best if you came here immediately. These are matters I don't care to discuss over the comm. He is in room 480."

"I'm coming over now." Zhandar ended the call, his hand shaking slightly. What in the world was going on? It must be something terrible, if Nalzhir was being treated at the medical center. And Trinity? What could have happened to her?

Zhandar didn't even bother to shut down his computer, but instead settled for closing the door to his office as he hurried out. Luckily, everyone else had gone home, so no one could see his haste or sense the worry that must be radiating from him.

The medical center was on the other side of town. Because he knew he would have broken all manner of laws against excessive speed if he drove, he left the car on auto and allowed it to guide him through the busy streets while he tried very hard not to stare at the chronometer on the dashboard and think of the minutes ticking past.

Eventually he did get there, practically bounding out of the car as soon as it had parked itself. He realized that running through the corridors of the medical center was probably not a very good idea, and so he forced himself to slow down, to walk at a brisk pace that would get him where he needed to go without attracting too much attention.

Room 480 was on the right-hand side at the end of the hallway. The door was closed, and Zhandar hesitated for a moment, then knocked.

"Come in." Rinzha's voice.

He pressed a gloved finger against the touch pad next to the door. It opened silently, and he took a step inward before he froze.

A hooded figure he guessed was Rinzha stood on the opposite side of the hospital bed, but that wasn't what had stopped him. No, it was realizing that the man lying in the bed did not have his hood pulled up, exposing him to anyone who might enter.

"A thousand apologies," Zhandar said at once, averting his eyes and preparing to exit the room at once.

"No," returned the man on the bed. Nalzhir, although of course Zhandar had never seen his face before. "You may look on me in my shame. It is nothing more than I deserve."

Something was very wrong here. Yes, it was an ancient custom to reveal oneself in this manner, if a person had done something truly beyond the pale. It was a way of saying that they did not deserve the honor and protection of the robes.

Unwillingly, Zhandar raised his head. A Zhore could not go pale, not the way a human could, but there was a taut look to Nalzhir's mouth, and heavy shadows under his pale green eyes.

"What has happened?" Zhandar asked.

Rinzha reached for a tumbler of water on the side table next to the bed and gave it to Nalzhir. He drank, then nodded.

"I will wait outside while you speak," she said.

She slipped past, dark and silent as a shadow. After she had shut the door behind her, Zhandar redirected his gaze to Nalzhir. It still felt wrong to look on him thus, but the other man had requested it.

"I failed her," Nalzhir said, and cold began to trickle its way down Zhandar's spine, moving out toward his limbs. It did not require a great leap of the imagination to deduce who the "her" Nalzhir was speaking of might be.

"What has happened to Trinity?" he demanded.

"She is gone. That man—that Gaian, Gabriel Brant—has taken her."

At the mention of Brant's name, the cold trickle became an icy flood, washing over Zhandar. He clenched his hands into fists, willing himself to remain calm. "How could he have taken her? Did he have the brazen nerve to come down here to Zhoraan to steal her?"

Nalzhir shook his head. His heavy black hair had been pulled back with a simple elastic band, rather than the elaborate metal holders the men of their people preferred. "No. We were on Kelzhar, for a meeting he had requested."

"Wait," Zhandar cut in, and held up a hand. "What meeting? What are you talking about?"

"Our diplomatic services bureau was contacted by this Mr. Brant. We all know that he is not an ambassador, but that was how he was presenting himself—with the backing of his government, which did not leave us many choices. They were accusing us of holding Ms. Knox against her will, and he demanded to see her in person. So I went with her to the second moon, to have this meeting and let the Consortium government know that she was here on Zhoraan voluntarily."

"And you allowed yourself to be gulled by such a ruse?" Zhandar asked, not bothering to keep the incredulity out of his tone. "Do you have any idea what Gabriel Brant is capable of?"

"A good deal, thanks to the information Ms. Knox has passed along. We knew it was a risk. But it also offered the opportunity to defuse the tensions, so to speak, and to let Brant and his superiors know that we would not meekly hand her over to them." Nalzhir let out a weary sigh then, and shook his head. "An outright refusal would have made matters so very much worse. It could have led to an escalation. I had guards with me, and we were technically on Zhore territory."

"All of which obviously mattered very little, since Brant got the better of you and stole Trinity away despite your precautions."

Nalzhir closed his eyes. To hide from what, Zhandar couldn't know. It wasn't as if the other man could see his expression. But perhaps the agent could feel the anger radiating from him. Zhandar wasn't trying very hard to block it. Not now, when this man had allowed Trinity to be taken by that beast Gabriel Brant.

"I am well aware of my failings, Zhandar," Nalzhir said at last. "And believe me, if I could somehow go back and change things, give up my life for hers, I gladly would. But that absolution is not allowed me."

"So what happened?"

"Some kind of gas in the ventilation system. It caused all of us to fall unconscious. Brant and his cohorts were prepared, of course, and put on masks. But it happened so quickly that there was nothing any of us could have done." He pushed himself up on the pillows, then coughed, an ugly rasping sound. "Apparently, the compound they used has some unpleasant after-effects, which is why I am here."

Once again a ripple of fear moved through Zhandar's veins. "He would use something so dangerous on a pregnant woman? I thought the child was what he truly wanted."

"No, from what the doctors have been able to ascertain, it affects Zhore more adversely than it does humans. Yes, Trinity must have been rendered unconscious like the rest of us, but she should not be experiencing any long-term effects from the gas."

That response should have made Zhandar feel a bit more relieved, but he wasn't. Not really. Because even if what had been done to her wouldn't send her to the hospital, she was still in Gabriel Brant's hands. From what Trinity had told him, Brant had no scruples. He would do whatever he wished to achieve his ends.

They had to get Trinity away from him.

"Where did he take her?" Zhandar demanded.

Nalzhir's gaze shifted to the window, where the sun had just dipped behind the building next to them. "I don't know, Zhandar. No one knows."

Her head was splitting open. Trinity put her hand to her forehead, then realized it hadn't literally broken apart…it just felt that way. With a groan, she opened her eyes, then immediately wished she hadn't.

Gabriel Brant was standing at the foot of her bed, watching her with greedy eyes. "Welcome back to the land of the living."

"Jesus Christ, Gabriel." She pushed herself upright, noting at the same time that she still wore the close-fitting tunic and pants she'd had on at their supposed "meeting." Well, thank God for that. At least he hadn't undressed her and put her in a hospital gown while she was passed out. "Where am I?"

"Back at the base. The anesthetic gas only would have knocked you out for a half-hour or thereabouts, so we gave you a dose of a little something extra to keep you asleep until we got you here."

Almost by instinct, her hand went to her stomach. If he'd given her something that would hurt Zhandar's baby—

His eyes seemed to follow her movement. "Oh, no worries, Trinity. It wasn't anything that could do any permanent damage. We wouldn't take that risk with our precious cargo."

She wanted to tell him the child wasn't "his" cargo, but realized she wasn't in any position to make that kind of argument. Instead, she set her jaw and looked away from him. This room had a window, and so she could see that same glowing nebula from a slightly different perspective. It was beautiful, but it did nothing to calm her soul.

Gabriel came around the side of the bed and stared down at her, gaze traveling from her still-flat stomach to her face. "I suppose congratulations are in order. But then, you did apply yourself to your assignment with a good deal of enthusiasm. Well done."

It was one of the hardest things she'd ever done, to keep looking up at him when all she wanted to do was tear her gaze away. Something in the way he gazed at her made her stomach begin to churn. She was back to her normal self now, and she couldn't forget the threat he'd made.

After this is all over…once we've returned you to your natural appearance…then I think I will want you very much.

Would he take that risk, though, while she was carrying Zhandar's child? Oh, sure, pregnant women had sex every day. Normally, it was not a big deal. But when the child involved was the half-Zhore hybrid Gabriel and his superiors wanted so badly…well, she couldn't even begin to guess. She'd thought she had most people figured out, after spending so many years reading their thoughts, but the way Gabriel's mind worked was something that continued to elude her.

Maybe that was for the best. She didn't know what she might think of her own mind and soul, if she could insert herself into his thought processes that easily.

Somehow she managed to force a smile onto her lips, even though her head was aching so badly she might have kissed Blake Chu if it meant he would give her a painkiller. "Well, Gabriel," she said, "you probably got the gist of it from the transmissions my implant sent out. But I have to admit that my Zhore was a spectacular lay."

His expression darkened. "Don't toy with me, Trinity."

"I'm not. I'm just telling you the truth."

And then she held her breath, because he bent down toward her. Oh, God—what would she do if he tried to kiss her? The mere thought of his lips on hers, after she'd known what it was like to be kissed by someone who truly loved her and wanted her, was enough to make her want to gag. But if she resisted…that could be worse. Much worse.

His fingers closed around her hair where it fell loose over her shoulder, and he yanked her toward him. Combined with the headache, the sensation was excruciating, and she let out a shocked gasp, clamping down on her teeth to prevent a whimper from escaping her lips.

Face inches away from hers, he said, "I'll take you when I want you. And there's nothing you can do about that, Trinity. Nothing."

Zhandar couldn't decide which would be worse— staying home from work and brooding over what might be happening to Trinity at that very moment, or going in to his office and having to pretend that nothing was wrong. In the end, he'd decided to go to work, mainly because concentrating on his day-to-day tasks had offered him some solace in the past, and he thought if he sat home alone with nothing to do, he might literally go mad. He had some time before the weariness and the heartache literally consumed him…days, perhaps a week, if he was lucky…but if Trinity was not returned to him before then, he would slip into darkness.

Leizha lingered in his office after she came in to confirm that he wanted the plans for their next retrofit sent on, now that they'd been finalized. "You are troubled," she said.

This was not a conversation he wanted to have right now, but sending her out of his office with no explanation would only make matters worse. He shrugged. "My mind is occupied, yes."

"Is it this Zhanna?" Leizha inquired, her tone studiously casual.

Ah, he should have known that would get back to her. His people were not known for being gossips, not in the way the Gaians or the Eridanis were, but they still talked amongst themselves. And no doubt "Zhanna's" precipitous departure had led to more than a few conversations among his staff as to precisely what had happened.

Still, he had no idea what he could say to Leizha now that wouldn't be an outright lie. He certainly couldn't tell her the truth. So he settled for replying, "There was some connection between us. But in the end it was not right, and she left."

There. All of that was technically true, if robbed of any accurate context.

Leizha nodded, then said, tone carefully neutral, "That is unfortunate."

More unfortunate than you will ever know, he thought. Ever since Nalzhir had told him of the way Trinity had been abducted, Zhandar had been castigating himself, wishing he had cast aside his pride and spoken to her, allowed her a chance to explain further. If only he hadn't allowed his anger to get the better of him, none of this might have ever happened. For if he had reconciled with Trinity, then surely he would have been able to persuade her not to go to that disastrous "meeting."

But while his people believed that careful reexamination of their actions might prevent a person from making the same mistakes over and over again, that certainly wouldn't do him any good in this situation. All the same, he couldn't help brooding over everything he had done wrong.

Now he would do anything to put it right.

Leizha still stood by the door, watching him from within her hood. Repressing a sigh, he told her, "Yes, it was a difficult situation. But I do not think her absence put us too far behind, since you came back and got us back on schedule.

A graceful tilt of her head in acknowledgment. "It was the least I could do."

His comm buzzed then, and he looked down at the display. This time he recognized the code—Rinzha, calling again.

This was certainly not a conversation he wished to have in front of Leizha, so he said, "I require some privacy for this conversation. If you would close the door?"

A sharp spike of curiosity seemed to move out from her before she could repress it. But she only said, "Of course, Zhandar," and moved out of the doorway, then activated the controls so it would shut behind her.

As soon as it closed with a soft hiss, he pushed a button on the comm. "Yes, Rinzha? Have you any news?"

"Not precisely. But there is someone that Nalzhir would like you to talk to."

"How does he fare in his recovery?" Zhandar asked, knowing that custom required him to make the inquiry. If pressed, he would have admitted that he cared very little for Nalzhir's well-being, after the mistakes he had made.

"Better," Rinzha said. A certain dryness in her tone told Zhandar that she knew all too well what he thought of her superior. "In fact, he has been discharged from the medical center and will be meeting you at your destination."

"My destination?"

"I will send the coordinates to your handheld. It is some three hours from Torzhaan, so I would advise taking the rail and then picking up a day car when you get there."

This was all sounding very mysterious. But if Rinzha and Nalzhir had found someone who could help them find Trinity, then Zhandar was willing to go to the other side of the planet to speak to them.

Or even the other side of the galaxy, if that was what was required.

"Thank you, Rinzha," he said.

"It is not a problem. We will see you in a few hours."

So apparently she would be going along as well. Perhaps Nalzhir was not quite as well as he thought, and so wanted her to come along to provide any kind of assistance he might need.

"Yes. I am looking forward to it."

They said their goodbyes, and he ended the transmission, then got up and began straightening his office as best he could. After that he shut down his computer and slipped out. Leizha was nowhere to be seen; it was the end of the day, and apparently she had taken his request for privacy as a signal that she might as well go home.

All the better. That way, no one would know for sure when he had left.

And even he didn't know when he would be back.

They must have given her something to sleep. Otherwise, Trinity didn't think she could have passed so many hours in dreamless slumber. Her mind had been tormenting her with visions of everything Gabriel could and would do to her, once he decided she'd had enough psychological torture and moved on to the actual physical suffering. They'd fed her dinner and given her water, either of which could have been laced with a soporific drug. She supposed it didn't matter one way or another.

The clothes they'd provided the last time she was here were still hanging in the wardrobe, and all the toiletries she'd used were still in the bathroom. Even though Trinity knew the room had to be under video surveillance, she went ahead and took a shower. What difference did it make? Gabriel had already seen her in the most intimate situations she could possibly imagine.

Although this was a bit different. At least when he'd been looking at her naked body before, it had been clothed in the Zhore skin they had given her. If he was watching her now, he would be seeing all of her...the *real* her.

A shudder passed over her, and she quickly pulled on the tunic and slim pants she'd laid out for herself. She didn't know who had chosen these clothes, but they fit perfectly, and were a soothing dark teal color. After so many weeks spent in black, her soul did feel just a little cheered by the return of some color to her life.

That was probably grasping at some extremely flimsy straws, but she didn't know what else to do.

The door chime sounded. Trinity couldn't quite prevent a mocking smile from pulling at her lips. After everything he'd done to her, Gabriel was going to scruple now at simply barging in on her whenever he felt like it?

She knew she would have to go ahead and answer that chime. If she ignored it, she was pretty sure he would let himself in, so she might as well exert whatever flimsy control over the situation that she could.

"Rested?" he asked as soon as she opened the door.

"Enough. Whatever you slipped me last night, it seemed to do the trick."

His smile didn't waver. Of course it wouldn't. He was enjoying this immensely. Trinity wondered what he did in his spare time for amusement. Pull the wings off flies? Or had he graduated by now to kicking puppies?

"Now, Trinity, we just felt it was important for you to get a good night's sleep."

"Mmm."

He moved past her into the room, and she shut the door behind him. At least the room looked reasonably tidy; she'd always picked up after herself, even as a child. No doubt a psychologist would have said that was her way of trying to create order in a chaotic existence.

Watching him, though, she could feel the anger rising in her again. Even though she knew she shouldn't provoke him, not when she had the baby to worry about, she planted her hands on her hips and said, "What exactly is your game, Gabriel? I mean, I understand about wanting a half-Zhore baby to study. Sort of, anyway. But all this other crap? The theatrics? The petty tortures? It's getting old."

His smile faded then, and his eyes narrowed. For a second, Trinity thought he was going to move toward her, but he stood his ground, hands knotted at his sides. "My *game*, Trinity? You think the future of the Consortium is a game?"

Oh, no, she wasn't about to let him get away with that. She lifted her chin and replied, "As I said, I understand why you'd want to know more about these Zhore/human hybrids. But this? The innuendo, and the glances, and the weird neck rubs and the kisses? I'm not sure what you're trying to prove, except that you're in control. But we both knew that already, didn't we? So again, what is the point?"

He remained very still, watching her. A muscle twitched in his jaw. Right then she was too aware of how he towered over her, how he had more or less complete command of this station. But she wouldn't let him intimidate her. She'd rather he did whatever he intended and got it over with, rather than keep dancing around the issue. If that meant sex, well, then, so be it. He wouldn't be the first man she'd slept with that she hadn't even liked. All right, in Gabriel's case, it was more loathing than merely not liking, but if you took your mind and heart out of the equation, it wasn't that big a deal. Just two bodies joining together. It wouldn't be like all the times she'd shared with Zhandar, those moments filled with the sort of bliss she'd never thought she'd be able to experience. They were two such different states of being that they really didn't have that much of a connection.

Then Gabriel seemed to relax slightly, and the smile returned. "Well, if you must know, it's because I've fallen madly in love with you."

She gave an ironic chuckle at that reply, one eyebrow raised.

"No? I thought that was what most women wanted to hear. Very well, then. No, I am not madly in love with you, but I think I might be slightly in lust. Wasn't really expecting that, if you want to know the truth."

This time her other eyebrow went up. "Gabriel, I doubt you would know the truth if it bit you in the ass."

There was something liberating about speaking her mind like this, of throwing aside her doubt and worry and fear. So far he'd done nothing in return but retreat into more verbal sparring. For all she knew, he'd been hoping that she might fight back, just a little, so he could amuse himself with their back-and-forth. After all, if he wanted to, he could stop it at any time.

The smile was still there, although something about it tightened a fraction. He said, "In my experience, truth is highly relative. For example, you believe yourself in love with this Zhore, this Zhandar. You've made that your truth. But is it really? He's an alien. You've known him for barely a month. Would any rational being recognize that love as being real or true?"

She wanted to argue. Of course she knew she loved Zhandar—and she had to hope that he loved her back, even if he was angry with her because of the way she'd been forced to deceive him. But she also knew, that if someone was looking at their relationship from the outside in, they would say there was no way they could have shared such a deep bond so quickly. Then again, an outsider wouldn't understand anything of *sayara*. That sort of connection couldn't be explained, only experienced.

"Probably not," she said frankly. "But I'm not trying to convince anyone else. I know what I know."

"I'm sure you do."

This time he did take a step toward her, and she forced herself to stand her ground. If he reached for her, tried to kiss her, or worse…well, she'd decide then what she was going to do. In the meantime, though, she wasn't going to back away, or look weak or frightened.

Something in her expression must have shifted, though, because he added in an off-hand tone, "By the way, we've been having some discussions, and we've decided that your gifts are simply too valuable to gamble on a high-risk pregnancy. We're looking for an acceptable surrogate, and once she's found, we'll transfer the fetus to her."

Trinity stared at him, aghast. He couldn't mean that. After all she'd gone through, they were going to swoop in and take her child from her before it was even born?"

He nodded. "You see now. You can try to fight me, Trinity, but I'll always be a step ahead." His hand reached out and grasped her by the wrist. "And once you don't have that little Zhore inside you any longer, I'll enjoy showing you exactly how little control you really have."

SIXTEEN

THE SUN WAS WELL BELOW THE HORIZON BY THE TIME HIS train stopped on the outskirts of a town called Tranzhir. Zhandar alighted and went to an automated day-car kiosk, where he entered his credit voucher information and picked up the fob for one of the day-use air cars parked in a lot next to the train station.

Once inside, he fed the coordinates for his destination into the car's onboard system and let it pilot him away from the station, down a road that led out of Tranzhir. The town was much smaller than Torzhaan, and he was out in the open countryside soon enough, moving at a good clip, since the car had analyzed the light traffic around them and determined that it was safe to go faster.

That was fine with Zhandar. He'd been restless all during the train ride, wishing it would go more quickly, although in truth, less than two hours had elapsed in the time since he'd left his office. And at least he was doing something, rather than wearing a dull spot in his floors with all his nervous pacing.

The car turned off the main road, moving onto a narrower lane that clearly led to someone's homestead. He couldn't see much in the dark, beyond what the car's lights illuminated in a ten-meter circle around them, but it was enough to know that this was rolling, gentle country, punctuated by a wood here and there. In the sunlight, it was probably brilliantly green. He knew this kind of land well enough, since he'd grown up on a homestead in countryside much like this.

Now the lane was curving, looping lazily as it wound through a copse of white-trunked trees. Once the car emerged into the open, Zhandar saw lights up ahead, coming from a large pale two-story structure that seemed to glow in the darkness. And as he approached and the car began to slow down, he saw that another car was already stopped out in front, a dark official-looking vehicle. That must have been the car that brought Rinzha and Nalzhir here. Wherever "here" was. Someone's home, by the looks of it, but exactly why they'd come to this place rather than anywhere else, Zhandar couldn't begin to guess.

His own car glided to a stop next to the other vehicle, and he got out before the engine began to even spin down. The evening air was cool and mild, smelling of *trazhar* lilies and a few other scents he couldn't identify. Then again, his childhood home had been a good thousand kilometers from here, so he supposed what grew here could be markedly different. One perfume was particularly enticing, and he made a note to ask what it was before he left.

The door opened even as he began to reach toward the button for the chime. A tall man stood there, his hood on a level with Zhandar's own. "Good evening, Zhandar. I am Lirzhan. Welcome to my home."

Zhandar pressed his hands together and bowed in the ritual greeting, even as his mind began to race. Lirzhan? Wasn't he the former ambassador who had formed the *sayara* bond with a Gaian woman?

That question was answered soon enough, because just as Zhandar stepped inside and Lirzhan closed the door, a human woman approached them, smiling. Her dark gold hair gleamed in the light, and she was quite beautiful.

And also, he realized as she came closer, extremely pregnant. Her draped dark blue robe couldn't conceal the rounded swell of her belly, and she moved with care. But her expression was serene for all that.

"Good evening, Zhandar. I'm Alexa, Lirzhan's wife."

He bowed to her.

"Come into the dining room," she went on. "I know it's a little late for dinner, but if you've been traveling all this time, you'll probably want something to eat."

"Thank you," he murmured, wondering if he had driven all the way out here for a dinner party.

She gestured for him to follow her, and so he did, going down a long hallway decorated with sconces of trailing plants and small delicate abstracts done in soft metallic paints. The effect should have been soothing, but Zhandar felt too on edge to truly appreciate his surroundings. He wanted to know why he was here. Something to do with this Gaian woman—who was also a former ambassador, he recalled—but how she could possibly help Trinity, he couldn't begin to guess.

Nalzhir and Rinzha already were seated in the dining room, which had the feeling of a lush grotto, with its grouping of indoor trees around a fountain set in the floor at one end of the chamber, and the vining plants that had been trained to grow up the walls and even across the ceiling. There was an open space next to Rinzha, and so Zhandar took that one, while Lirzhan helped his wife into her chair before seating himself beside her.

The ambassador lifted a pitcher of water and poured some into the footed glass that sat in front of Zhandar, then handed him a plate filled with the sorts of things that would be easy to consume during a meeting—pieces of fruit, and bits of cheese and bread, and his favorite, mushroom turnovers. It all looked quite good, but his appetite seemed to have deserted him in the midst of his anxiety.

"Forgive the secrecy," Lirzhan said, "but after hearing of how our planet's security was breached by agents of the Consortium, we thought it better to have this discussion in private."

"Exactly how private?" Zhandar inquired. It seemed as if Lirzhan was implying their own government was not involved, but Zhandar didn't see how that could be so, not with Nalzhir and Rinzha in attendance. He needed a clearer idea of where they all stood.

"Private enough," Nalzhir said then. "To put it this way, while our government recognizes the need to take action and do what we can to rescue Ms. Knox, officially, it is attempting to stay neutral. Ms. Kreg here of course has a good deal of knowledge of the Consortium's various agencies, because of the post she formerly held, and Lirzhan also has far more experience of Consortium practices than most of our people."

Although he desperately wanted to believe that they could help, Zhandar had no idea how they could be of any real assistance. While he didn't pretend to understand the twisted workings of the darker parts of the Consortium's government, he did know that the Gaians were excessively good at hiding what they didn't want to be found. And he had a feeling that Trinity was someone they *really* didn't want found.

"Is it all right if I speak in Galactic Standard?" Alexa Kreg asked. "I'm slowly mastering Zhoraani, but this could get complicated, and it would be easier if I stuck with GS, since I know all the Zhore have to learn it as a second language."

"Of course," he replied. He understood the language better than he spoke it, but he could manage.

"We all understand your distress, Zhandar," Alexa said. Her voice was smooth, controlled; he could see that she was used to speaking in front of others, and knowing that they would listen to her. "And from what I've heard so far of this Gabriel Brant and the people he's working for, you have every reason to be concerned. However, Trinity is also valuable to them, or they wouldn't have risked so much to retrieve her. The task at hand is to narrow down where they might have taken her."

She paused. But the others just nodded, clearly wanting her to continue. And since Zhandar had nothing to contribute yet, either, he inclined his head slightly and picked up his glass of water.

"They'll want some distance between here and wherever they've gone to ground," she said, ticking off the options on her fingers. "But at the same time, they wouldn't take her anywhere near the Gaian system. If she's right in their backyard, so to speak, their deniability goes out the window. Someplace like Iradia might work, except it's just a bit *too* lawless, and so risky. True, there are lots of inhabitable planets that could work as a base of operations, since they haven't been settled, and so no one's paying any attention to them."

For some reason, she paused there, her gaze flickering toward Lirzhan as she smiled slightly. He didn't seem to react, although Zhandar got the impression that he might also be smiling within his hood.

"However, based on the statements that Trinity made to Nalzhir, it sounded as if it was roughly a nine-hour subspace jump from wherever they performed the surgery on her to this system. That doesn't narrow it down much, but according to the charts Lirzhan and I looked at, there are no Gaia-class worlds within that range. So...."

"So," Lirzhan continued, "we are guessing that this Gabriel Brant's base of operations is not on a planet, uninhabited or otherwise, but on a space station of some sort. That sort of structure is relatively easy to hide, especially if it's located in a system that has been catalogued but not settled."

"That is something," Zhandar agreed. "However—and correct me if I am wrong, as I am only a simple horticultural architect—wouldn't the odds of finding a space station in so vast an area be, well, astronomical?"

To his surprise, it was Nalzhir who answered him. "That is true, but there are still ways to narrow it down. A space station is never completely self-sustaining. It must have ships to bring it supplies, changes of personnel, that sort of thing. That kind of traffic can only be hidden up to a point, even as good as the Consortium is at concealing its tracks."

Zhandar set down his glass of water. "That may be, but who would be tracking it? I understand that on Gaia and some other worlds, there are people who are specialists in this sort of thing, but on Zhoraan we have no need of...hackers." He said the last word with some distaste, glad that no equivalent existed in his own language.

Alexa's lips pursed in amusement. "Perhaps, but they can be useful, especially when they decide to use their skills for good."

At that remark, Zhandar could only tilt his head to one side. "I fear I don't understand."

"I know someone. He was in and out of Eridani when I was with the Consortium consulate there. At the time he was also working for the government, but in the last few months he's gone dark, so to speak."

"'Gone dark'?" Zhandar repeated, mystified. Perhaps his grasp of Galactic Standard wasn't as good as he thought.

"He decided that working for the Consortium wasn't such a good deal after all. When the stories about Hunan Province leaked…." Alexa let the words trail off, and she shook her head.

That name sounded vaguely familiar. Zhandar wasn't one to pay much attention to any sort of news, let alone anything involving the Consortium, but it seemed there had been some sort of scandal that the Gaians had desperately tried to hush up. He just couldn't recall the particulars of the incident. Now probably wasn't the time to ask for an in-depth explanation, however.

"Anyway," she went on briskly, once she seemed to realize that neither Zhandar nor any of the others were going to require more clarification, "that sort of soured him on the whole thing. He left the Consortium service and went undercover. I have no idea why he got in contact with me, but I received a message from him a few months ago."

"What was the message?"

This time she didn't just smile. She grinned, and something about the expression softened her features immeasurably. Yes, she was a lovely woman, but Zhandar had thought her rather cold. If he hadn't known she shared the *sayara* bond with Lirzhan, he probably would have never believed it.

"The message said, 'I like what you did, or what you tried to do. Anytime you want to give the Consortium hell, you just let me know.'"

Lirzhan chuckled, but once again Zhandar found himself mystified. Judging by the faintly puzzled aura surrounding Nalzhir and Rinzha, it appeared they felt the same way.

Seeming to take pity on them all, Alexa said, "The Consortium didn't much appreciate one of its ambassadors defecting to marry an alien. I compounded the transgression by trying to call them on some very underhanded research they were conducting. So Jackson was commending me on that. How he knew, I can't say for sure, but he's a very good hacker, so he must have caught a whiff of what was really going on and decided to investigate for himself."

"Jackson?" Rinzha said.

"His name is Jackson Wyler. I'm sure if I contact him and tell him what we're looking for, he'll do the rest."

"How quickly?" Zhandar asked, hoping he didn't sound too anxious. It was obvious that Alexa and Lirzhan were offering any help they could, but at the same time, he couldn't prevent himself from thinking about how the moments were slowly ticking past. Anything at all could be happening to Trinity while they sat here talking.

"I don't know," Alexa replied. Her voice softened as she spoke; clearly, she understood his concern, but there was only so much she could do. "I'll contact Jackson and give him our parameters, then see what he has to say. He's spent the last fifteen years hacking systems that couldn't be hacked and analyzing data at a level I doubt any of us could fully comprehend, so if there's anyone who can find a solution for us quickly, it's him."

That sounded a bit better. Zhandar knew he was very good in his own specialized field, but he used computers as helpful tools, not as weapons...or as scalpels. If this Jackson Wyler was a skilled as Alexa seemed to think he was, then they might have a fighting chance.

"In the meantime," Lirzhan said, "let us all eat our fill, and do our best to keep up our spirits. Zhandar, do you think it is feasible to take a short leave of absence? We have ample space for you to stay here, and that way we'd be able to act quickly if Jackson does find something for us."

Zhandar couldn't help sending a dubious glance at Alexa's swollen belly. While he wasn't overly familiar with the various stages of pregnancy, it looked as if that baby was about to make an appearance any day now.

"It's quite all right," she said, sounding amused. "I'm not due for another two weeks. I'm sure we'll have all this worked out by then."

He hoped so. Because he didn't want to contemplate what might happen to Trinity if she ended up being held by Gabriel Brant for such a horrendous stretch of time.

Not that he, Zhandar, would even still be alive by then to find out.

The chronometer on the wall couldn't make a ticking noise like the antique clocks she'd seen in historical vids, and yet in her mind, Trinity thought she could hear every second going by with excruciating slowness. Gabriel had left her alone after making that last threat. At first she was relieved that he'd found something else to occupy his time, but she realized he hadn't done so out of the goodness of his heart. No, this was just another one of his petty little tortures.

Meals were left for her at regular intervals, and she forced herself to eat. Not because she was experiencing anything close to hunger, but because of the life growing inside her. The life Gabriel wanted to take away.

If they'd been on a base on some uninhabited world, she might have contemplated thoughts of escape. Surely trying to survive on an alien planet would be better than simply waiting around until Gabriel's minions found an acceptable surrogate. But on a space station, her options were a little more limited. Even if by some miracle she managed to get out of her rooms and to the station's shuttle bay, she didn't know any more about piloting a starship than she did solving a differential equation.

She didn't have anything to bribe anyone with, and even if she did, the only person she'd been allowed to see besides Gabriel was Blake Chu. And the odds of subverting Blake to her cause were probably…well, math had never been her strong suit, but she had a feeling those odds were awfully high.

What if she threatened to hurt herself, hurt the baby? No, she doubted she could bring herself to even pretend to do that. Anyway, merely by agreeing to the original mission in the first place, she'd proven to Gabriel that she had a fairly healthy sense of self-preservation. She doubted he'd buy any martyr acts from her now.

The door chimed, and she stiffened. Had Gabriel finally decided he'd had enough of leaving her alone and thought it was time to come in and torture her a bit more?

If he had, there wasn't much she could do about it.

"Come," she said, glad that her voice was steady, even though her heart had begun to beat faster the second the door chime sounded.

It wasn't Gabriel who entered, however, but Blake Chu. The smirk he wore looked positively Gabriel-inspired, however.

"How are we doing today?" he inquired.

"*I'm* fine," she said.

He squinted, as if attempting to look at her more closely. "Hmm. You're looking a little tired, actually. All this sitting around getting to you?"

"Are you kidding?" she shot back. "After having to play secretary for the past few months, this is being in the lap of luxury. It was very thoughtful of Gabriel to make sure that all the latest entertainment feeds were sent to my console."

Well, not all, actually. There was a conspicuous absence of anything resembling news. Just fluffy entertainment in various forms. It was better than nothing—watching the melodramas the vid writers cooked up helped to divert her thoughts, if only in short bursts—but she had to wonder what was going on in the larger galaxy.

Blake shrugged. "Well, good, I guess." He paused then, and she could almost feel him poking at her mind, trying to find a chink in the mental armor she'd erected.

Good luck with that, she reflected. After spending a month among the Zhore and having to keep those barriers up at all time, dealing with Blake's blunt-force approach was almost laughably easy.

"What did you want, Blake?"

He smirked. "Oh, right. Gabriel sent me along to let you know that they've found an acceptable surrogate. She should be here sometime within the next thirty-six standard hours."

Trinity's stomach clenched. But she knew her barriers were still in place, so Blake shouldn't be able to sense any of the roiling dread that had overtaken her. A standard day and a half before Zhandar's child was stolen from her forever.

Yes, she'd known the surrogate might appear at any time. And really, considering Gabriel's ruthless efficiency when it came to making something he wanted happen, thirty-six hours was almost glacially slow.

The question was, could she come up with a plan to thwart him within the next thirty-six hours?

"Great," she said carelessly, hoping that her hesitation hadn't lasted long enough for Blake to notice. "The sooner they get this thing out of me, the better."

I'm so sorry, Zhandar...I didn't really mean it.

Blake gave her a nod of grudging approval. "Yeah, I can't say as I blame you. Bad enough that you had to... you know. But then to have to carry it for nine months? Nasty."

She wanted to tell him that the really nasty thing was his VR girlfriends and the various apparatus he used to get off while engaging in those virtual encounters. But since it seemed as if she almost had him on her side right now, the last thing she wanted to do was antagonize him.

"I know," she replied, then gave a mock shudder. "You'd think Gabriel might have thought of that from the beginning. Then we could have performed the transfer as soon as I got back here."

"Well, I don't think he was counting on...." Blake seemed to stop himself then, as if he'd been about to reveal something he shouldn't.

Gabriel wasn't counting on…what? Being "slightly in lust" with the woman he'd chosen to be his secret weapon? Well, that made sense. If he hadn't want to sleep with her, Trinity doubted he'd be worrying too much about letting her carry the child to term, no matter what he might say about risking her talents. It was the child who couldn't be risked. Neither he nor the doctors and scientists he was working with really knew enough about Zhore physiology to say whether sex during pregnancy was safe.

She wasn't going to admit to Blake that she knew all about Gabriel's plans for her. It was clear enough that the two men must have shared a few confidences…or maybe Blake was a little better at getting into Gabriel's head than her handler wanted to acknowledge. Either way, this was one time when it was probably better to play dumb. Especially since she'd just begun to have an inkling of a plan.

"Oh, yes, I got the feeling that he wasn't expecting me to get knocked up that quickly," she confessed, giving Blake what she hoped was a half-sly, half-embarrassed look, as if they were sharing a confidence.

"Yeah, that," he responded at once.

There. Relief. He was relieved that she hadn't pressed the issue or asked any awkward questions. She remembered how she'd gotten in all the way during their training sessions, by letting her thoughts become an invisible mist, one that slipped quietly through all the defenses he'd so carefully created.

"So," she said, "how do you even find a surrogate? Put an ad on the local e-board?"

"Of course not," Blake replied. "I don't know the details. But obviously it's something we needed to be discreet about."

"Oh, right." Good. Now he was thinking of her as stupid and silly. And if he considered her to be a foolish young woman who didn't know what she'd gotten herself into, then he wouldn't believe her to be any kind of threat. Certainly not the sort of opponent who could take him on, let alone best him. Being Blake, he was so confident of his own superiority that he'd conveniently erased that one instance where she'd slipped into his thoughts without his even realizing what she was doing.

Trinity sank into his mind then, getting every useful piece of information she could extract. The station was out in the middle of nowhere—she didn't even recognize the sector designation—and while, because of security reasons, its staff didn't seem to rotate out on anything like a regular basis, they did have a supply ship come out every three standard months to bring food, equipment, spare parts, and whatever else might be needed.

That ship was not technically a Consortium ship, but a private vessel subcontracted for the job. And it was going to be here tomorrow.

Was it bringing the surrogate as well, or would she be arriving by a different ship? Trinity guessed the surrogate must be on board, because otherwise that would have been too much of a coincidence. Either way, it didn't matter all that much, because she realized that the supply vessel was her only true hope here. Somehow she would have to find a way to get on it, and be away before anyone even noticed that she was missing.

No problem.

She wanted to grimace, but couldn't, because Blake was saying, "So I guess once she's rested after her trip here, they'll do the…procedure."

"Great." She paused, then asked, "Do you think it'll hurt?"

He gave her a scornful look. "That fetus isn't even the size of a fingernail yet. Of course it won't hurt. You won't even notice a difference."

Except that Zhandar's child will have been taken from me. I think I'll notice that a good deal.

"Oh, yeah, you're right." She slanted a look at Blake. His expression was fairly neutral, but she noted the slightest lift at one corner of his mouth. It didn't take a mind reader to guess what he was thinking right then.

He was thinking about what Gabriel was going to do to her once he didn't have to worry about interfering with the half-Zhore child's development.

Trinity swallowed. She had to find some way to sneak on that shuttle tomorrow. Or else….

Or else Gabriel would have won. And after that, she wasn't sure if she'd still have the strength to resist him.

SEVENTEEN

Lirzhan led Zhandar to the room where he would be staying. It was large and airy, with a fountain in one corner surrounded by lacy ferns. He might not be able to rest while he was here, but that wouldn't be because the room wasn't comfortable.

Apparently picking up on some of what Zhandar was thinking, Lirzhan said, "I know it's difficult, but do what you can to get some sleep. I will bring some necessities for you and leave them outside your door."

"I thank you for your hospitality," Zhandar said formally.

"It is yours for as long as you need it," Lirzhan replied. He hesitated for a second or two, then went on, "Believe me, I know what it feels like to have the woman you love in the hands of those who appear to have no morals, no scruples. I know nothing of this Gabriel Brant save what I have been told, but I do know he values the child that Trinity carries. He will not do anything to endanger either one of them. That may be scant comfort to you, but scant comfort is better than none at all."

Actually, Lirzhan's words did reassure Zhandar somewhat. Brant clearly would do anything to get what he wanted, but now that thing he wanted was a human/Zhore hybrid to study. Doing anything that might hurt Trinity would only damage his prize as well. No, for now she was probably safe enough, if chafing at her captivity.

"Thank you for that," Zhandar said. "Trinity is a resourceful woman, and intelligent. I am sure she is doing what she must to bide her time until help can come to her."

"Precisely. So sleep now, and with any luck, we will have some news for you soon."

Zhandar nodded, then bade Lirzhan good night and shut the door to the guest room. He had not brought a change of clothes, but perhaps that would be part of what his host had said he would provide. In the meantime, it was enough to take off the heavy robes and drape them over a side chair, then pull the clasp from his hair and shake it loose. After having it pulled back tightly all day, it felt good to let it fall over his shoulders, free at last from the confining clip.

Then it was time to remove his boots, and lie down on the bed. He tried not to think of Trinity, but the more he attempted to force her from his mind, the more she was there—the pleading in her blue-green eyes the last time they had spoken, the worry and the fear that she had tried to barricade from him. At the time, he had thought himself completely justified in his anger, but now he could only berate himself once again, wishing he'd been able to look past the hurt and the betrayal and be just a little more understanding.

Right then, he would have given anything to be able to hold her in his arms again. He could only pray that his stubbornness hadn't stolen the one thing he realized was more precious to him than anything else.

It was still quite dark when the door chime sounded. Zhandar sat up in bed, blinking at his unfamiliar surroundings. For a second or two, he couldn't place where he was. Then he remembered—Lirzhan and Alexa's homestead.

His host's voice came from beyond the door. "My apologies, but Alexa has some information for you."

That was the only spur Zhandar needed. In a flash, he was out of bed and reaching for his cloak. He'd barely finished fastening it around his throat and pulling the hood low before he was pushing the button to open the door.

"What is it?" he asked, then stepped out into the corridor.

"Good news. Come with me."

Hoping—and wondering if he was foolish for allowing himself to hope before he'd heard anything else—Zhandar followed the other man down the hallway to another room, clearly an office. Alexa sat at a desk, facing a comm, although the screen was dark. Nevertheless, a man's voice was coming from the speaker.

"…always think they're so clever, but they're not as good at covering their tracks as they think they are. Especially if you know where to look."

The voice was clearly Gaian, speaking Galactic Standard. The man's tone had a faintly ironic quality, the words drawled, as if he were simultaneously bored and amused by the current topic of conversation.

"So anyway, yes, there has been an unusual amount of money funneled into a station in Sector 1754, including a good deal of appropriations for medical equipment. Why someone would need that kind of equipment for a space station out in the middle of nowhere, one that's not servicing a colony or a fleet or something along those lines, I have no idea." The voice paused, then continued, "Well, actually, I think we all have an idea."

"So you're sure that's it, Jackson?" Alexa flicked a brief glance over her shoulder to acknowledge Lirzhan and Zhandar as they came in, but quickly turned back toward the comm.

"Am I one hundred percent positive? No. But I'd say we're in the ballpark of around eight-five percent. And if I were a betting man, I'd bet on those odds."

"You've found her?" Zhandar murmured.

"We think so," Alexa replied. "That is, Jackson did the analysis, and there's just nothing else out in that range that's showing any kind of activity. In Sector 1759, there's some mining going on in a system with a number of satellites that contain unusual concentrations of heavy metals, but it was fairly obvious that Trinity was on a space station, not a planet. Anyway, all the traffic in Sector 1759 is above board and accounted for. But in Sector 1754, which is supposed to be completely empty—there are only two systems that even have planets in that sector—he's tracked traffic that has no business being there."

"Yes," drawled the voice from the speaker. "And more to come. There's a supply ship—the *Cote d'Ivoire*—that's on its way there right now. ETA is around 22:00 hours their time tomorrow."

"We'll have to intercept that ship," Zhandar said. Surely if they were able to stop it, board it, then they could use the supply vessel as a way to get into the space station.

"Two steps ahead of you, cowboy," Jackson Wyler said. Bemused by the Gaian's off-had tone, Zhandar wondered what in the galaxy a cowboy was. He didn't have time to pursue the question, however, because Wyler was speaking again. "I've already sent the coordinates to Alexa, along with the codes to show that you're with the Gaian Defense Fleet and have orders to board their vessel, due to its carrying contraband."

"But"—Zhandar looked from the empty screen where Jackson's face should have been to Alexa, who seemed more or less unruffled by his declaration—"if this supply ship is carrying cargo for a Consortium space station, why would the Gaian Defense Fleet have any reason to stop it?"

"Typical bureaucratic snafu," Alexa said. Then, appearing to take pity on his continuing confusion, she went on, "The Consortium is so large, and so complex, that contradicting orders are given all the time. Since the supply ship is piloted by subcontractors, they're not going to be totally sure of what's going on. They'll be a lot easier to intimidate and board than an actual ship of the GDF's support corps."

Lirzhan spoke for the first time. "I hope you're not planning on being one of those who intend to intimidate and board that supply vessel."

Alexa sent a rueful glance in the direction of her swollen midsection and chuckled. "No, I don't think I would be very effective. And obviously neither you nor Zhandar are going to pass muster, either."

"I don't care anything about 'passing muster,'" Zhandar protested. "But if you think I am going to stay here when I should be going to Trinity—"

"Hold your horses," Jackson broke in. "I know some people who can help. I'll set up a rendezvous just outside Zhoraan's system. You can meet there, and they'll take you in the rest of the way."

"People?" Zhandar wasn't sure he liked the sound of that. Yes, Alexa had said they could trust Jackson, that he was no longer a servant of the Consortium. Even so, he didn't like the idea of completely handing the rescue mission over to a group of strangers.

"Trained professionals who'll be able to extract your girl. You ever attempted a rescue of someone held in a Consortium facility, Zhandar?"

"Of course not," he replied, liking even less the aura of subtle sarcasm that seemed to pervade Jackson's words.

"Well, then. I'm not saying you can't go along, but you'll have to keep yourself safely hidden until the time is right. Last I checked, the GDF didn't have any Zhore on its duty rosters."

The hacker had a point. As much as he hated to admit it, Zhandar knew he was more than conspicuous. Even if he sacrificed his privacy, rid himself of his bulky robes, and put on a stolen uniform, he could never pass himself off as a Gaian.

"I understand," he said stiffly.

"Great. Then I guess we're all good to go. I assume you can arrange passage from Zhoraan to the coordinates I've given you?"

"Yes," Alexa replied. "I've passed the word along to those in the government here who are helping us. They'll have a ship standing by."

"Okay. Twenty-two hundred hours their time gives you"—a pause while Jackson apparently did a few calculations—"a little more than twelve standard hours to get to your destination. You have a little slop time, but not much. So don't waste it."

"We won't." Alexa paused, then added, "Thank you, Jackson."

"Thank me later, after you've gotten your girl back. In the meantime, give 'em hell."

The transmission seemed to end there. Alexa swiveled her chair back toward Zhandar and Lirzhan. "All right, we have three hours. Nalzhir is already on his way here with a shuttle, and there's a ship at the base on Kelzhar that's being fueled and readied as we speak. They'll take you to the rendezvous point."

"You were able to coordinate all that already?" Zhandar supposed it wasn't outside the bounds of possibility, but something about Alexa's smooth efficiency was a little intimidating.

"Well, most of it was Nalzhir's doing. I just sent him the latest updates, and he got things moving along the proper channels."

"Still—"

She waved a hand. "It's the least I could do. Anyway, there's no time to waste. As Jackson said, it's time to give 'em some hell."

Trinity knew they had surveillance cameras covering every inch of the suite where she was confined, and so she had to make sure she didn't do anything that would attract any particular attention. Whoever was watching the feed wouldn't see much right now, since she was merely sitting on her bed with her legs crossed, eyes shut and her hands resting lightly on her knees.

To an outside observer, it would simply look as if she was meditating, but anyone who knew her well would have also known that she didn't meditate. Then again, no one did know her well. Not even Zhandar. He loved her, or thought he did, but he didn't truly know her.

That was all right. Some days, she didn't even want to know herself.

This was something she used to do back when she was first coming to terms with her gift, with what it could and couldn't do. Most days, all she'd wanted to do was push it as far back in her mind as she possibly could, because it was all too overwhelming. All those thoughts, all those minds, beating at her. What person could possibly put up with that?

But she'd also learned that if she sat very quiet and very still, didn't fight those intruding thoughts but instead allowed them to flow through her mind, she could learn a great deal. That was how she'd discovered that her mother truly didn't know who Trinity's father was—she'd thought it was a man named Dominic Alton, but it could also have been Roman Cole, since their coloring wasn't dissimilar, and….

Trinity had shut down that particular thought tendril, because the last thing she'd wanted was to discover any more sordid details than she already had. Since she resembled her mother except for her coloring — Acantha Knox was blonde, with hazel eyes—Trinity knew the particulars of her features wouldn't provide any clues as to who her father actually was. She could have tried to track down those two men and attempted to learn for herself after her mother was gone, but in the end she'd decided it didn't matter. Neither of them had been around to see her grow up, so why should she bother now that she was an adult?

It wasn't just her mother's thoughts she'd sensed in that moment, though, but everyone in their building: the Tsao family next door, the Garcias down the hall, the McKenzies and the D'Ambrosios and everyone else. Tom D'Ambrosio was cheating on his wife. The oldest McKenzie girl, who was a year older than Trinity and always seemed impossibly worldly and glamorous to her, was two weeks late for her period and freaking out that she might be pregnant, even with the hormone shots. And so on.

The intensity of the experience always wrung Trinity out, and so she tried to avoid casting her thoughts so widely unless it was absolutely necessary. In fact, she hadn't done it for years, more out of self-preservation than anything else. Most of the time, there wasn't much useful to be gleaned from delving into so many people's minds, unless discovering sordid details about their lives was something a person like Blake might find amusing. Trinity never found it amusing, though. Sad and scary and overwhelming was more like it.

Now, though, ranging through the station and attempting to learn where everyone was and what they were doing might offer Trinity her only chance of escape.

She caught the echo of someone who had to be Blake. His thoughts were impenetrable; clearly, he kept his guard up at all times, not just when he was in her presence. That discovery didn't surprise her too much, since she did more or less the same thing. It was the only way to stay sane when you were gifted—or cursed—with psychic abilities.

And then there were the medical techs, including the doctors who'd operated on her. It seemed they were in the process of analyzing her blood. Trinity didn't even remember giving a blood sample, but she'd been knocked out for a good long while when she was brought here. It could have easily been taken from her then. There were ten in that group, from what she could tell, but it also seemed as if they generally didn't venture far from the level, three down from where Trinity now sat, that had been designated as the med center.

Guards, too. She'd never seen any of them, but there were twenty assigned to the station. A small support staff—two people working in the kitchen, three technicians whose jobs entailed making sure the systems regulating the station kept operating efficiently. Since she couldn't sense anyone else, she guessed that all other duties, including janitorial, must be handled by mechs of various types.

And then…Gabriel. He was on the level above hers, but almost on the opposite side of the station. At the moment, he didn't appear to be doing anything to mask his thoughts, probably because both she and Blake were far enough away that Gabriel must have decided they couldn't offer any kind of threat.

Right then, Trinity wished he still had his barriers up, because her handler was thinking about her. And not in a logistical sort of way, such as contemplating the details regarding the surgery that would hand off her child to the surrogate who was about to arrive, or how long the recovery time afterward would be. No, in that moment he was indulging a fantasy of forcing her to her knees, then holding her by the hair while making her suck his cock.

Bile rose in her throat, and her eyes opened. The concentration—the trance, or whatever you wanted to call it—was gone. She made herself take a breath, and then she unfolded her legs and got up from the bed. A glass of water certainly wasn't enough to erase that image from her mind, and yet right then, it was the only thing she had.

So she fetched a plastic tumbler from the small cup-board above the sink, and poured herself some water. It tasted tinny and strange after the pure, sweet water she'd drunk on Zhoraan, but at least it was wet. Also, the act of getting herself the water helped to steady her nerves a bit. Yes, if she allowed herself to dwell on it, the bile would resurface, but she could control it by not allowing that hideous image to resurface in her mind.

It wasn't the oral sex. She'd always sort of enjoyed that. Certainly she'd loved doing it to Zhandar, feeling those delicate, tiny scales slip against the surface of her tongue. Her disgust now arose from the realization that Gabriel was just as aroused by the thought of forcing her to do something sexual to him—*anything* sexual to him—as he was by the physical act itself.

I have to get out of here.

Of course she already knew that. Now, though, the need for escape seemed so much more urgent. She had to save her child, but she also had to save herself. Maybe she'd been fooling herself by thinking that all Gabriel wanted was merely sex. She could have handled that. She might not have enjoyed it, but she could have lived with it. But now that she'd seen he wouldn't be satisfied with simply bedding her, that he'd need to debase her first in order to show who had the power here...well, she knew she wouldn't be able to survive that. It might not take a day, a week, or even a month, but sooner or later, after being continually used in such a way, Gabriel would break her. And then she, Trinity, would be gone, and the only thing left would be a shell of a body that he would continue to use as he wished.

She would die before she allowed that to happen.

Certainly Zhandar had never imagined his first trip into space would be like this. To be fair, he'd never really imagined going into space at all, because he loved Zhoraan and saw no need to leave his home world, but even so....

A shuttle had come directly to Lirzhan and Alexa's homestead to retrieve him. On board were Nalzhir and several silent men Zhandar assumed must be guards. Why Nalzhir had them there, Zhandar wasn't sure, because they only accompanied them to another, much larger ship that they docked with in the dark spaces just outside Zhoraan's solar system. Zhandar was handed over to the newcomers, and then Nalzhir and his escort departed in the shuttle, presumably to return to their own world.

The new ship was manned entirely by Gaians, but they clearly had no official loyalties to anyone. Their vessel was unmarked, and they were dark gray jump-suits with no badging, no patches, none of the various identifying accoutrements he had heard the Consortium military and its adjuncts so loved to place on their uni-forms. Their leader, a man with skin almost as black as Zhandar's own, had introduced himself only as Ejiro, informed Zhandar that they would reach the space sta-tion's system in approximately eight and a half standard hours, then disappeared back into the cockpit.

There were fifteen of the soldiers or commandos or whoever they were. None of them seemed inclined to speak, although Zhandar noticed one or two giving him sideways glances when they thought he wasn't looking. He couldn't blame them; he doubted either of them had seen a Zhore this close up before. Not that there was much to see. Even so, behind a layer of steely self-con-trol that was admirable for a human, he could still sense ripples of curiosity, and even unease. Not about the mis-sion, per se, but merely to be involved in something that involved such secretive aliens. Apparently infiltrating a secret Consortium base was all in a day's work for them, but to have a Zhore on board their ship? That was something else entirely.

Conversation with any of the men seemed to be out of the question, so Zhandar had to content himself with merely looking out the window, which was interesting at first. The stars had never seemed brighter, and the other planets in the Zhoraani system were like gleaming jewels in shades of gold and pearlescent white and rusty red.

Then the ship shifted into subspace, and the colors outside the window were no longer quite so lovely, but seemed to shift and shimmer into shades that made his stomach want to turn. He pushed the button to lower the shade. Across the way, one of the soldiers cocked an amused eyebrow but didn't say anything.

Well, I suppose you are used to going into space, but I am not. And though Zhandar had read brief accounts of what travel through subspace was like, those accounts did not come anywhere close to describing what it was actually like when experienced for yourself. For many reasons, he would be very glad when this journey was over.

Oddly, he dozed, probably because he had only slept for half the night the evening before. Just as well, because otherwise the journey would have seemed twice as long as it already did. The shudder of the ship as it dropped out of subspace woke him. All around, the soldiers seemed to have gone on the alert, checking and double-checking their weapons, eyes now hard, intent.

Zhandar wished he had similar preparations that he could occupy himself with. But he was only a passenger here, allowed to come along because apparently no one thought he would be too much in the way. Well, and probably because Alexa had insisted on it. Even a squad of mercenaries might be intimidated by a woman like her.

The next moment, Ejiro emerged from the cockpit. Now he wore a flat black cap on his bald head. His hand rested on the sidearm in the holster he wore, but he looked relaxed and calm, with no hint of worry about what they were facing.

"We wait here," he said.

"Wait?" Zhandar demanded. "Wait for what?"

"You think we were going to go in there all guns blazing?" Ejiro returned, looking singularly unperturbed. He had a soft singsong accent, one that under other circumstances, Zhandar might have found soothing. Now it just seemed to grate on his nerves. "They're sweeping the system. This ship has no clearance. We've got to wait for the supply shuttle to show up. It'll come out of subspace close to here, outside the gravity well and beyond the range of their scans. We take the shuttle and use that to go in. It's already got the clearance. Understand?"

"Yes," Zhandar said, although he wasn't happy about the delay. To think that Trinity was probably less than an hour away, and yet they had to sit here and wait….

"Good," Ejiro said. "They won't be expecting us—they're just civilians, makin' a run to a place that isn't supposed to exist. And they'll be confused an' worried when we I.D. ourselves as a GDF vessel. It'll be over before they even know what's happening."

Zhandar had to hope so. Then again, Jackson Wyler had sent this team because he trusted them to do what was necessary. They had to have a good deal of experience with this sort of thing. How precisely they'd acquired that experience, he had no idea, but he was finding that there were a good many things he had no idea about. Zhoraan had sheltered him well. Perhaps too well.

The minutes ticked by. Or at least Zhandar assumed they did. There was no chronometer visible in the cabin. All he could do was sit there, silent and tense, and force himself to wait to see what happened next.

Then the ship shuddered. Not the same sort of shudder as when she'd emerged from subspace, but a sharp jolt. Zhandar grasped the hard edge of his seat to keep himself from sliding forward, but none of the men around him so much as reacted.

"Got her," Ejiro said with some satisfaction.

"Got her…how?" Zhandar asked.

"Just like reelin' in a fish," Ejiro replied with a chuckle. The men around him seemed to get the joke, because they nodded, and a few even smiled.

Well, they might all understand, but Zhandar was even more mystified. Seeming to take pity on him, Ejiro said,

"Tractor beam. Small one. Only works on ships the same size as this one, or smaller. But it gets the job done."

So such things actually existed? "How—" Zhandar began, but Ejiro held up a hand.

"No time. It's experimental. Let's just say a friend gave it to me." His expression sobered, and he went on, "Team Alpha, handle it."

Half the strike team headed toward the back of the ship, where the access hatch was located. They weren't wearing pressure suits, so Zhandar wondered what they actually planned to do. But then there was a hollow *thunk,* and the ship shivered again, although more faintly this time.

"What…?"

This time, Ejiro stopped Zhandar with a shake of his head. "You ask a lot of questions, Zhore. We pulled the shuttle up against us so the team can take the umbilical to go over there. They'll have it all handled in less than two minutes standard."

That sounded like an optimistic estimate to Zhandar, but he didn't bother to protest. And it seemed that Ejiro knew exactly what he was talking about, because in a remarkably short amount of time later, one of the strike team members reappeared in the passenger compartment.

"All handled, sir," he told his commander. "Four crew members, all subdued and taken to the holding area."

"Excellent. I'll bring the passenger over."

By "passenger," Zhandar assumed Ejiro meant himself. Good. He'd worried that he might be left behind on the commandos' ship, but apparently he would be allowed to ride along on the hijacked supply vessel, even if he couldn't actually set foot on the space station.

"What are you going to do with the captives?" he asked. If they had been actual Consortium personnel, he might have been less concerned about their fate. But they were only subcontractors, here to do what they thought was a simple job. They didn't deserve to meet with any misfortune because of that.

"Not to worry," Ejiro replied with a chuckle. "We'll give them back their ship, soon as we're done with it. A' course, they'll have to explain to their bosses what happened here, but that's no concern of mine." The amused glint left his dark eyes, and he went on, "A'right, then. Time to go. Step lively, and remember to stay out of the way."

With that, Ejiro was moving toward the rear of the ship, heading for the umbilical that connected them to the captured vessel. Zhandar did as he was told, following the Gaian, with more of the commandos bringing up the rear. Although he was willing himself to be calm, he could feel his heartbeat speeding up. So much closer now. Things were falling into place. In less than an hour, Trinity would be in his arms again. He would have to apologize, tell her how wrong he'd been to turn away and be so unforgiving.

And then he'd have to hope that she would be more forgiving than he.

EIGHTEEN

AFTER FOCUSING ON THE STATION FOR THE BETTER PART OF an hour, Trinity thought she had a fairly clear idea of where everyone would be at any given time. The only wild cards, really, were Gabriel and Blake; the rest of the station's staff seemed to stick to their set routines. Even the guards, who moved around the hallways rather than staying in one place, had patterns to their movements that were easy enough to detect, once she had concentrated on those movements for a little while and then filed them away for future reference.

All right. Everyone present and accounted for. Now came the hard part.

This was something Trinity hadn't attempted for years, mostly because the implications of her actions had scared the hell out of her, even as a teenager who'd at first was only looking to have some fun. Back then, she'd been invited to a party, but her mother, in a rare fit of responsibility, had said Trinity couldn't go because she'd caught wind that the party-thrower's parents were traveling, and therefore "anything" could happen.

Acantha Knox had probably been right about that. But Trinity, only wanting to fit in, had railed against her mother's intractability. And then she had an idea.

For the past five years, ever since she'd turned twelve, she'd been able to see into people's thoughts, sometimes in a distressingly detailed way. Doing so didn't require any great effort on her part. In fact, it was harder to keep their thoughts out of her own mind rather than to look into the thoughts of others.

But what if she used the power of her mind to actually force someone to do something?

She'd sat on her bed and thought as hard as she could at her mother, *You want to let Trinity go to the party. It's okay if she goes to the party.*

And so on.

Less than an hour after that particular experiment, Acantha Knox had appeared at the doorway to her daughter's room and had said, somewhat waspishly, "All right, you can go. But you need to be back here by eleven."

Ecstatic, Trinity had jumped up from her bed and hugged her mother. And she'd gone to the party, which was awful, because there was absolutely no supervision, and everyone got more or less drunk, and Bradley Lassiter cornered her in the bathroom and tried to stick his tongue down her throat. Trinity had escaped home well before her eleven o'clock curfew, feeling chastened.

Her mother was already in bed, apparently trusting that Trinity would be back when she had promised.

Which she had been, but at the same time, guilt began to assail her. She'd basically reached into her mother's mind and made her do what she, Trinity, wanted. And that was just wrong, on so many levels that Trinity didn't even want to count them.

She'd never reached into someone's mind in that way again.

Well, until now.

She decided to make Blake her puppet, for two reasons. One, like Gabriel, he seemed to have the clearance to go wherever he wanted on the station. No one would question his coming to her room, because he'd already done so on Gabriel's orders. Second, she'd reached into his mind before. She knew how to get past his defenses. But because she'd never mentioned this one particular facet of her talent to anyone, she also knew Blake wouldn't be expecting her to pull anything like this.

Closing her eyes again, Trinity let her thoughts range out through the station. It was getting late in their artificial day—her evening meal had been brought to her hours ago—and so she knew Blake would be in his rooms. Hopefully not jerking himself off with his latest VR girlfriend, but if that turned out to be the case, she'd just have to shake him out of it, disgusting as that notion might be.

Luckily, though, he was just closing down his computer for the night. He hadn't begun to get ready for bed, which meant he was still dressed. Even better. This would be easier if she didn't have to make him jump through a lot of hoops before he even got out the door.

She let herself sink into his thoughts, which, thank God, were mostly innocuous right then. Whether he should hit Gabriel up for a raise, now that the whole Trinity Knox thing seemed to have worked out pretty well. Or, failing that, at least get an extended leave someplace where he could lie on a beach and try his luck with some real women, the kind he could have fun with for a week or two, no strings attached.

It was a tiny seed she planted. Just the suggestion that he needed to go out and check on Trinity. She'd been acting a little strange, and although it seemed as if she was okay with having that Zhore embryo removed, maybe it was better to check that she didn't do anything drastic, especially with the supply ship arriving with the surrogate in less than an hour….

Blake got up from his desk and moved to the door, then let himself out. His rooms were located two levels above Trinity's, so he went to the lifts and summoned one. It seemed to take an excruciating amount of time before the elevator arrived. Eventually, though, the lift gave a half-hearted *bing,* just before the door opened.

At that hour, the elevator car was empty. Trinity knew she didn't have a lot of time, though, because one of the guards was due to sweep her floor in approximately five minutes, and she needed to have Blake get her out of there and on her way to the station's hangar before the guard appeared.

But in less than a minute, he was on her level, walking down the corridor to her room. She got up from her bed and went over to the sofa in the little sitting area, then turned on the vid. It was late, but not so late that he should think it strange that she was still up and watching a show.

The door chimed, and she said, "Come." That wasn't too bad. Her voice hadn't shaken at all.

Blake came in, looking both sort of blurry and unfocused, and yet cheerful. "Hey, Trinity."

"Hey, Blake," she replied. "Did you need something?"

"I, uh…." His words trailed off, and he shook his head. "I thought I did. But now I can't remember what it was."

She gave what she hoped was a sympathetic nod. "That's too bad. Why don't you come sit down and watch the vid with me? Maybe that'll help you remember."

"Um…sure." He came toward her and then settled himself down on the couch.

"Comfy?"

"Yeah."

"You know, if you don't like this show, you can change it." That was the tricky part. She needed to leave him here so she could head out to the hangar, but she also knew she couldn't devote the entirety of her concentration to keeping him rooted in this spot. Once she was roaming the hallways, she'd need to focus as well on making sure she avoided the guards.

"Oh, okay. Thanks." Blake turned away from her and directed his next words to the vid unit. "*Scarlet Dawn*, episode forty-seven."

Somehow Trinity managed to prevent herself from rolling her eyes. *Scarlet Dawn* was an extremely bloody serial that focused on the exploits of a crack team of GDF special ops. The violence probably wasn't the only reason Blake enjoyed the show—one of the leads was a demolitions expert with enormous boobs.

Whatever floats your boat, Blake, she thought then, before saying, "Well, you have fun with that. I need to check on something. Okay?"

"Okay," he said absently, attention already focused on the screen. Trinity supposed she couldn't blame him too much—those breasts were pretty distracting, and she wasn't even attracted to women.

As Blake's eyes seemed to glaze over, Trinity got up from the sofa and tiptoed out the door. He didn't stir, and she murmured a silent thank-you to the universe. One part of her mind was still hovering over his, just in case he should rouse himself from his stupor enough to realize that their valuable captive had just slipped out from under his nose.

The rest of her, however, had to focus on getting away from the level where her room was located and over to the hangar, which was at the very bottom of the station and on its opposite side. She didn't have a chronometer, but she knew the guard should be coming along at any moment. In fact, as she reached out with her mind, she could feel him riding up in the elevator.

Damn. She wouldn't be able to avoid him if she stuck to her current course. Luckily, there was an access stairwell just around the next corner, so she slipped in there and began hurrying down the steps. It would be a slog, as the space station comprised some fifteen levels, but at least she was headed down and not up. And really, this was probably better in the long run, since no one seemed to use the stairs at all. From what she could tell, the guards came this way every once in a great while, just to show that they were policing every section of the station, even the ones that weren't used all that often. However, they only did that when directly ordered to.

None of them seemed to be coming this way tonight, though, and so Trinity was able to slip down into the very bowels of the space station undetected. When she reached the bottom level, she paused next to the door and took a breath to gather herself, while at the same time dipping more deeply into Blake's mind. His thoughts felt muddied and tired, almost as if he was about to fall asleep. That would be even better. And if Gabriel somehow came upon him there, passed out in her room…well, those would be some explanations she'd love to be around to hear.

But she wouldn't be there. By then she would've slipped aboard the supply ship and gotten safely away. It would be tricky, but she was fairly sure she could convince the crew of that ship—using a little extra mental persuasion—that she was supposed to be there. After all, they'd brought one woman to the space station, and had come to take another one away. It all made perfect sense.

First, though, she had to get on board. And that meant making her way through the corridors that led to the hangar area without drawing any notice. The hangar itself had two guards permanently stationed there, along with a couple of technicians to oversee the atmospherics and the calibration of the membrane that kept air in but also allowed a ship to come and go.

Trinity paused around a corner and focused on the hangar. Only one guard seemed to be present at the moment; maybe the other one had gone off to take a leak or grab a drink of water or something. Likewise, a single technician accompanied the guard. They were discussing the prospects for the upcoming low-G football tournament back on Gaia's moon and didn't seem particularly engaged. Good. That meant they were bored and probably not paying much attention. She would have thought they'd be a little more on the alert, since the supply ship was due to arrive at any moment, but maybe they'd been stationed here long enough that even the prospect of seeing a few new faces, however briefly, wasn't that big a deal.

Suddenly, though, a sort of whooping siren filled the hangar, and Trinity stiffened. Had her absence been detected?

Poised to flee, she listened with her mind, realizing almost at once that the whooping noise was merely the station's proximity alert, letting the personnel on duty in the hangar know that a ship was approaching. She let out a breath and began to creep closer, pausing just outside the heavy double doors that opened onto the hangar itself. Not too much longer now.

A few minutes later, the floor seemed to shiver slightly under her feet. That must be the ship itself, settling itself on the surface of the hangar bay. Trinity reached out with her thoughts, wanting to know how many crew people were on board the supply vessel. She hoped it wouldn't be more than three or four, because the more of them there were, the more difficult it would be to keep all of them under her control for a flight of eight or ten or even twelve hours.

But then she stopped, her heart hammering in her chest. It couldn't be…no, that was impossible. And yet somehow, she knew the touch of that mind. Familiar, comforting, like a warm blanket she wanted to wrap around herself.

How he'd come here, she had no idea, but Zhandar was on board that supply ship.

"This shouldn't take too long," Ejiro told Zhandar. "Jackson located your girl on Level 10. So we'll take the team and fetch her. You'll stay here, along with our pilot."

Zhandar gave a resigned nod. By now he'd come to terms with the idea of having to wait while the commandos went to rescue Trinity. He certainly didn't have any training in close-hand combat. And even if he had, he was far too conspicuous to be allowed along on such a mission.

Something in Ejiro's manner seemed to relax slightly. Perhaps he'd been expecting his Zhore charge to protest. But he didn't waste any time after that, directing the men under his command to follow him into the hangar. Zhandar watched them file out, then began to reach out to close the hatch…right before he paused, his heart beginning to pound away in his chest. There was a touch on his mind, familiar, soft, for some reason reminding him of the fragrant night-blooming flowers whose scent he'd admired so much back at Lirzhan and Alexa's homestead.

Trinity.

Somehow, she was nearby. Zhandar was sure of that, because although their bond was strong, he still couldn't sense her if she was too far away.

Which meant that Ejiro and his men had quite possibly gone off on a useless quest.

But he couldn't worry about that right now. Pausing at the open hatchway, Zhandar dared to peek out into the hangar bay where the stolen supply ship now rested. All seemed quiet and still. For a group of fifteen heavily armed men, Ejiro and his commandos moved with surprising stealth. Then again, going about their business as quietly as possible was probably a necessary part of their training.

There must have been personnel of some sort guarding the hangar, but there was no sign of them now. Ejiro's squad must have already subdued them and moved on.

Judging it safe enough to step out of the ship, Zhandar had just put his booted foot on the gangway when he heard a single syllable in his mind.

Wait.

He froze. That was Trinity, he was almost sure of it, but they had never communicated in such a fashion before. Zhandar had no idea such a thing was possible, but then again, he didn't have a very clear idea of exactly what her psi powers entailed. No one among the Zhore had those sorts of gifts.

And a few seconds later, she appeared, quietly inching her way into the hangar, casting furtive glances over her shoulder as she did so. Zhandar longed to run down the gangway and go to her, but he did as she'd instructed and remained where he was. At least he knew that she was unlikely to be caught at this point, since Ejiro's men had already taken care of the guards, but even so, Zhandar could feel himself tensing as he watched her, so conspicuous with her bright brown-gold hair and tunic and pants in a dark blue-green that matched her eyes.

Eventually, though, she came to a place where she could no longer hug the wall. She dashed away from its spurious cover and came straight for him, light footsteps tripping up the gangway. And then she was in his arms, and he was holding her, inhaling the sweet scent of her hair, feeling how incredibly real she was, and yet so slight and delicate at the same time.

"Trinity, how—" he began, but she silenced him by going up on her tiptoes, then pressing against him and placing her mouth on his.

She was all sweetness and fire, and he never wanted to let go. His anger now seemed like a pale thing, compared to the reality of her.

But after a few seconds, she did pull away. "Zhandar, how are you even *here?*"

"Because I couldn't bear to think of you in his hands. And because it turns out we both have friends we never even knew we had."

Her expression was puzzled, but she nodded. "Which is wonderful. But if you have some way of calling those friends back—"

"I'll let the pilot know." He turned to head back into the ship. Her fingers slipped into his, though, and he looked down at her.

"You're—you're not still angry with me, are you? I suppose I could go into your mind to find out, but I need to hear you say it."

Her eyes stared up into his face, shimmering blue-green, pleading. In answer, he bent down to her, reaching out to pull her against him again.

But a man's ironic tones interrupted them. "What a touching reunion."

Trinity stiffened at once, radiating sharp-toned worry. She squared her shoulders and said, "I think you've lost, Gabriel."

Gabriel. Zhandar's eyes narrowed as he stared at the man who confronted them now, standing a few yards away from the end of the gangway. He was tall and dark-haired. No doubt many would have thought him handsome. But something about the way he stared at Trinity made Zhandar's flesh crawl.

The Zhore way was one of nonviolence, but in that moment, Zhandar wanted nothing more than to plow his fist into Gabriel Brant's jaw.

Brant said easily, "Oh, I don't think so, Trinity. Granted, it seems as if your freakish friend here is a bit more resourceful than I'd imagined…and you, too. But it's time to make a decision. Come with me now, and he gets to keep breathing. Otherwise…."

The sentence died away into the air, but Zhandar didn't need any more words to understand what Gabriel Brant was trying to say. No, his point was perfectly illustrated by the pulse pistol he held, pointed directly at the center of Zhandar's forehead.

No. Trinity stared at Gabriel, at the squat, evil-looking gun he held with such cool authority. With some people, she might have said they were bluffing, but she knew Gabriel didn't bluff. Either she stepped away from Zhandar, or the man she loved would be killed here and now.

True, there were the men who had come here with him, but she couldn't count on them returning in time to be of any help. Now she was cursing herself for not stopping them as they left the hangar. At the time, she had sensed them, had realized they weren't the crew from the supply ship, but she'd been having a hard enough time keeping Blake quiescent from this distance and couldn't delve into any of the strangers' minds to discover exactly what they were up to. And right now she could also sense the presence of one of them, still in the cockpit of the stolen ship, but he was communicating with the team that had just left, and not paying any attention to the drama playing out just a few meters from his ship.

"All right, Gabriel," she said, then moved away from Zhandar so she stood in the center of the gangway. He reached for her, clearly trying to stop her, but she was too fast, and slipped out of his reach. Raising her hands, she went on, "Promise me you'll leave him alone."

Gabriel chuckled. "No, Trinity, I don't make those kinds of promises. What I will promise is that your Zhore will have a nice hole in his forehead if you don't get off that gangway right now."

Son of a bitch. She knew she didn't have much of a choice, so she continued to walk away from Zhandar.

His footsteps sounded on the metal ramp behind her. A second later, a pale blue pulse bolt flew over both their heads. Trinity let out a half-scream, then whirled to look behind her. Zhandar seemed all right, but he had stopped almost mid-stride.

"I mean what I say." Gabriel lowered the gun so it was once more trained directly on Zhandar's forehead.

That last shot had clearly only been a warning one. Good thing that pulse bolts couldn't wreak the same havoc on metal hulls as they did on human flesh, or they'd all be starting to breathe vacuum about then.

"Yeah, kind of got that," Trinity countered, then wished she'd kept silent. Her voice had sounded entirely too shaky. But she couldn't change that now, so she just walked the last few steps to the end of the gangplank, then touched down on the hangar floor.

At once, Gabriel's free hand snaked out and caught her by the bicep, pulling her toward him. Zhandar let out a muffled sound of anguish.

Something about hearing that groan, of feeling his pain and frustration at not being able to do anything to help her, made Trinity's rage come boiling up from deep within. He'd come here to help save her, and now Gabriel was pointing a gun at Zhandar's head and smiling. And although he had said he wouldn't pull the trigger if Trinity came to him, she knew then that he was lying. Maybe it was because his barricades had finally slipped a little, now that he was about to experience his moment of triumph, or maybe it was simply that exercising her powers the way she had during this past hour had sharpened something in her mind, but she could see it in him then. Gabriel wanted to kill Zhandar. He wanted him dead because Trinity had dared to intimate that she thought the Zhore a better man than Gabriel himself would ever be.

Seeing that, knowing that Gabriel intended to do, she realized she had no options left to her.

Except one.

This time she couldn't make her thoughts a mist. That was fine for settling into someone else's mind without their knowing what she was doing, but the current situation called for something a little less subtle. It was time to bring in the sledgehammer.

Her thoughts crashed into his, breaking on them the way a battering ram might have splintered a castle's wooden door, once upon a time. He cried out and took a step backward, but he hadn't dropped the pistol. It wasn't trained on Zhandar anymore, but pointed directly at Trinity's chest.

"Bitch," he gasped. "What the—"

She wouldn't let him complete the sentence. Once again she flung the full force of her mind against his. This time he staggered, looking like someone who had just received a blow from an invisible fist, then fell to his knees. The gun slipped from his fingers.

That seemed to be all the encouragement Zhandar needed. While Trinity stood there, not quite believing the evidence of her own eyes, he rushed past her in a billow of black robes, then bent and retrieved the pulse pistol. With it pointed at Gabriel, who was breathing raggedly and blinking, as if not sure what exactly had just happened, Zhandar moved over to stand next to Trinity.

"Are you unharmed?" he asked her.

"I—I think so."

"What did you do?"

She shook her head. "I'm not sure. That is, I just thought *at* him, used my mind to get in." She didn't know if she wanted to explain anything other than that. Zhandar was not an easily ruffled person, but she still hesitated to explain that she'd more or less used her psi talents as a weapon.

"And if we'd known how effective that was, we might not have been in such a hurry to rescue the damsel in distress," came a man's voice with a singsong West African accent.

Trinity turned and saw a tall black man, followed by a group of fairly hard-looking cases, come into the hangar area. "Sorry," she replied. "This time, the damsel decided maybe it was time for her to rescue herself."

He laughed, then waved at two of his commandos. "Get that one wrapped up. Put him in with the others."

The two soldiers hurried forward and each grasped Gabriel by an arm, hauling him to his feet before dragging him off toward what looked like a small control room some ten or so meters away.

"The 'others'?" Trinity asked. Her head was swimming a bit—both at what she had just done to Gabriel, and because she was wondering how in the universe Zhandar had ended up here with a group of men who wouldn't have looked out of place as extras on Blake Chu's beloved *Scarlet Dawn.*

"The guards and the technicians stationed down here in the hangar bay," the leader of the mercenaries—or whoever they were—replied. "Got 'em stuck in a supply closet. We'll put a time lock on it so they can get out after we're safely away." He turned toward Zhandar, grinning. "Never thought I'd see the day when one of you Zhore would be pointing a gun at someone."

A lift of his shoulders, broad under the flowing robes. The hood swiveled in Gabriel's direction, seeming to watch intently as the man was gathered up by a couple of the commandos and hustled off toward the hangar's control room. Once they were out of sight, Zhandar surrendered the gun to the commandos' leader. "I would prefer to not have to touch one of those again."

"Well, we'll see you safely back to Zhoraan, and then likely you won't." The commander's dark gaze was keen—perhaps a little too keen—as it traveled from Zhandar to Trinity and back again. She didn't even have to poke into his thoughts to know what he was thinking. All he said, however, was, "And I'm assuming that's where you'd like to go, too?"

"Yes," she replied, and went and wrapped her arm around Zhandar's waist. He stiffened for just a second—from shock at the public display of affection, nothing more—and then curved his arm around her as well. She leaned against him, feeling the strength of his body, the unseen embrace of his love and affection. "I can't think of anyplace else I'd rather be."

NINETEEN

The transfer back to the commandos' ship took place without incident. No doubt the actual crew of the supply vessel would be dining out for weeks on their story of being hijacked out in the middle of nowhere. Or perhaps not. They could be facing their own particular set of repercussions, although Zhandar couldn't see how even the most unjust government wouldn't understand that a crew of four subcontractors wasn't really equipped to prevail against a hardened team of more than a dozen mercenaries. Even so, he wished the best for them. Perhaps it might be time to ply their trade in a sector not quite so dominated by the Consortium.

Barely a half-hour into their return flight, Trinity leaned up against his shoulder and fell asleep, the last bit of worry smoothing itself from her face as she allowed herself to slip into slumber. Looking down at her, Zhandar thought he'd never seen anything so beautiful, or so precious. And yet he'd almost thrown her and her love away, simply because he'd been unable to look past his anger to understand why she'd done the things she had.

If any of the men who shared the passenger compartment with them were made uncomfortable by his obvious intimacy with Trinity, none of them showed it. And although he couldn't read minds the way she could, he couldn't sense anything except satisfaction with a mission well done. Maybe one or two seemed just the slightest bit annoyed, but their irritation appeared to stem from the object of their rescue mission not staying put where she was supposed to.

For himself, perhaps Zhandar would admit to wishing Gabriel Brant had met a more fitting fate than being locked up in a supply closet. Then again, when he contemplated what the man would probably face once the truth of Trinity's escape got out, he thought that perhaps it was better that Ejiro had left Brant to the tender mercies of the Consortium's own investigative teams. At the very least, he would probably be demoted and sent back to Gaia in disgrace. And if his own handlers were sufficiently annoyed, the man might be sent to that very same MaxSec prison on Titan that he'd used to threaten Trinity.

Zhandar couldn't summon the will to be terribly concerned about what might happen to Gabriel Brant after that.

What he did think about, however, was the way Trinity had quite publicly come to him and put her arms around him. While the men under Ejiro's command didn't seem the type to gossip, even so, the story might begin to get out.

And would that be such a bad thing? Perhaps his people's obsession with privacy sometimes worked against them. If they'd been more open about their population problems, and then allowed that in rare cases the Zhore and humans could interbreed, perhaps a plot like Brant's would never have gotten past the planning stages. Surely the Eridanis, long allies of the Zhore, would have offered their assistance and support.

Zhandar looked down at Trinity again. A tendril of gold-streaked brown hair had fallen over her cheek, and he reached over with a gloved hand to brush it away.

A gloved hand.

He stared at his leather-encased fingers for a long moment, considering the thoughts that had just passed through his mind. Perhaps too much secrecy was not such a good thing after all.

Before he could stop himself, he grasped the fingertips of the glove and pulled it away, revealing the glinting rainbow shimmer of his bare skin. There, that was better. Now he could feel the softness of Trinity's hair against his fingers. She stirred, and her eyes opened. Bleary at first, and then she seemed to focus on him, on the way his hand was exposed to everyone in the cabin.

A sharp tingle of worry, followed by a warm rush of understanding. She nodded, straightening in her seat.

Zhandar was aware of the watching eyes of the commandos, of the way they were trying to stare without staring at the revealed flesh of his hand. He knew he must do this thing now, before he lost his nerve.

With shaking fingers, he clutched the edges of his hood and then pushed it back so it lay against his shoulders. Black hair fell free against the black fabric of the robes.

Inside the cabin, all was deathly still, except for the faintest vibration of the ship's passage through subspace. Zhandar could feel all those eyes on him, even as he sensed the strength of Trinity's approval and admiration, clothing him in the very moment he felt most unclothed.

Then Ejiro stepped forward, and clapped a hand on his shoulder. "Welcome to the galaxy, Zhandar," he said, smiling.

And Zhandar smiled in return.

Trinity wasn't sure she would have believed it if she hadn't seen it for herself. But no, there was Zhandar, pushing back his hood in front of all those men, proudly bearing the brunt of their shock and surprise, even though in general they were certainly not the type to gawk.

Afterward, lacing her fingers through his, she murmured, "Why?"

"Because it's time," he replied quietly.

And she couldn't argue with that.

They were quiet the rest of the way back to Zhoraan, their hands still clasped in one another's. The ship landed at a facility out in the woods somewhere, clearly a private 'port. And Nalzhir was there waiting for them.

As Zhandar had begun to disembark, he raised the hood once again. Trinity lifted a questioning eyebrow at him, and he said, "While I might be willing to start a revolution, I also understand that I cannot change the world overnight."

"Oh, I don't know about that," she responded, but she thought she understood. What he'd done on the ship had required a level of bravery she wasn't sure she entirely comprehended, but even so, that action had only involved revealing himself to outsiders, to people who had no true conception of the utter privacy and secrecy the Zhore maintained in all levels of their public lives…and even their not-so-public lives.

He'd squeezed her hand, then led her from the ship. They'd already said their thanks and made their fare-wells, so almost as soon as their feet touched the soil of Zhoraan, the ship was lifting from the ground and head-ing back toward the sky.

And what a sky that was, deep cerulean tinged with green, and with high, high clouds streaked across it like the finest of antique lace. Trinity stood there for a moment, breathing in the fresh air, realizing that she was safe, that Gabriel Brant could never hurt her again.

Or…could he? After all, he had stolen her right from her apartment there in Torzhaan.

"You are troubled," Zhandar said, even as Nalzhir emerged from the shelter of the spaceport's office complex and began to head toward them.

"That's a strong word. I suppose it's just that I'm not sure Gabriel won't try something again."

"His actions do speak of a certain level of desperation. However, I think he will be spending a good portion of his near future trying to explain how you got away. I will admit that I don't have a firm grasp of the inner workings of Consortium government agencies, but I would imagine that kind of incompetence isn't the sort of thing they like to reward."

Zhandar's words soothed her a bit. True, the government didn't tend to be too forgiving of those who failed it, especially on such a spectacular level. It would probably be a long time, if ever, before Gabriel was entrusted with anything of more importance than overseeing the trash-hauling schedules for Luna City.

Nalzhir approached then, radiating relief. "Ms. Knox, welcome back to Zhoraan."

"Thank you," she said politely. "It's good to be back." And it was, although right then what she wanted more than anything was to go to Zhandar's apartment and spend a very long time reacquainting herself with every square inch of his body. Well, right after she had a decent meal, anyway. They'd been given water pouches on the mercenaries' ship, but no one had mentioned food.

She couldn't see his face, but she thought Nalzhir smiled then. "I also sent word of your return on to Lirzhan and Alexa. They were somewhat occupied, as apparently she went into labor early, but—"

"Is she all right?" Zhandar asked, concern obvious in his voice.

Alexa. The former Gaian ambassador, who now had a Zhore husband. Hers would be the second Zhore/human child born. Trinity listened, anxious now as well.

Nalzhir raised a gloved hand. "She is fine. The baby has already been born. A healthy girl."

Thank God. So that seemed to be two for two when it came to these hybrid children. Trinity touched her own stomach briefly. *And you—you'll be fine, too, despite everything,* she told the tiny baby sleeping within her.

Zhandar seemed to understand what she was thinking, because his fingers twined themselves around hers once again. "That is welcome news. Then I will save my thanks to them for later, when they are not quite so busy."

"Perhaps that is for the best. But now, I believe you would wish to return to Torzhaan?"

Yes, thank God, went through Trinity's head, even as Zhandar replied, "I can think of nothing else we would rather do. I suppose at some point you will need our report, but if we can be allowed our rest first…?"

"Of course," Nalzhir said.

Rest, Trinity thought. *I'm not sure what we're going to be doing is precisely resting, but….*

Something of her thoughts must have transmitted themselves to Zhandar, because his fingers tightened on hers, and he murmured, "Soon, my love. Very soon."

She just hoped it would be soon enough.

Nalzhir had muffled Trinity in some borrowed robes, but as soon as she stepped into Zhandar's apartment, she pulled them off and draped them over the back of a chair. "Your turn," she said.

He followed suit, piling his hooded cloak on top of hers. They stood that way for a moment, regarding each other, not speaking. Then she said,

"When you let those men see you. It was brave, but…."

"But you are wondering what my end goal is." He went to her and kissed her on the cheek, gently, marveling at the velvet softness of her skin. "Some *zhir?*" he asked.

A little sigh escaped her lips. "Love some." The Zhore liquor had such a low alcohol content that she knew a small amount couldn't hurt the baby.

He went to the refrigeration unit and pulled out a bottle, then retrieved a couple of glasses and poured a measure of the pale gold liquid into each. Trinity came to him in the kitchen and lifted one of the glasses.

"To the future."

"That is a good thing to drink to." He raised his glass as well and drank, savoring the dry mineral taste of the liquor as it drifted over his tongue. Slanting a look down at her, he said, "And I believe you were wishing for some food?"

She arched an eyebrow. "I though I was the mind reader here, Zhandar, not you."

"Let us just say that I've begun to understand something of your thought processes." He went over to the robes he'd just removed and extracted his handheld from an interior pocket. A few swipes of his finger, a few taps on the screen, and then he set the device down on the dining room table. "It will be here shortly."

"Wonderful." She paused for a few seconds, obviously thinking something over, then asked quietly, "What *is* your end goal, though? Those mercs don't seem like gossips, but I'm pretty sure word will begin to get around."

"Good." He paused, then drank some more of his *zhir*, a healthy swallow that almost emptied the small glass. After this glass, he would have to stop, because he did not want any memories of this time with her hazy and blunted by the alcohol. "When the Eridanis first came to Zhoraan, they were surprised by the way we hid ourselves, but they accepted our customs. They did not try to change us. And as we began to have more contact with the galaxy, instead of opening up, we became that much more reclusive and clung to our practices that much more tightly. It is true the robes serve some purpose, in that they can help to protect us from the emotions of others, but the real truth is, Trinity, that we are taught from an early age to keep those emotions to ourselves so that we don't inflict them on others. So in many cases, these robes only serve to keep us separate from one another. And that is something we cannot afford. Not with what we are facing now."

"But what about those of us who aren't Zhore?" she asked. "It's not as if most people are trained to have the kind of mental barriers someone like me might have. That's got to be tough for you."

"It can be," Zhandar replied. He set down his glass and came to her. Seeming to understand his intention, she also placed her glass on the table and then let him take her hands. Her fingers felt so fragile in his, but he knew how strong she truly was. "But there are very few of us who venture out into the greater galaxy. Some, yes. People like Lirzhan, who was an ambassador. Or this Sarzhin, who met his Gaian wife on a colony world. Even fewer who travel because they want to see stars and worlds that are not their own. It is not that difficult to stay at home and enjoy the beauties of Zhoraan, and be surrounded by those who know how to politely keep their emotions shielded. Better, I think, to catch a stray drift of someone's worry or fear or anger every once in a while rather than have the entire galaxy thinking we are all some kind of hideous monsters under these robes."

Trinity opened her mouth, as if to protest, then stopped herself. Sounding rueful, she said, "I was about to tell you that we do no such thing…but it's true. If you could find it in yourselves to let everyone else know what you truly look like...." She stopped herself then, and chuckled slightly, blue-green eyes dancing.

"What is it?" Zhandar asked, puzzled by her reaction. Surely nothing he had just said was that amusing.

In response, she went up on her tiptoes and kissed him on the cheek. "Oh, I was just wondering what was going to happen once the word gets out that you Zhore are not only gorgeous, but empathic and amazing lovers as well. Every single woman on Gaia is going to be hopping a ship for Zhoraan."

That seemed rather terrifying to him, and certainly not a cause for amusement. But Trinity's expression told him she was teasing, at least a little. Also, he realized then that the mass defection of Gaia's women might have one beneficial side effect. "Ah, well," he said then, "I suppose that will be all right, especially if it has the end result of teaching your men that they should treat their women a little better."

She laughed and pulled him to her, and they kissed, her lips so soft, so full, that he could feel himself stiffening at once. But then the door chime sounded, and he had to pull away so he could relieve the delivery mech of its burden and bring their food inside.

It was only the work of a moment to take everything he'd ordered to the living room, where they sat and ate, speaking little, both of them knowing that they only partook of this food now so it would give them the energy they needed for what was to come next. Truly, he didn't know when Trinity had last eaten, but for him it had been more than a day. Perhaps he should have been more weary than this, considering all that had transpired over the last thirty-six hours or so, but he knew he couldn't be tired, not with Trinity sitting next to him on the sofa, her knee brushing against his, the soft lights in his apartment catching shimmers of gold and even deep copper from within the masses of her hair.

She looked thoughtful, though, the teasing light of earlier gone from her eyes. "But what will all this mean for Zhoraan's women? Gabriel seemed to think that the fertility problems were all theirs...but are they?"

He didn't reply at first, considering her question. Truly, he did not know for sure. It was obvious that he had no difficulties fathering a child, but how much did that truly mean? "I cannot say, Trinity. It is something we will have to consider. One would think that if a woman of your race can share the *sayara* bond with a man of the Zhore, then a woman of my people should be able to bond with a human male. It just has not happened yet." Something in him found that difficult to believe, but then he told himself not to be so narrow-minded. Simply because Gabriel Brant was such a despicable specimen of humanity didn't mean all Gaian men were like that. Ejiro, now—he seemed like a good enough sort. Perhaps his adventurous spirit was the sort of counterpoint that calm, cool Leizha truly needed.

The thought made him smile, and Trinity's mouth quirked in response.

"I think you're playing matchmaker," she said. "Which I've heard is a sign of a man who's happy in his current relationship."

"Oh, I am happy," he replied. "Indeed, let me show you how happy I am."

He reached out to her, taking her fingers in his. At once she rose and let him lead her to the bedroom.

There was no need for speech. Not now. Slowly, carefully, he undid the unfamiliar fasteners of the tunic she wore—buttons, he thought the Gaians called them—and then pulled the garment away. Underneath she wore a breast support of some lacy fabric, very different in appearance from what the women of Zhoraan might wear, but with the same basic purpose. This one seemed almost calculated to be enticing, though, with the way her creamy flesh was cupped by the material and at the same time revealed by it.

Trinity seemed to notice where he was staring, and gave a humorless laugh. "Trust Gabriel to leave some sexy lingerie for me." She used the Galactic Standard word for "lingerie," since Zhoraani had no real equivalent. Undergarments among his people were strictly utilitarian. "Thank God he didn't have a chance to actually see it on me."

Neither did his people believe in a universal deity, the way some Gaians did, but from what he could tell, many of them seemed to evoke this "God" when giving thanks—or cursing—even if they didn't seem to be people of faith otherwise. But although Zhandar didn't share that belief, right then he found himself thanking God as well that Trinity had been rescued before Gabriel could get make any further progress in his nefarious plans for her.

"I do enjoy seeing you in it," Zhandar told her, then bent and trailed a line of kisses from her collarbone to the curve of her breast. Again, the velvet softness of her skin entranced him. She let out a soft, hissing breath and arched her back slightly, pushing herself into him.

Ah, that lacy garment was entrancing, true, but what it hid was far more delectable. He located the hooks at the back and undid them, then dropped the scrap of fabric to the floor. His hands closed on her bare breasts, stroking them, feeling how her nipples hardened under his fingertips.

There was nothing for it but to take one into his mouth, to run his tongue over the pebbled flesh and hear her cry out. She was so very responsive, as if every nerve ending in her body had been attuned to his. Perhaps it had. After all, she was *sayara*.

Then they were falling to the bed, her fingers tugging at his garments, pulling them away. She pressed her naked body against him, as if she wanted to feel the whispery sensation of his finely scaled skin against every centimeter of her form. He couldn't blame her for that, because he was also marveling at the smooth suppleness of her body, the exquisite texture of her skin. Perhaps when he had first looked upon her in this form, he had thought her alien, but now she was only herself, perfect in every way, every curve seemingly designed to fit against him. And when he finally slid inside her, it was as if they had been made to lock together, their bodies the light and dark of the universe, of wholeness, of creation.

He could ask for nothing more than that.

She slept beside him for hours and hours. So much so that when Trinity woke up, she felt almost dizzy.

Then Zhandar's hand was on her shoulder. "Good afternoon, my love."

"Afternoon?" she echoed, sitting up and rubbing at her eyes. The bedroom was quite dim, the shades almost fully drawn, but she thought she could see the faintest traces of bright light seeping around their edges.

"Yes. You've slept for almost twelve hours." His hand moved to her hair, stroking it, and she almost purred at his touch. Even now she could feel herself begin to tingle and come alive, her body needing him. Craving him.

Seeming to sense her arousal, he moved his hand lower, stroking her. She cried out as his fingers buried themselves in her sensitive flesh, and she rocked her hips in time with those delicious strokes, knowing that the orgasm would hit her very soon, partly because she'd already been so relaxed, so satisfied, to begin with.

She clung to him as she came, and even as the shudders were still rippling through her, he lifted her and set her down on him so he could fill her again. Ah, that was it—that was perfection, Zhandar inside her, their bodies moving together, no words, only their need and the one thing that would satisfy it.

This time he climaxed first, but only by a few seconds. Gasping, she let herself collapse on his chest, feeling the shudderingly delightful sensation of all those tiny scales against her naked breasts. For a long moment they stayed that way, until their breathing smoothed out, and they were quiescent. Trinity knew she'd have to get up soon, go take a shower, do whatever else she needed to do to get ready for the day, but this felt so good that she didn't want to move.

"I didn't know it could be this perfect," she said at last, her voice barely above a murmur.

A long pause. Then Zhandar replied, "Neither did I."

Something in his voice seemed to catch at her. Very gently, she pulled herself off him, then lay down at his side. She pushed a long strand of night-black hair away from his face. A sort of hidden pain seemed to pulse from him, although she couldn't tell exactly what had caused it. Taking a breath, she said, "It's—you don't have to say that if it's not the truth."

"'Not the truth'?" he echoed, his tone genuinely incredulous. He stared into her face, his silvery eyes a cloudy gray in the darkened bedchamber. Then he shook his head. "Oh, my love. That is not what I meant at all. It is only—" The words stopped there, as if he was turning them over in his mind, attempting to find the best way to arrange them. When he spoke again, his voice was so low that she had to strain to hear it. "After Elzhair, I had thought there would be no one else. It is very rare, you know, for someone to have the *sayara* bond with two different people. Not impossible, but it also does not happen very often. So to have it with you, and then to realize…." He paused again, and Trinity forced herself to remain silent, knowing that this was very difficult for him. "…to realize that what I share with you is even more than what I had with Elzhair…."

Once again words seemed to abandon him. Trinity pressed against his side, molding her body to his. "Zhandar, it's all right. This is not a betrayal. This is only affirming that life goes on. You will always love Elzhair. But you love me, too. Love isn't something finite. You can have as much love as you need for everyone in your life."

For a long moment, he said nothing. Then at last his hand slipped over the contours of her form, going from thigh to hip and then resting there. Finally, it moved to her belly, still flat, showing nothing of the child growing within. At last he spoke, his tone filled with wonder.

"Yes, life does go on."

EPILOGUE

GABRIEL BRANT KNEW, FROM THE LOOK OF GLEE ON HIS coworker's face, that Eli Turner had some piece of news or other tidbit that he wanted to torture him with. After six months here, Gabriel still couldn't decide which was worse—being demoted to data analysis in this windowless hole of an office, or being forced to share said windowless hole with Turner, who seemed to delight in his office mate's fall from grace.

It could have been worse, he supposed. At least he wasn't coordinating waste removal in Luna City.

Yet.

"What is it, Turner?" he asked, voice as even as he could make it. Letting that little bastard hear even the slightest edge of irritation was enough to set Eli off on ever-increasing rounds of petty torture.

"You might want to see this, Brant," Eli said, making the vowel in Gabriel's last name as flat and nasal as he possibly could. It was an affection that had made Gabriel begin to hate the sound of his own name.

"We're on a deadline."

"This'll only take a minute. Besides, it involves your last mission. Sort of."

Despite himself, Gabriel scowled. The last thing he wanted to be reminded of was that complete cock-up of a project. And that stupid bitch, Trinity Knox. How could someone who looked that innocent and big-eyed and sweet be such a conniving wench? Every once in a while, in the darkest hours of the night as he lay awake, rehashing what had gone wrong and what he could have done to change it, he might have admitted to himself that wanting to screw her senseless could have impaired his judgment a little. Still, how was he supposed to know that the Zhore could have mounted anything like that assault on the space station where his little breeding experiment was supposed to take place? Those scaly bastards were supposedly complete pacifists. What the ever-loving hell were they doing hiring mercs to do their dirty work?

"I'm busy, Eli."

Grinning, Eli pointed his handheld at the screen on the opposite wall. It was supposed to be used only for official business—projecting charts and graphs, watching the occasional "motivational" vid—but Eli used it for his noon entertainment, mainly because he knew that Gabriel hated the mindless shows that he watched.

What appeared in the next moment, however, was not the sort of vapid entertainment broadcast or rerun of an adventure serial that Eli usually chose. Instead, the screen showed a background of blue, blue sky, the sort of blue one never saw on Gaia any longer, and waving fronds of lacy blue-green trees that looked alien, although Gabriel would admit that he was no expert on botany, alien or otherwise.

That wasn't what drew the eye, however. In the center of the screen was a very pregnant Trinity Knox, looking glowing and radiant and happy, despite her bulk. To either side of her were two women that Gabriel also recognized, although he had never seen either one of them in person. One was the coolly beautiful former ambassador, Alexa Kreg, and the other was Annika Jespers, the colonist's daughter from Lathvin IV. Alexa held a sleeping infant in her arms, an infant with the glinting rainbow-scaled skin of the Zhore, while Annika was wrestling with a similarly complected little boy, almost two standard, who clearly wanted to get down and run around.

And standing behind them were three tall Zhore, similar in appearance at first glance, although their eyes were all different. The one with Alexa was the tallest, the other two just a shade shorter.

All these observations passed through Gabriel's mind in an instant. Then his thoughts caught up with his eyes, and he had to prevent himself from doing a double take, because Eli would have enjoyed that too much.

None of those Zhore males were hooded. They wore high-necked tunics in shades of black and dark gray and the deepest green, but that was all. And they stared into the camera steadily, showing no sign of discomfort that they were so revealed for all the galaxy to see.

Trinity was speaking, her voice clear and steady. "… change comes to everything, even Zhoraan. We wanted the galaxy to know our stories, and those of our families. The Zhore are not monsters, but merely another humanoid race, like the Eridanis and the Stacians. One that we can join with, and mingle with, if our hearts and minds are compatible." She paused for a second and smiled, and the Zhore behind her—who must have been Zhandar—laid a hand on her shoulder.

They both looked ineffably happy, and Gabriel wished he somehow had the power to reach across the light-years that separated them from him and punch them both in the face.

The camera shifted to Sarzhin. "Too long we have kept ourselves separate, but, for many reasons, that time is now at an end. We want our children to be citizens of the galaxy, to be part of a greater community, and not locked away."

Annika smiled up at him, nodding, even as the camera moved once again, this time focusing on Alexa Kreg, who apparently had just handed her sleeping infant off to the Zhore male behind her. Damn, she was gorgeous. How was it that those scaly-skinned freaks could somehow attract the best-looking women?

When Alexa spoke, her tone was cool, matter-of-fact. And damning. "But our stories are not the only ones that need to be heard. For decades…centuries, really…the Consortium has been involved in the very worst sorts of activities—extortion, illegal research, kidnapping, false imprisonment, intimidation on every level. Some of these activities began to come to light with the scandal in the Hunan Province last year, but that, I assure you, was only the tip of a very large iceberg."

Gabriel couldn't believe what he was hearing. Oh, sure, he knew the Consortium's hands were dirty, and didn't much care. Business was business. But how the hell was this signal not being jammed at the source?

He shot a sharp glance over at Eli, who had rocked back on his heels and had his hands jammed in his pockets. "They're going to cut this off at any second."

"I don't think so," Eli replied, sounding way too cheerful. He was the type who couldn't resist a bit of *schadenfreude*—even if said delight in the misery of others involved the possible downfall of the very government that employed him. "It's coming in on all channels. It's flickered once or twice, like they're trying to kill it, but whoever's pushing the transmission through obviously has a lock on the entire communications network."

Which meant they were good. *Really* good. The smallest tendril of worry began to worm its way down Gabriel's spine. He'd always thought of the Consortium's citizens as sheep, stupid, easily led, and ready to be exploited, but if someone slapped them in the face hard enough and woke them up….

"But you don't have to take my word for it," Alexa went on. "Accompanying this signal is a data feed with information on the murders they've covered up, the treaties they've reneged on, the people they've sent to rot in prison for no crime other than trying to expose the Consortium's own criminal activities. We urge all of you to analyze this evidence and see for yourselves, then make your own decisions. The power lies in your hands, for this government—in word, at least, if not practice— is a democracy. You can change it. If enough of you will this change into being, then it can exist." She stopped then, gray-blue eyes seeming to bore into the camera, and said simply, "Don't let the Consortium make you its slaves any longer."

She stepped back. After panning across the faces of those in its field of vision, human and alien, but all determined, all willing to put their privacy on the line to show that a fundamental shift had just occurred, even if most of the galaxy hadn't realized it yet, the screen went dark, except for one word written in Galactic Standard.

Change.

For a few seconds, neither Eli nor Gabriel said anything. Gabriel's mind was racing. Then he said harshly, "Was she telling the truth about that feed, or was that just a line of bullshit?"

"I don't—" Eli blinked and looked down at his handheld, then swiped his finger across it. "Holy shit."

Gabriel didn't bother to ask what he was seeing. Instead, he pulled his own handheld out of his breast pocket. The alert on the home screen was flashing, indicating that he had a new message.

How someone had managed to send a simultaneous transmission to every device in Consortium space capable of receiving it, he had no idea. Not the Zhore. The Eridanis? Maybe. They'd always been in bed with the scaly freaks.

With a shaking finger, he swiped across the screen, downloading the message. Almost at once a parade of images began to flow across his handheld. Worlds he'd never seen. Faces he didn't recognize. Bodies being processed in a facility that he guessed was in Hunan Province. Documents and contracts and treaties and lord knows what else. All of it there, just ready to be dissected for the damning evidence it contained.

He looked up from the handheld's screen to see Eli staring at him, the first traces of fear obvious in his pinched face. "What does it mean?" he asked at last.

"The end," Gabriel said heavily. Maybe it wouldn't happen today, or next week, or even in the next month. But the change Alexa Kreg and her compatriots had called for was coming, sweeping in with the inexorable power of the tide.

And Gabriel knew that he, and many others like him, would probably drown in that tide.